THE GODS AWOKE

MARIE VIBBERT

Journey Press
journeypress.com

Vista, California
Journey Press

Journey Press
P.O. Box 1932
Vista, CA 92085

CREDITS
Cover design: Sabrina Watts at Enchanted Ink Studio

First Printing September 2022

ISBN: 978-1-951320-22-5

Published in the United States of America

JourneyPress.com

For Mary Grimm and Mary Turzillo,
who taught me everything.

Contents

Chapter One: Epiphany 1

Chapter Two: Congregations 20

Chapter Three: Families................................38

Chapter Four: Visitation..............................53

Chapter Five: Tests......................................71

Chapter Six: Annunciation............................87

Chapter Seven: Rites 101

Chapter Eight: Petitions 115

Chapter Nine: Canticle 134

Chapter Ten: Venal Sins..............................147

Chapter Eleven: Penance 159

Chapter Twelve: Mortal Sins 174

Chapter Thirteen: Confessions....................188

Chapter Fourteen: Passion Play 202

Chapter Fifteen: Scriptures........................215

Chapter Sixteen: Martyrs............................233

About the Author... 244
Acknowledgments 245
About the Publisher... 246

Chapter One
Epiphany

The young man, Illoe, caught my attention first. He stood on a threshold, an archway between two rooms, with a tray in his hands and two emotions pushing at each other in his mind. It was this tension which fascinated me. He wasn't aware, of course, that I was there.

Two women sat at a table near him, also unaware of me. They were very aware of him, and he of them, with sight and sound and the pressure of physical *being*. The two women bothered him. Illoe couldn't talk to the one with the other there, and even if the other were gone, there was something about the words that had to be said that made them impossible, and kept him on the threshold of speaking.

The woman he wanted to speak to was Hitra, a priest. From where he stood the morning sun painted a golden outline around her, marking out the tiny springs of her hair in a way Illoe found beautiful, and she found unflattering. The dining room had been built where it was to catch the first light of the morning as it spilled over the mountainside. The temple gardens and the city below were dark, a rumor of shadows in the window glass, punctuated by the slender white chimneys of factories reaching to touch the morning as it poured into the valley, tall weeds that accentuated the flowers of stone and glass buildings.

Illoe stepped up into the room.

Hitra studiously avoided looking at him. She had words of her own she wanted to say, but was wedded to not saying them. Though he was indentured to her and a fair number of years her junior, Hitra could never quite command Illoe.

1

Hitra sweated in her robe. The calendar dictated autumn dress, but it was not autumn yet. She stretched her toes as far as she dared, in the unseen space under the table, not wanting to brush Maede's boney shins and expose herself as less than priestly, less than comfortable.

Conversation wavered between Hitra and Maede, her guest. It was a forcibly amicable discourse between acquaintants that called themselves friends because it was convenient for both to do so. Hitra liked Maede for her habit of donating large sums of money to the church whenever a temple needed to be repaired or a shrine rededicated. Maede was fond of Hitra for her very good taste in donors, and for the legitimizing sound of the words "my friend, a priest of Temple Mount."

Illoe leaned between them, extended one arm to set his tray down. "There's more bread, ladies, and jam."

"What you've brought will be fine," Hitra said, not quite looking at him. "Her ladyship would like more tea, I think, but that will be all."

He decided, then, to abandon what he should do, and what he could or ought to do, and disrupt things for the sheer chaos of it. "Talking about men?"

I fell in love with him then.

Maede's eyebrows raised practically above her hairline. She set down her teacup harder than necessary. Even in exaggerated shock there was a blankness to her primness, as though she didn't quite understand what was going on, and had only picked up a clue that she ought to be insulted, as though a prompter had whispered it to her.

There was a connection, a stirring of the hearing centers of the brain, between Hitra and Maede. Instinctively, and with more physical effort than was actually necessary, Maede made words in Hitra's mind.

It wasn't as simple as all that, but I don't know if you can appreciate it from my point of view. Their minds were mostly opaque to each other, though I could see both of them so easily. For them, there were pinholes, through which they squeezed a narrow wavelength of energy, guided by a metaphor they were taught as children, of making connections like the pipes carrying water through the city.

But I'm holding up the story. Maede's words were heard only by

Hitra and by me. *Is this how your boy talks in front of guests?*

Hitra's smile tightened at the corners.

Illoe looked from one woman to the other, guessing the gist, if not the precise content of their secret words. He raised the empty tray over his head like a torch and triumphantly retreated down three wide steps to the main area of Hitra's chambers.

To his mistress, silently, he said, *The best part is that she proved me right, and doesn't realize it.*

Hitra's response was automatic. Words she had sent many times before, sitting ready in a corner of her mind, like a stencil. *Why must you bait her like that?*

Because she makes it so easy. These words, too, were customary. The connection between them was strong and easy, and utterly undetected by Maede.

Just put on the tea, Illoe, please?

Hitra pretended to be intensely interested in the selection of sliced breads. "He really is quite a good assistant. I'd be lost—"

"You should get rid of him. You're too young, and more importantly, *he* is too young. It looks questionable. Young, single women should only have older male servants. Or women. But I'd never tell anyone how to live their life." Maede puckered her lips over her tea, and after a second's refreshment, continued talking in the same tone, "The Ritual Celebrant has committed a crime against sense and decency."

Illoe supplied his own interpretation from the next room: *Someone trampled a gilly-flower on High Street.*

Hitra felt a conversational whiplash, and took a moment to realize the subject of discussion had altered. *Illoe! No eavesdropping.*

Illoe continued to eavesdrop, as amused as I was. Hitra set her cup carefully in the center of her saucer, so as not to spill or make a clatter. "What has Reha done?"

"You know, Hitra, I have no time for politics or political people. But that's what this is. A political attack." Maede's eyebrows tilted sharply. "She wants to eliminate the Ministry of Flowers." She flattened her left hand so her four rings hit the table simultaneously. "Eliminate it. Completely. Reha says it's unnecessary. Unnecessary, that's what she said, to my face! And now, in the harvest season, when we have so many bulbs and bushes to prepare for winter."

Hitra kept her face studiously concerned, though a need to smile tightened the back of her throat. "I'll talk to her. There has always been a Ministry of Flowers; the pilgrims and tourists expect the temple district to be arrayed appropriately."

"Not just that, Hitra! As a priest of the earth, you must agree that we have a responsibility to these small lives. We can't just abandon them to the ice and, well, the ice!"

Hitra wondered what the real story was. "The Ritual Celebrant was probably trying to antagonize you. Your ministry isn't even under her regulation."

"I've tried appealing to the crown, but you know how the Queen is—if it isn't the end of civilization as we know it, she'll send you to talk to the city officials. But the city assembly listens to the church, and Reha is the church, and she is determined to ruin me."

"Why would Reha want to ruin you, Maede? Honestly?"

In this case, I could see from Maede's mind that "ruin" involved not allowing her volunteer committee to levy fines. Maede did not offer up this explanation. She suspected it would not be appreciated as the attack it was. "I have no idea. What have I ever done to her? Politics, Hitra! Politics and political people are ruining the temple and this city."

Hitra looked out the window, over the shadowed lawn of the temple's residence complex. The high, expansive view she'd worked hard to earn. The sun was over the mountain at last, the city storefronts painted with light. Hitra could feel she was watching over all of the district, down to the tiny pinpricks of movement on the docks, a sail barge skimming like a splinter toward port.

Looking at the view was something to do while thinking of what to say to Maede. She had almost formed a correct, polite answer, when a column of fire as wide as a well fell from the heavens, hitting an unimportant point on the lower terrace an easy stone's throw from her seat, just beyond the intersection of two paths. There it hung, casting the watery luminescence of dawn into darkness behind it.

Illoe was the first thing to catch my interest, as I have said, but the pillar of fire was a close second.

Animal panic simplified the layered and preoccupied minds of every person who witnessed it. Even I wasn't sure what to make of it. Fire played over Hitra's dark face, a weaving of light, occasionally rising flecks of shadow. Maede leaned forward, confused by Hitra's expression, and the two ladies were mirrors for a moment, jaws hanging loose. Maede's cheek twitched and then she blinked. There were two false starts before she turned her gaze behind her and saw the fire, filling fully a quarter of the view, twisting shapes within it like glowing intestines, a perfect line of blaze in the lush and manicured gardens of the temple complex.

Hitra's sleeve dragged utensils off the table as she rose. She pressed her hand to the curved window glass and flinched from its unexpected cold. Hitra took one shaking step backward. She took another.

Hitra and Maede, both trying not to run and only barely managing to jog, passed Illoe in the sitting area. He'd heard their conversation stall and was coming in hope that a subtle question like, "Is the youth committee meeting today?" (it wasn't) would open the way for Maede to leave so he could finally ask Hitra about his contract. He held a teakettle, its handle wrapped in a green cloth. "Is something wrong?"

Hitra lifted her hood with both hands and settled it over her hair. Her eyes met Illoe's, a visual communication far better than their trick with minds. Yes, something was wrong. Very wrong and she did not know why. "I'll be back," she said, and followed Maede out the door.

I didn't like being as lost as they were. As confused. I couldn't remember being confused before.

Firelight flickered over the glass tiles of Hitra's sitting room in odd angles, nothing like Illoe's memories of times when the fire pantry hearth was blazing and the lanterns lit. The three steps up to the dining room cast fanning shadows onto the rug, making the room seem alien and new to him. Illoe started toward the dining area, but then looked to the open front door and set the teakettle down on an empty clay floor-tile.

He closed the apartment door and went back to the fire-pantry with the kettle, which he set on the firebricks, then he shook his head at himself and set the pot on the sideboard. Teatime was over.

He walked carefully across the sitting area, enumerating in his head all flammable items adjacent to the bay window. Grass, a low tanglewood shrub...he reassured himself that the outside wall was glazed brick and whatever it was would not catch the building on fire. He went back to the pantry for a tray to clean up the abandoned tea things. He could gawk at the fire later, he thought, with disdain toward everyone doing so right now. Vultures, pulling entertainment from someone else's tragedy.

What an unexpected lack of curiosity! "Look out the window, already," I said. He turned at the sound of my voice, toward where I suppose I had imagined my presence to center. He didn't see me. I felt him worry at the phenomenon, that he had definitely heard a voice, a woman's voice, not a random mind touching his, but sound, and now it was gone. He examined the walls of the room. He must have walked right through me. I realized I hadn't a clear idea where I was.

Illoe paused, staring at the oil lantern just inside the front door. The flickering flame highlighted his lone silhouette, cast by the larger flame outside, above it. He'd heard that voice, my voice. He felt a prickle of fear. Someone, he thought, was in danger.

With careful steps, like a priest carrying a precious offering, he took his tray up to the dining nook.

At last, he beheld the flame in the window before him. It played over his skin, caresses of orange and yellow. He looked at the surge and ebb of color on the translucent porcelain and shining brass tea forks. It was beautiful. He felt privileged to see something so destructive, but safely behind glass.

He carried the tray to the window and studied the scene before him: people running, black against the light, like the sailing curls of spent kindling. It didn't look like the fire was spreading or anyone was hurt, but it was so strange. He felt for Hitra's mind. *Boss?*

There was no response. He tried again. *What in the name of Wenne's sacred tits...*

Stay inside. Everything is...it's fine. Wait for me. The connection closed as quickly as it had opened.

Illoe began to worry that there was something important he had missed.

☽O☾

Outward from the temple, shock, terror, and confusion jolted minds from their concerns. The unexplainable column of flame sent ripples through the city. Merchants ceased to worry about thieves; thieves ceased to worry about merchants; parents ceased scolding their children. While beautiful in their progression, the reactions got repetitive from my perspective, until one little mind caught me, like a reed dragging against the rippled pond. His thoughts were different.

He'd expected this.

I hadn't expected that, and I was pretty sure I knew everything.

The column of flame was a line, fuzzy like yarn, when viewed from the poor neighborhoods of the low city. Arel, full name Arelandus Nereshore, pressed his cheek to the plaster-caked corner of his house. The roar the flame created in the walled gardens of the temple district wasn't even a crackling here on Hopeful Street. He could hear, however, the calls and bells of the city watch, the organized panic of professionals. He was calm, with an edge of excitement. He was prepared.

Arel felt the vibration of his wife pulling the iron latch on the window. Her palm was distorted by the thick glass as she guided it out, obscuring his view. She set her hands on the sill. "Arel, do you see it?"

"It will burn until all have seen it." He lifted his cheek from the reassuring roughness of the house. He was aware of how self-assured he sounded. He reminded himself to be humble.

"You'd better come in. Jana's here. She ran all the way from Sorrow's Market."

Despite his nod of agreement, they stood together a while longer, neither wanting to let go of the strange sight before them. Throughout the city, people gathered on rooftops and at intersections where the vantage was clear. Even those that fled did so with their heads craning behind them. It wasn't hard to see, the temple district being at the highest point of the city, backed by dark mountain stone. Arel wondered where the pillar of fire was relative to the buildings of the temple — whether it was near the path he took every day as an acolyte, from the residence buildings to the seminary. It was right of center, in front of the lower buildings, the administrative ones, he thought. It was hard to see the ordinary shapes of white stone. Though the arches were as thin as hairs glittering in the sun from this distance, everyone knew the shapes of the temples, could pick out a poor rendering in a mural. The sugar-confection of the temple architecture was the backdrop of the city, and now it sank from sight against the bright light in front of it and the watery shadows that cupped the mountainside behind.

Another head appeared in the window. Jana's profile lined up perfectly with Arel's, turned in the same direction. "Speaker Arel, I come to tell you about this. Aja, Mel, and me were in the market. We think it's a sign. Don't you? Don't you think it's a sign? You tell me, Speaker. I'll go tell them."

"It's a message," Arel said, and the far-off fire blinked out.

The three of them—Arel, his wife Debha, and the visitor Jana—stared after its trace, at the diminishing line of false color created by their own retinas. They all felt his words had caused the light to vanish. Arelandus Nereshore hardly trusted himself to draw in his next breath.

But he did, and then his mind was just another muddle of fear and confusion. Had he been wrong? He thought the fire would burn a full day. Unless everyone in the city had seen it already and it winked out just then, but that would imply his words were mere coincidence, and he didn't believe in coincidence. Not for himself.

What an idiot. He thought he completely understood the gods, understood *me*. I went to poke him in the gut, and discovered that I had no idea how to touch things. At any rate, nothing happened and he didn't feel my presence.

Arel and his wife and his guests sat down around a low table and started a discussion where they all repeated each other.

"We should have a meeting."

"The Ritualists will claim this is their sign, because it was at the temple."

"It doesn't belong to the Ritualists."

"Of course not!"

"They'll say it does, though."

"The congregation will want a meeting."

"Yes, a meeting."

Something so simple, a mere column of fire that didn't even last an hour, had affected the entire room of people, but they had no idea I was there. More than one worried that Senne, that evil trickster, had caused the fire, or caused it to go out. I was Senne, I knew that much, and I hadn't done any such thing, but I couldn't make my presence felt, much less clear my name.

Who had upstaged me with that column of fire?

☽◯☾

I went for answers to the highest seat of power. The sun shone with summer intensity into the office of the highest religious official in Chagrin City, the Ritual Celebrant, Reha, High Priest of Wenne. A large number of high church officials crowded the usually ample room. Tall windows provided shafts of gold, offsetting the dark floor, the dark walls, the pristine white robes of the aged Ritual Celebrant herself, who rested her weight on the windowsill and said, "There are many things in nature that are beyond our knowledge."

The assembled priests were not the leadership council, whom she'd asked for, but rather every member that had been nearby, and those one or two steps junior to a member who had been in the courtyard or near enough to hear the summons. Some were in casual dress, others stood like trees in full regalia, the thick folds of their gowns hiding their limbs and making them appear to grow out of the floor.

Hitra stood near the back. She had seen the temple groundskeepers throw water at the column, and when that failed, sand. She had run to the windows with the rest of her peers when it was announced that the flame had gone out. She had seen the pristine grass and the arbiters pacing and gesturing as they argued over where exactly the flame had been. She had been a part of the huddled crowd watching, and disdained it, thinking herself somehow more academic in her staring.

Hitra was irritated. So far, the meeting had consisted only of urgings not to panic. Hitra was not about to panic, and she did not need a meeting. Hitra herself was a member of the leadership committee, and wondered that anyone who wasn't had volunteered for this.

A late arrival slipped in the door. A male priest. One of his brothers rushed to greet him. "Is everyone in your area all right?"

The male priests squeezed hands, both secretly delighted to have been close to disaster. "Everyone's a little shaken, but we're fine. What about you? Is Nahne all right?"

Hitra rolled her eyes. It was very small, how her colleagues interpreted any strangeness only as possible danger to themselves. Hitra had thought theologians above that. Still the holy leaders of the city whispered and touched, spreading confirmations of safety in rooms, hallways, streets, neighborhoods. The Celebrant held still, giving her people leeway to be distracted.

A junior priest of Wenne asked, "Where's Hitra? Did Hitra see anything odd with the grass?"

Hitra wondered, not for the first time, why people assumed a priest of the harvest god Revestre was automatically a botanist, but she tried to answer diplomatically. "I couldn't tell the spot where it had been, save for the sand and water the gardeners had thrown. There was not a single singed blade of grass. I don't believe it was a form of lightning."

A woman sputtered at Hitra's tight-lipped statement. "Lightning? Are you blind?"

"I said I don't..."

Only an atheist, the woman thought, would be looking for natural explanations. "Lightning isn't even a consideration!"

Reha held a hand up to calm the growing tide of argument. When there was absolute silence, she let it hang for a second untouched, and then spoke with deliberate calm. "I believe that was Hitra's opinion as well." How a statement was easier to hear when spoken by authority! "Be still, daughter of Senne."

Senne? This was my priest? I studied her with new interest. She was older, thin, and dressed in a casual under-robe. She'd missed her breakfast and was trying not to think about it.

Reha straightened to her full, rather modest, height. "No more of this. We are not going to assign meaning. We are not going to endorse panic. We," she strafed the room with a glare, "are going to maintain business as usual. We all still have jobs to do. If your faith can't handle a little unexplained event, I suggest you take a good long look at the sunrise every morning."

The priest of Senne was annoyed to have the discussion tabled, but glad Reha had brought up sunrises, as she was locked in a constant fight against the heresy that the properties of the sun were explainable by science. Reha would have hated to realize she was interpreted that way, because she did believe in the science, she just thought the sun itself was an unknowable body.

I easily flew up through the ceiling, the atmosphere, and the vacuum beyond. The sun was a fiery ball of gas, not rising or falling but orbited by the ball that included the city and its temples. How silly their interpretations of the phenomena were! Feeling smug, I returned, centering myself at Hitra's side.

Hitra knew there were too many in the room being silent who would later complain that no one had spoken up, and so she took in a deep breath and released it slowly. "Your Eminence, people will demand a response from the church."

"And they will get one: a personal one, from each of us as we address the fears and concerns of our parishioners. Let the people know that we are open to listen to them and to console them. I'm asking everyone to hold extra office hours as long as needed or as long as your will to do so holds out."

A cascade of mental groans, barely suppressed. Most of the priests had hoped to have no office hours. Surely no one was more affected, more in need of time off to process this, than theologians!

Reha made a brushing motion with her hand, moving the topic on. "Her Highness has assured me that the Assembly are appointing a team to investigate. Naturalists and the like. The Adept of the Academy are meeting as we speak, and are expected to support the Adept of the Crown in the investigation. I hope, after we have a formal meeting, as soon as possible—my aide is scheduling it—we may declare the Adept of the Temple are united with them." Reha clapped her hands and leaned forward. "Now is the time to be thankful we live in a society that has the luxury of supporting theistic scholarship. No one and no thing has been harmed. If faith itself is to be harmed by this, it will have to be our doing. Sona, aren't you leading the sixth hour ritual? Better get cracking on it. I suspect attendance will be up. Go, all of you. Fight panic, don't spread it."

Hitra stepped to the side, to let the others file out before her. The sun was in her eyes, and that was the only reason she lowered her head. She was furious. If Reha could give the priesthood a performance like that, she could do one for the public who would appreciate it more. *Eminence, you have to make a statement, even if it is just what you said here. The public expects it, and it is your duty.*

Reha strolled around her desk. *I've made my decision.* She pressed down the curling edge of a parchment and pretended to read it.

The priest of Senne was one of the last to leave. She hung on the thick doorframe for a moment, looking anxiously back at the Ritual Celebrant, hoping if she waited long enough, she would be gifted a clear plan of attack, some itemized list of duties. She was rather stupid. Who'd ordained her? More importantly, how did I go about picking a high priest for myself? I cleared my throat, or tried to. I didn't have a throat.

Reha didn't hear me. I tried again.

The heavy door fell into place, locking out my priest and the others. Hitra was still there. She had waited for this moment. "I'm not sure you've made the right decision."

"The Legend of Elintar." Reha lifted the parchment she was studying. The sun shone through it, making it glow — the lines of text on the other side a fuzzy pattern. "This is the Lowland version, popular with Hushers and apocalyptic sects. 'And in the place of her coming the god Wenne drew a line of fire upon the air that joined the sky to the ground and burned one hour, until all in the city had seen it.'"

Reha let the parchment fall. "Do you want to tell all of Casu that the world has come to an end?"

"Eminence, I don't believe it has."

"Good. Neither do I. But the real power of my job, Hitra, daughter of Revestre, is the word 'no,' and I have to be very, very careful when I use it. If I call this fire divine, it is not natural. If I call it natural, it is not divine. And I honestly do not know what it is. Saying nothing while speaking is a job for politicians, not me."

"Others are going to find that prophecy. Others are going to interpret it. Your job is to tell people what to believe."

"My job is paramount on my mind. Trust me to do it?" She sat down in her chair and turned her gaze once more to the scroll. "The priest of Wenne has no official statement at this time."

Wenne. I had no memory of meeting her, but I knew who she was. My nemesis. The sun to my moon, all goodness and light and not-having-fun. Of course she'd do something like this, just to irritate me. I had to find her. I spread out, over the city, until I felt I'd break apart. I poked my nose into the government Assembly and the Academy Hall. Workmen were back to their tasks on the piers, loading and unloading ships, angry that they weren't allowed to gawk and talk longer, like the warehouse workers along the rooftops. A glassmaker offered a prayer of thanks to the goddess of the sun that his fires hadn't diminished while he was distracted.

Wenne wasn't there to hear this prayer to her, but she had to be somewhere.

☽○☾

Illoe wanted to kick Maede. He'd picked his spot: the corner of her mouth, where the flesh was loose and made her lips seem sunken. Unlike most noble women, Maede wasn't plump enough to be beautiful; she was a sort of deflated balloon of a person.

He wasn't sure if he could reach the exact spot, but maybe if he pushed her out of the chair first, he could land a solid blow with his heel and, he hoped, hear her teeth clatter together like broken ceramic.

I adored the specificity of his violent fantasy, though he had no real intention to harm anyone. The thought kept him entertained while she chewed her way through the entire supply of Hitra's biscuits. "I'm sure she's not coming back soon," he said, not for the first time. "Hitra would have sent me a message."

Maede had been stout in her youth, but meetings and speeches and worrying about meetings and speeches had withered her. However, she assumed against all reason that Illoe was attracted to her, to her position and power. Men were not as focused on the physical as women. That was because men were more physical. It was their brute strength that made them ideal for housework and not thinking.

Maede boiled. Her robes were hot, her thighs slick with sweat where they met, and she fancied her heart itself burned, a chemical state wrought by her emotions. Maede *wanted*. She wanted to throw off her robes to the cool air. She wanted distraction and calm and to be told what to think. She wanted so much, yet she just sat there and let herself smolder.

Much like Illoe wanted to kick her, or at least for her to leave so he could stop holding a polite look on his face. The two of them were tinder waiting to start a flash fire. I wanted to strike a spark.

"Really," Illoe held his hands out, assuming a placating stance. "She always lets me know when to expect her. I'll have her call you."

Maede stuck an elongated fingernail into the folded corner of her mouth to dislodge a soggy clump of biscuit. "Young men are more attractive when silent."

If Hitra were within his mental reach, Illoe would have passed along a witty retort about how attractive he wanted to appear to this woman. He told the retort to himself, anyway. It wasn't that good. He switched his hands from clasping right to left. "I could send you a message as soon as she returns. Directly to your home. You won't miss anything."

"I am not here to keep from 'missing' anything. Your mistress will want to talk to a trusted confidant as soon as she gets home. If you were the least bit skilled with people, you'd know that."

Somehow, Illoe kept his face impassive. "Of course, Lady Faydehale. I'll get you more tea, then."

"Don't you dare, young man. You'll be gone another hour."

Illoe was pretty sure he hadn't enjoyed more than five minutes away from the horrid woman the last time he had refreshed the teapot. It had been barely time enough to contact the temple kitchen and place an order for lunch.

Someone struck the door-chime and Illoe almost jumped. He could tell by Maede's glare that she saw his relief. "Excuse me, Lady," he bowed.

"Don't even think of it! Your mistress isn't home. You don't know who that could be."

The tension was gone, and I had done nothing with it.

Illoe skipped down the steps to the main area, and bounded past the sitting couches in three strides. "A moment!"

He pulled both doors open together and stood with arms spread before a strange man with pale skin. He had one hand still resting against the copper chimes. Illoe lowered his head in lieu of a bow as he let go of the door handles. "What can I do for you, sir?"

The man, one Forthright Jeje, glanced nervously over Illoe's shoulder, where Maede stood with crossed arms. "Holiness?"

Maede being mistaken for Hitra was a joke too precious not to share. Illoe tried to convey his utter amusement in expression alone. "Her Holiness is not at home. Would you care to wait?"

Maede shrieked. "Absolutely not!" She stomped up to Illoe, and he felt the annoyingly soft texture of her sleeve on his arm as she pointed over him. "State your business and go; there will be no strange men loitering in a priestess's private chambers!"

Jeje shrank back. "I... I'm sorry."

"Don't be, please," Illoe said, seething inside, because all the civility in the world couldn't cover up the raging water-beast behind him. "Leave your name and location; my mistress will contact you when she can."

Jeje touched his forehead, remembering a hat that wasn't there. He never wore his cap on Temple Mount, because it identified his ethnicity and aroused the police. "I... no, no location code, I'm, well, I'm Sanadaru, so she couldn't.... This was bad, coming here. I... I'll try at the youth center."

Illoe closed the doors and turned to see Maede standing less than a step behind him, her arms crossed, her dark, floral gown rising and falling with her heavy gasps. "Lady," he began, and then was startled by a sudden, sparkling pain against his cheek. He blinked and took a moment to realize that she had slapped him. He touched his face. "Lady Maede," he said, louder than he had spoken to her ever before, "you must leave."

Maede felt the futile smallness of the slap, the absence of any release from her anger and frustration. I was jealous of the warmth on her fingertips. She rolled her shoulder back and this time he caught her wrist as her hand flew toward him. His fingers were hard against her skin, as no one's had been since she had gotten her first job as head of her mother's company. And him, a commoner! She jerked away. "I think I'd better."

Maede felt, strangely enough, like she was punishing him by leaving.

☽○☾

Hitra came home so late that Illoe had to light a fire and reheat the supper that had been delivered from the kitchen. She pulled off her outer robe and let it fall in the foyer. "What a day," she said, and laid down on the nearest of the two sitting-couches.

Illoe brought the flint striker in to light the lanterns. "Dinner will be ready as soon as you can drag yourself to the table."

"I'll have it for breakfast then." She rubbed a hand over her eyes. "Messages?"

Illoe shook out the reed. "Too many." He gathered up her fallen robe. "Pretty much every parent with a child in your choir called to ask if practice is still on. I told them it was. Maede was here until fifth hour. I almost killed her."

Hitra knew how much Illoe hated Maede, but rather than the apology she felt she said, "You would do well to be nice to her. She knows a lot of people."

"She's a skrok." He folded the robe over the back of the couch and reached down to brush a stray lock of hair off his mistress's face. "And that makes you a skrok-herder if you keep her around."

"Language, Illoe."

'Skrok' wasn't considered bad language down in Illoe's neighborhood, though on Temple Mount it was scandalous. He carried the robe into the bedroom. "She's a skrok. Her kids are skroks. Her mother was high priest of Skroktar!"

This Skroktar, God of Filth, wasn't real, but invented by a playwright generations ago, and morphed into popular consciousness to the point where there were songs, poems, and even a few sincere worshipers for him. More mortal impudence.

Hitra tried to smother a laugh. "You're not making me laugh. I spent all day in meetings or reorganizing meetings I had planned weeks in advance." Half to herself, she continued, "No one wants to schedule anything. People are fleeing the city. Actually fleeing the city. They almost evacuated the mount, for Darian's sake. The mount!"

Illoe folded her outer robe on the airing rack, calling from the bedroom, "Yeah, I got a couple messages about that. The kitchen actually did shut down for an hour, and the laundry sent everyone home at six." He set the cold dinner he'd gotten for her in a pan to reheat and looked to see if anything else had been left lying about the front room. He could see her, lying on the couch in her silk under-robe of translucent saffron, the hair under her arm visible as a darker spot as she scratched her scalp.

"You can't imagine the chaos out there. Some people think this is the wrath of the gods come upon us. Others think it's some hidden poison in the air. I saw no fewer than five adepts with their hanging sleeves tied over their noses."

Illoe watched the movement of fabric folds over Hitra's breast and thought it was rather a shame all the priests under a certain age didn't wear under-robes exclusively. He shook his head and bent into the fire-nook to check on the food. "Yeah, Oke told me it was crazy in the kitchens. We need to talk business. Are you up for that?"

"Ugh. No, not now, Illoe. Can it wait?"

He poked cubes of meat with a stone spoon. "It can wait an hour. It can't wait two weeks."

"Tomorrow, I promise we'll talk tomorrow. Today is just shot, out of the question."

"So, what do you think it was? Oke tells me there's a powder street magicians use that burns up in a flash and doesn't leave any evidence."

Hitra's eyes unfocused. "That burns white to yellow," she said. "This was redder. Like a wood fire."

Illoe set the cover back on the pot and hooked his pot-holder back on its hook. "So," he repeated, with raised eyebrows this time, "what do you think it was?"

"An unexplained natural phenomenon," Hitra quoted without inflection. She pushed herself up to sitting. "There are many things in nature that are beyond our knowledge."

"That's the only reasonable answer." Illoe carried Hitra's dinner over to her. "Though it could be some new chemical someone discovered. One of the glass colorists, maybe. They're always talking about some new experimental mix. I bet it was an accident. No one's sick enough to pull a trick like that on purpose."

She looked up at the wooden tray he held above her. "There is a small possibility, Illoehenderen, that this was the work of the gods."

It was about time someone said that.

The tray teetered slightly as Illoe shifted his grip. "You don't really believe..." Her eyes stopped him. He set the tray down beside her, on the soft surface of the couch. "Sorry."

Hitra had to reach quickly to keep the stew bowl level. "I can't believe you almost asked that."

"I meant just about the fire. I know you're for real, Hitra. I know you believe all this stuff." He cringed, inwardly, at his awkward phrasing.

Illoe helped Hitra move the tray into her lap and she waited to speak until the stew was safe from tipping, her hands on either side of the bowl, her face over it, smelling the savory steam. She knew she should maybe not speak at all; to push someone toward belief was almost always to push them away. "You shouldn't call it 'this stuff.' The gods are what you make of them, and if all you make of them are disposable words, what does it say about your spiritual health?"

Illoe muttered something he hoped she could interpret any way she wanted, halfway between 'yes' and 'sure.'

She didn't buy it. "I swear, sometimes I think you're an atheist."

Illoe was, in fact, an atheist. He took a step back. He raised one shoulder. He changed the subject. "Something happened today."

She raised her head.

He didn't want to say the something that had happened, that Maede had slapped him. He knew he should report it, that it was the only way to prevent Maede doing it again, but he also didn't like how weak it made him seem, so instead he said, "A Sanadaru was here. He didn't leave his name or why he came."

"A Sanadaru?" Hitra couldn't recall knowing any Sanadaru. "Perfect. I insult the Ritual Celebrant and then heathens are seen in my home." Now it was her turn to cringe. "No, no. I didn't say that. He must be a relative of one of my youth outreach students or something. He might even be a convert. I'm not going to panic about that now."

Illoe thought there were plenty of Sanadaru better than some priests he knew and decided to punish Hitra with the truth. "And Maede hit me."

Hitra snickered. "Oh, she did not."

"Yes, she did. Across the face. I told her to leave and she stormed out."

"Ah, me." Hitra scooted forward to hand the tray back to Illoe. "Put that on the dining table, please."

He nodded. As he stepped up to the darkened eating nook, he said, "Do something about it. File a complaint. Tell her spouse. I don't know. I don't care if she knows I told you. Maede can hate me all she wants; she's not going to stop liking you."

Hitra pressed her thumbs into her forehead and concentrated for a moment on the pressure and release. "Maede is an important person."

"If you happen to be a flower."

"Her family is important. I just... she really hit you?" She was sure he'd offer some detail that made this a misunderstanding, an accidental brush of bodies.

Illoe felt, like a constriction, the inevitability of Hitra dismissing this. He felt helpless.

So did I.

The flint striker snapped as he lit the oil lanterns. Soon the round dining platform was warm and bright, curtained with the flat black of an unseen world outside. Illoe leaned against one of the columns. *I should tell her about the contract*, he thought to himself, *while she's feeling guilty*.

Instead he said, "Hitra, get up here and finish your dinner. You want me to apologize to that she-skrok, I will. The soup's getting cold and I'm not going to heat it up again."

"Yes, sir." She smiled, getting up, despite how tired she was. She enjoyed his nagging and he enjoyed nagging her; it was a comfortable game they played, and it made the strangeness of the day fade.

Chapter Two
Congregations

Reha knelt in the pre-dawn shadows of her bedroom. It was a simple room, formerly that of the Ritual Celebrant's secretary. She'd insisted on moving to it when she took office and found the Ritual Celebrant's traditional chambers both too far from the office and too opulent. She let her secretary sleep in them.

The floor here was plain wood, unvarnished and silvery, meant to take chalk, but she used a prayer matt of painted leather in consideration of the clean-up. She drew a line in front of her knees. She was proud of her drawing ability, a necessary offshoot of priestly duties, and usually lavished time and attention on her private meditations. She did nothing fancy today, just a straight line, even chalk on the dark prayer mat: the line of clarity. "As it has been since the covenant of peace, I pray first to Wenne, Queen of Gods, Law-maker, Lady of Wisdom, the Sun at Zenith," she paused, and, her mouth curling slightly, added an obscure name for the god to her litany: "Lady of Fire, teach me what I must know." Her hand hovered over the end of the line, but no, she decided, no flourish. She stood, bowed, and turned her back to the line she had drawn. She bowed again, to the south, and knelt down to draw a parallel line. "Secondly to Senne, the Hidden Moon, Lady of Power, Darkness, Trickster, you have my respect, the token is continued, do not turn on me."

Kind of rude. I am also god of art, wit, magic, and water that flows underground. That ties me tangentially to technology and to stars: all the very interesting and pretty things are mine.

A quarter-turn, another bow. She connected her first and second line. "Revestre, Harvest-mother, Golden One, I pray to you, guardian of this season." Unlike a layman, Reha would not dream of switching which hand held her chalk, but twisted to finish the box, caging herself in self-consecrated space. "Dioneltar, Ocean's Daughter, Sacred of the Mountain and Rock, I pray to you on this, your day." Her meditative task finished, she bowed her head. She thought a while about the best thing to say to four summoned gods, wanting to make a short prayer. Too many words, she mused, say less than just enough, and gods weren't exempt from being distracted or confused. She took a breath. "Guide my actions to the greater good." She held still, perfectly still before us, humble and silent.

Us?

There were others in the room, like myself and yet not. Wenne had formed a face, just an outline of fire that nodded in time with her disciple's thoughts. She avoided my gaze, which made me realize, with joy, that I had one.

Who was that, that vagueness to my left? Revestre? Or was it the sea-god? Maybe. One god out of four was missing. Revestre or Dioneltar. I rather hoped it wasn't Hitra's god, who was, in a way, in charge of Illoe. What did the daughter of stone and sea look like?

Wenne and whoever-it-was had to be there for the same reason I was: looking for answers from the woman who prayed just as she looked for answers from us. Despite really, really wanting to, Reha could not detect our presence.

"Wenne," I called to her. Her name hung around her and inside her, like a cloak or like intestines.

"Trickster," she said. She glanced my way and then pointedly away again.

I was annoyed at the rebuff but at the same time I wanted to live up to Wenne's expectations of trickery. I wasn't sure how. It seemed the sort of thing that ought to come naturally.

Reha offered more ritual prayers, for the harvest and the weather and the people, like ticking boxes to keep the bureaucracy of myth moving forward, her mind already half on her day that was about to start. This was awkward, painfully so.

"Did you create the fire?" I asked Wenne. "Were you doing that stupid prophecy? The one about the world ending? How did you do it?"

I felt Wenne think that of course she had sent the column of fire, why was everyone asking that like it was in question? Her fire-face scowled. Her lips moved. No sound came.

"Speak up," I demanded.

More mouthing and glaring. She was trying to make sounds, to warn her priest about me, and she had no idea how sounds worked. She hadn't paid attention, hadn't seen the air compress and expand.

"I've done the work of being heard; clearly, you could return the favor."

She vanished into a rude symbol.

Reha slipped backward and wiped her chalk lines with a specially prepared whisk. "Go and be well," she bade us. Her knees ached, and she yearned to return to bed. Still I waited, while the formless some-one melted away and Reha pulled her outer robe on and sighed. She was sure the drama and novelty of the fire would burn itself out in a week.

Good. That would serve Wenne right.

☽○☾

I returned to Hitra, who had spent the morning at her desk in her bed-room reading her seminary textbooks, which she'd had Illoe fetch for her from the high shelves over the bed. He'd bring one down; she'd take it, look up sheepishly, and ask for another.

He obliged. Passing her a tome on the history of prophecy he asked, "So, that business I mentioned last night?"

Hitra turned away from her work and gave him that intent look she had, that the acolytes and congregations loved so much—the one that said, for you, and you alone, I will stop the world. For one min-ute. Because one minute was all Hitra ever had. She took his hand earnestly in hers and said, "Not now, please, Illoe? I have to get ready for this. We'll talk soon, I promise."

Illoe believed her, mostly. What else could he do? Hitra was un-stoppable when she had a plan. Illoe fetched her things and went back to the fire pantry. He had decided to clean the oil nozzles on the stove. They were ceramic, delicate little sea creatures of unpainted clay. Most people let them get gunked up and then broke them off and bought new ones, but Illoe had kept the same four nozzles working since he'd moved in, and he was proud of that, and how nice they looked coming out of the vinegar he soaked them in.

He got his domestic skills from his father, he knew, and he was embarrassed by the thought. His father was why he had to talk to his boss.

Hitra thought he was talking about Maede and was determined to wait him out until he forgot about it. She slipped past him with her blue incense dish clutched to her chest — the fire pantry was also the corridor linking Hitra's bedroom to the main area of the apartment, the legacy of impractical designers who must have thought no priest would ever actually eat in her chambers.

"Can you not do that right now, Illoe? Guests are going to be here any minute."

He let the nozzle in his hand fall back into the bowl of vinegar. It spat out a bubble of air and sank. "What do you want me to do?"

"Are the snacks ready?"

A cold tray had been delivered from the kitchens and set on a water bath in the dining nook to keep it fresh. "Yes."

Hitra adjusted the incense burner on the sitting-table, and then surveyed the room, pointing from the pillows to the curtains, checking off a list in her head.

Left without a purpose, Illoe took the bowl of vinegar back to his room.

Temple priests were not supposed to have live-in servants, and so the temple architects had not planned for any. Illoe's room at the back of the apartment had been meant as a rear entrance and boot-parlor. Low storage boxes doubled as benches, for winter-arriving servants to remove their wet shoes.

He liked it. The back wall was nearly all window, cheerful and sunny when it wasn't too cold. He had his bed, plenty of room for his clothes, and very little need for privacy. His untouched prayer mat held his shoes and the lumpy pottery he'd made when Hitra had dragged him to the youth art festival. One of the acolytes had stamped holy symbols in the simple bowls while they were drying, and Illoe had unsuccessfully tried to scrape them off, leaving the edges lopsided and rough. They'd waited ever since for a trip down to the seminary art school, where Hitra promised she would show him how to make them smooth again and glazed. Illoe didn't bother Hitra about it. When enough time had passed that she was sure to have forgotten, he planned on breaking the bowls apart and giving the pieces to his mother, who could always use more clay.

From his memories, it was clear he didn't do much in his room besides sleep and make Hitra's Harvest Home and Summer Festival presents every year, but today he lingered, mine alone to enjoy. He flopped onto the bed without a care for how his tunic landed askew, exposing a firm young thigh and a wide expanse of shoulder. Illoe thought it was ridiculous how the priests were using this fire-column event—miracle or not—as an excuse to disrupt daily life. Like food wasn't still being prepared and laundry washed by those with less time on their hands or less power to shirk.

Feminine voices filtered back to him through intervening walls and rooms, just a texture of sound: whispers, the movement of furniture, the clink of glass. The guests were arriving. He pressed his feet against the wall opposite his bed and rolled a scroll open and closed over his face.

He couldn't read it that close, but he knew what it said:

> *Letter of Indenture of the Casu-born male Illoehenderen Middlemount, second son of Loata Middlemount, citizen in good standing of Chagrin City*
>
> *To*
>
> *The Casu Lady Hitra Hautridge, daughter of Counselor Hautridge and Lord Helaunteret, herself an Acolyte of Revestre, on this day Graduate of the Seminary of Temple Mount in the Temple of All Sacraments, City of Chagrin, Land of the Casu.*

It was handwritten, as anachronistic a thing as the outdated institution it represented. Indentured servants were a thing of the past, of a world lit by smoking candles and populated by nobles in trailing gowns. The delicate, pressurized world of Hitra's old money noble heritage, a world that carried on in its own little circle, somehow even more insular than the temple, heedless of the city and technology around it, writing out writs and encasing them in brass.

The important part, the relevant part of his indenture to the present crisis wasn't at the top, it was almost at the bottom: "Changes to this agreement must be made after the anniversary of the indentured's birth and before the morning dawns on Harvest Home."

Illoe, the indentured, needed to make a change to the agreement.

The scroll had sat, ignored but not forgotten, for four years, in among Hitra's other papers that were only important themselves as objects: her diploma from the seminary, her commission as a priest. Illoe and Hitra never talked about the indenture, and sometimes they both forgot that he was anything other than Hitra's very accommodating live-in friend. But two weeks ago, on his nineteenth birthday, Illoe had taken the time to open the case and look at it, in anticipation of next year's birthday and the end of this chapter of his life.

There were four weeks between his birthday and Harvest Home, and so he had read very thoroughly, with a lawyer's care, and found, in the section on 'compensation to the family' a throwaway little clause. "Marital disposition of the indentured shall be the sole responsibility of the contract holder, and shall be determined by the closure date."

He played the sentence back and forth in his mind, tricked apart the meaning of each individual word, but in the end, he had to admit there was only one translation. Hitra had to find him a wife before releasing him. He was getting married in one year. At the moment he looked forward to eagerly as the start of his dating life, his parents wanted him to get married.

It wasn't like he wanted to rush out and proposition women on High Street, but he felt he'd been more than patient, waiting for his contract to end so he could be free to date without complication. Maybe even meet some girls who didn't want to be priests.

He'd put off talking about it on his birthday, because it was his birthday and Hitra had forgotten, but he didn't want to remind her in case she hadn't. It was silly, but he never put his birthday on her calendar. It didn't seem like it ought to be his job.

He put off telling her about it the next day because it was an awkward subject to bring up on top of a reminder that she'd forgotten. Then he had put it off because it was the weekend and Hitra was busy. And then he had put it off because he should talk to his mother about it first. Except he didn't want to talk to his mother. And then weeks had gone by. Now he had ten days. And then, because, he mused, the universe personally hated him, a purported miracle, or at least a very distracting phenomenon, had landed just outside his hedges.

What he wouldn't give to insert a sixth day in every week. There were enough gods; the calendar makers could have had longer weeks if they cared.

And now the house was filled to bursting with Hitra's ritual assistants, acolytes, neophytes, and youth sponsors. They were sitting in a circle around Hitra's front room with the curtains drawn and the candles lit, hunched over their knees, "opening up to each other." It was the same crap Hitra had organized when one of the acolytes had lost her father in a boat accident the spring before.

In Illoe's opinion, the current meeting was an insult to that death, which, while no excuse to sit on the floor and burn incense, was at least a real event. He had degraded the fire column that much in his memory. As lovely as it was, he saw nothing more in it, no hope of a romantic explanation—nothing more than some build up of gasses. He had heard about gasses under the ground down in Longlee Valley that had to be burned off before the rock oil underneath could be gotten. It had to be something like that, a natural spurt, like the oil coming out of the burners on the stove.

He had a short tolerance for religious discussion, and it took all of it to keep smiling and quiet when he contacted Hitra's peers to arrange appointments.

He let the scroll spring back into a tube. It was just going to have to wait another day. Maybe it didn't matter. Maybe it would work itself out. He looked up at the ceiling and had a profound feeling of knowing exactly how much longer he'd be seeing it. One year minus ten days, and his life was going to start over again.

He tossed the scroll up and then panicked when he missed the catch, falling onto his side to fish it off the floor. It wasn't damaged. He slipped it back into its case.

He stretched on his stomach and closed his eyes. He reached out with his mind, felt for Hitra's presence, which was all he could do, his power so much less than hers. She was there, in range, not listening. I tried to put myself in his way, so he would touch me with his mind. I was as insubstantial to him mentally as physically. He felt Hitra's lack of attention. He reached out further, to the local router, and with his help, to his mother. She wasn't listening, either, though he thought he felt something deliberate in the silence. That was his imagination. Illoe didn't have the gift to feel such things.

Loata Middlemount was outside her usual routing area, negotiating with a clay-seller down by the west river. Illoe's mother never refused a call from him. She was rather the type to not-so-subtly hint that he should call more often.

He touched the router's mind again.

Put me through to location code 62.

Name please?

Just Router 62, please.

His brother's mind was almost unrecognizable in its business-like lilt. *Location 62, how may I direct your call?*

Ele, it's me.

There was a pause, and Illoe worried he'd lost the connection. *What, did someone die?*

Illoe mouthed the 'no' to himself and rolled over onto his back. His tunic was now bunched around his waist and his short trousers were riding up. His body was strong and fresh and full of energy. I could perfectly picture my hand on his thigh, but he didn't feel it.

I tried to call Mom, but she's not home. Could you have her call me? It's about my indenture and it's urgent.

I'm not your secretary. And I'm not supposed to take personal calls at work.

When you get home, tell her to call me. It won't kill you.

There was no reply.

Ele had not cut him off. He was merely silent. Ele listened to his brother's mind, half-formed thoughts breaking and reforming: heard Illoe give up and tell his local router to close the connection. Ele even heard Illoe try to think of someone else he could call. It was the most Ele had heard from his brother in four years, and he wondered why Illoe didn't have the decency to say something personal to Ele himself, instead of using him as a message service for their mother.

Ele was two years older than his brother, muscular, and not as pretty. He opened the eastern blind on his tower and let some air in, but it smelled of the market below, of rotting cabbages and gutted fish. He closed his eyes and ran his fingers over the routing tables that were carved in the sill around him. It helped.

Opening his mind, he felt others throughout the city: people whispering secrets, people demanding responses from estranged loved ones, people ordering fish-ball soup to be delivered. Wordlessly, he pushed thoughts to their destinations. The local arbiter, the baker on Laud Street: these were minds as familiar to him as his own. The hard part was keeping calm. He could not make an impression on the traffic, just pass it along, touch two minds and let them talk to each other. Boost the ungifted by repeating them. If he got emotional, the gifted would feel it and his supervisor would be contacted. If he got distracted or took too long, everyone in the chain would feel it and his supervisor would be contacted. His job was grueling and the only satisfactory performance was one no one noticed.

Illoe didn't understand that, and probably never would. Ele was good at his job. It took more than an adept's talent. It took patience, intelligence, a quick memory. And all of it came from within. Ele was nobody's creation, no one's man but his own.

That was what he told himself as he went back to his exhausting job. He never even thought about moving a message to the wrong mind or broadcasting juicy bits of gossip. He was disappointingly submissive.

☽O☾

Hitra sat against the wall in her sitting room, her robe tucked under her feet. The faces of her staff—young, serious—glowed in the candlelight. "Most scholars believe Elintar's line of fire represents the rising sun, that it's an allegory. In the Adept Council yesterday, it was proposed that Elintar had seen a natural phenomenon, something that would have occurred without divine force, but that the gods used as a sign. Did you all read the essay I told you about? 'Does Wenne Make the Sun Rise?'"

They watched her. They took in the words. They looked around the circle, wanting to see if someone else would speak first. Many of them had not read the essay, which started out with a dry chunk of astrological math explaining the rotation of the planet. One girl gave in and spoke, though she had just skimmed to the end. "Well, when I read the essay, I thought it was about how, um, you know, everything is a miracle in a way?"

Another girl perked up. "Yeah, I thought that, too. Like, knowing how a thing works doesn't make it less magical."

Hitra felt good. That was exactly the point of the essay! And her students were opening up, talking about important things: nature and spirituality and the divine. She waited for a lull to ask the next question, the important question. "Was the column of fire yesterday a sign from the gods?" Hitra held her breath, waiting. Unlike Illoe, she wanted, even needed, for answers to be more beautiful than banal. The possibilities, while unspoken, were perfect, enchanting, complete. Words would break them down, but—she hoped—through words something more beautiful would be created.

There was silence, eyes moving back and forth as each student tried to see what the others thought before answering.

"You're allowed to have an opinion. You all have as much right as I." Hitra turned to one of the acolytes, a recent and promising seminary graduate. "Jante, why do you suppose Wenne created her sign for Elintar? What was she trying to say?"

Jante rested her chin on her knee and said, "In the story, it's a warning. You can forget the gods, but the gods will not forget you."

One of the youth choir members rolled her lips inward, and Hitra prodded her to speak. "Well," she drew the word out slowly, a little afraid she'd be judged for her opinion, "I thought it was more about the Sanadaru and the Casu, about what makes us different. I mean, that's how my dad always talked about that story. The Sanadaru weren't punished for ignoring Wenne, the Casu were, because, you know, we're the ones who ought to know better."

"We have a special duty." Hitra held back the urge to say more. They had to come to their own conclusions. "That's right. What is our duty?"

Jante suppressed an urge to roll her eyes as the younger girls exchanged blank looks.

"To pray every day," one suggested.

"Jante?" asked Hitra, feeling her acolyte's irritation.

Do I have to answer this? It's humiliating when you want me to repeat your own words for you. Make someone else.

Hitra forgave Jante, having been in her shoes, and it had been a cheap tactic. She made sure to address the room, not Jante. "I know this is a basic lesson, but the first lessons are the most important. Let's look at what we learned as children, not what we've read in the latest broadsheet."

Jante gave in and spoke with lack of interest, "When Senne gave the children of Cassia the power to speak to the gods, she warned that we were indebted to use that power. Most people interpret that as needing to pray regularly, the Hushers say it means you're only supposed to use your mind to talk to the gods. The liberal sect—our sect—thinks it means we have a duty to advance science and knowledge."

Perhaps I was more naïve than Jante, but I had a feeling Hitra and her students would tease out exactly what was going on through questions and answers, one logical step at a time. I just had to wait, and listen.

A breeze fluttered the candles as the curtain separating the rest of the apartment from the front room drew back. Illoe's long leg stepped over a girl's outstretched foot. "Excuse me," he said, and proceeded to step stork-like over and between the gathered church youth.

A gentle ripple of giggles, appreciation, and whispers spread through the room along with an explosion of mental traffic. Illoe's presence drew more acolytes to Hitra's gatherings than the priest knew. The devout young women were urging each other to reach under his tunic, to trip him, to embarrass him and themselves in the fevered delight of humor and hormones.

You can practically see all the way up to his butt!

"Illoe, why don't you join us?" Hitra asked.

Fervent, explosive prayers of thanks fluttered from mind to mind, that Hitra had thought of that.

Fat chance, boss. He didn't need to be able to hear the thoughts bandying around him to know they were there. "I have to get some shopping done." He held his tunic against his thigh and stepped around Jante. "You're out of chalk."

"It can wait," Hitra said.

Illoe turned in place to give her the briefest and shallowest of bows. "It can't," he said. "I'll be back soon." *Do not force me to take part in this, Hitra. You won't like what I have to say.*

She grimaced at the edge in his thoughts. "All right," she said. "We'll talk later."

They are definitely lovers, Jante thought, bitterly.

Across the room, another girl yearned for Jante to look at her the way she looked at him, unaware that her best friend, sitting next to her like they always did, was thinking the same thing about her.

Illoe closed the door behind him, containing a room full of teen girl hormones. He had only a brief moment of relief before his eyes fell on another sign of danger.

There were arbiters hanging around the gardens, leaning on the low fences, their purple sashes shining in the sun like water. Illoe craned his head to see what the problem was. A crowd milled about the grass, some holding lanterns despite the bright sun. One man held a placard on his chest with a quote from scripture, "Her fire will seek out the abodes of sin." He was looking dourly at another man who carried a banner (badly draped) that read "Welcome The God With Joy." Both thought the other was incorrect in his interpretation of events and doctrine and were boiling with their inability to change the other's mind.

The center of the confusion was a circle in the grass, marked in orange paint. Small piles of flowers and paper icons littered the walks around it, but everyone had superstitiously avoided placing anything inside the circle. There was an argument between two arbiters and a knot of people holding candles. The question was whether a path should be kept clear for people wishing to see the circle and if so, which path. Illoe shook his head. He suspected they were the self-same fools that had fled the city the day before.

He cut through the gardens to the temple plaza, avoiding the thronged walkways by slipping between the flower boxes that blocked off the wide steps that ended — or began — Penitence Street. No one in the area thought it odd that a street should lead to steps, and that those steps should end in flower boxes. They'd all seen it too many times and so they'd stopped seeing it, but the unfinished look bothered me. No one around had a memory of why the stairs ended at nothing, why they were blocked off. Since they didn't know, I didn't know, and the realization of that was upsetting.

The acolytes' desires, the tourists' frustrations, they were clinging to me, like a hangover, or perhaps like still being drunk.

Illoe's mind was calm, prepared for the walk through the city, contemplative, like the minds of the laborers carrying burdens across the high square. A row of pillars prevented draft beasts from befouling the temple mount and everything the temple ordered from the city had to be carried by men.

The cobbles of Penitence follow a covered streambed; the water that once flowed overland now swept through masonry vaults underfoot. At the narrowing of the road, where it dipped sharply to the plaza below, the underground passage narrowed as well, to force the water through a wheel that powered Chagrin City's primary uphill transport, called the Water Car.

I could feel it — the tense water squeezing its way under stone in its passion for down. I felt it in a way none of the people walking above it could. A few were aware of the vibration under their feet, some excited by it, but most had traveled this road often and had long since stopped noticing. The water was powerful and dangerous. I felt the edge it gave even to unnoticing minds. I was moved to be passionate. I recalled the hunger for touch the girls had felt, unexplored cravings for untested flesh. I was hot with impatience and impotence. I wanted to touch, move, change. Was I a god or not?

I felt myself pressed on all sides, tight and fast and narrow. I brushed Illoe's cheek. The down of his young skin bent against my briefly-formed fingertips. The world froze in that moment, and I could count the hairs I'd touched (twenty-six) and I had had two fingertips. It was the briefest, gentlest touch.

Illoe toppled like a broken reed, the rough pavement tearing cells from his skin.

The sting of injury, however minor, drew Illoe into an unreasoning rage, jerking his limbs to strike imaginary foes. Bluster kept the tears back. He swore on "Revestre's Golden Tits" to beat the twelve bodily humors out of whoever had bumped him. He wanted, desperately, for someone to come forward, for a reason to hit and hurt. No one was near him. No one but me, and his fists passed through me without impact on either of us.

People were staring. He stood out on Temple Mount, in his secular clothes. It wouldn't take long for someone he knew to hear about him swinging at air and yelling at nothing. He wished the ground would swallow him whole.

But I'd touched him!

He stomped his way down to the market, feeling more embarrassed and less angry with each step. I had touched him. It just took focus. I flew with this new knowledge, expanded like steam. All the city was mine. I could touch things!

I poured myself back toward Illoe, who was bumping shoulders through the plaza to get to the water car. A woman "accidentally" brushed his leg, a subterfuge neither of them believed, and I was reminded how he'd fallen, and hurt—his wounds still smarted on his palms.

I should try someone I liked less, first.

$$\mathcal{D}\mathcal{O}\mathbb{C}$$

Arelandus Nereshore was having an argument with his wife, from an emotional distance. He felt his faith had been destroyed, and so it seemed a small thing that his wife looked at him with pursed lips, or turned her back on him after pouring tea. These small things would normally have driven him to distraction, he observed, detached, imagining himself insubstantial, cut off from all meaning. *He* felt he was broken apart from the world—the cheek! He had a luxury of touch I couldn't imagine. He sat, depressed the cushion under him, and his fingers sweated against his knee.

He'd been Mr. "I Know Everything" only one day ago.

Boda, the priest of their congregation, kept a neutral point between Arel and his wife, speaking to both though they did not speak to each other. "It's always been very kind of you to open your home to the community." She looked first to Arel, then to Debha. "It's your own decision, whether or not you want to do so in the future. No one is expecting you to always be available."

The harder I tried, the more my fist sailed through Arel. How had I done it with Illoe? Was it my emotional state, or my concentration? I had been fully invested in the surface of him.

Oblivious to my mounting frustration, Debha set the teapot in front of her husband. "We can host. This is just a temporary thing."

"No," Arel said, quieter. "No, I don't want meetings anymore."

Debha glared at Arel. Arel tried to look aloof. I hated them, how caught up they were in pettiness while I had a real problem. All three of them knew that Debha would not be asked to lead the study sessions without him. She was not loved by the community as he was. No one wanted to say it. She wanted to point out how she allowed the meetings at first as a concession to his ambitions, at a cost to her own. Because of it she was mocked, called husband-ruled, but bringing it up would be an argument against continuing the meetings, which was what she wanted.

It was all about their own self-importance. All of them. Arel was upset because it had been a full day and no gods had contacted him, personally. Debha was upset because she wanted to be prominent in the Husher community, and she couldn't do that while her husband was throwing a sulk. Boda needed them to get along so that she could continue to draw on Arel's fame as if it were her own.

Boda leaned forward and laced her fingers together. (Fingertips. Yes. I formed two, modeled on hers, carefully and slowly.) They all knew what she wanted to say, if not the exact words, so there was a feeling of friction to be gotten over before she got them out. "We haven't talked about the…protest."

She curled her lips inward and paused before her last word, expelling it out with a special gathering of courage. She wasn't sure if it should still be called "the protest" or some other, more significant word. Emotion spiked in the other two, though they made no move to show the big, ugly fears they shared but wouldn't acknowledge. Fears they couldn't articulate to themselves clearly enough for me to understand.

The protest. I was not there; I could only see it in their minds, and memories are fractious things. A blue shadow on white stone, a dog's bark: these things were clear, but the words on the sign he carried were forgotten. The sun shone its blessings with all the vigor of early spring, the cold days of winter fresh enough in mind to add an extra piquancy to the warmth. It was hardly past dawn, but already the shadows had lost their night chill, and he was hot from the long walk up to the temple district, to Uptown Square, eager for the cool press of stone, cobblestones dirty at the edges, columns marked with scrapes at the height of vendors' carts. These things he remembered clearly, and imbued with a glamor of importance. It was a historic day. The most historic.

I'd lost myself in pursuit of the memory, and lost my carefully won fingertips.

Boda continued to speak. "We talked before about the possibility of failure, remember? How the act itself was brave, the outcome not important? Some of us may have hoped our actions would change the world, but what we did changed how people think of Sectarians, and that is a victory, wouldn't you agree? We made them notice us."

Arel had been so sure they would succeed. He was a leader, his people were following him—his perfect, simple idea—and he was bursting with his own pride and belief. He was quiet when they spoke of caution and low expectations: failure wasn't a possibility. He'd turned his face up, toward the sun, felt its warmth, saw the red glow through his closed eyelids. He felt the uneven cobbles beneath his knees and the minds of his compatriots, of Boda and all the Adept Sectarians, their minds joining his, a chorus, a togetherness. They reached outward, borrowing each other's power, and probed past the familiar speech of Casu, past the simple thoughts of mountain sheep, far, far, farther, feeling for the minds of the gods. The only proper use of the gifts of Senne.

...In his opinion, anyway. As Senne, my opinion should matter more, having given telepathy to humanity, and I felt it was perfectly fine to use your mind to order fish balls. Fish balls have to be gotten somehow. There was something dark and violent in the way the sectarians thought of propriety... that life should be narrowly defined, that ordinary, quiet errands could be imbued with evil.

Debha looked directly at her husband. "I think it's important, in light of what has happened, to keep up appearances, keep up activity. We don't want people saying the fire on the mountain was a sign of the gods' approval of Ritualist ways." She turned to the priest. "Frankly, I think we should claim it as a sign of our own."

"It's not that easy," Boda was half panicked, realizing this was her responsibility, as the only official priest in the room, "putting words in the mouth of Wenne. What if blame falls on us? What if this isn't..." she struggled to find the word, "benevolent?"

Arel raised his head. "It wasn't a sign. It didn't feel right."

His wife narrowed her eyes at him, but spoke to Boda, "I'm not saying it was a sign or not, but if it was, there's nothing that says it was in support of the Ritualist sect."

Boda fussed with her teacup. "I and the church leaders have all been studying our scriptures for occurrences of this sort. There's a very similar column of fire in Elintar's scripture, marking the place where Wenne would meet the prophet and give her the four laws. While a similar fire appearing on Temple Mount might be taken as a sign the gods approve of the priests there, the lowland translation includes a warning that Wenne would come to earth again only at the end of days, and in a place of great sin."

"A place of great sin!" Debha clapped her hands and gestured like she was clearing the subject off the table. "It couldn't be clearer. The gods are on our side, and they want the corrupt church to fall. Someone should write a broadsheet. Arel could help."

Arel tried not to look at his wife. "The fire in Elintar's story marked the location at which the god would meet her chosen prophet. Wenne would be announcing that her next prophet will meet her on the grounds of the Ritualist temple. Even if I thought we could explain this so easily, I wouldn't want that interpretation."

Though, he started to think, if it was an invitation to meet the god, someone—he—could go to the temple. He shied away from the thought, disgusted with his own egotism.

"There are other fires in scripture," Boda said. The others looked at her blankly, and she shifted in her seat. There had been another, hadn't there? A good one. Her memory was fractious as well, recalling clearly the feeling of certainty, as she discussed and read with her colleagues, but not what was written on the pages before her. "Well, in Feyate's final apocrypha, there's an encouraging account of Senne sending fire down as a punishment."

Arel squinted at the priest. "Feyate's fire destroyed a temple."

She hated how fast he'd answered. She'd hate it more if she knew he hadn't studied the night before like she had. "True, but it is a reference where fire was used as a negative sign."

Debha stood, reached for the teapot, realized it had not been touched and therefore did not need replenishing, and so waved her hands over it. "We should have the community talk about this. We'll host the scripture meeting. Arel's just feeling beside himself. Once everyone is here, he'll feel better."

Arel shook his head. He didn't care about the meeting, or the column of fire, which seemed such a flimsy thing now that it didn't suit his beliefs. "We tried to touch the minds of the divine, and we felt nothing. Nothing." Like a child reaching under the bed, expecting fur, claws, the slither of a tentacle, all imagination was not so horrid as that nothing. Either there was nothing, or it was something they could not, could never, perceive. He'd hoped the fire was a repudiation of that horror, but now it had come and gone.

"But I'm here," I said. I waved at them. I might have been a breeze. Arel looked distractedly around, sensing something. I was close. I needed to concentrate.

Boda cast a pitying glance at Debha, who was caught wanting that pity and also detesting it, fiddling with the tea things and trying to come up with some other subject of conversation. "Well," Debha said, "with Harvest Home upon us, it should be easier to find candy in the shops. We should have a sweets-hunt for the children, don't you think?"

Boda and Arel were momentarily united in disbelief and annoyance, but there was no going back. Debha continued to outline a series of activities around the coming holiday in a loud and artificially chipper voice until there was nothing to be done but for Boda to agree to put it forth to the congregation if Arel would agree to discuss it in the meetings of the laity.

My fingertips poked and prodded, unfeelingly, at Arel's stubbled jaw. This was getting nowhere. Perhaps I could only be sensed by Illoe.

Chapter Three

Families

I found Illoe about to turn onto his parents' street, Angletide, a narrow walkway with an unreadable sign. No one knew or cared where Angletide was but the people who lived along it.

I wanted to touch him again, but I didn't want to rush it and drop him on the pavement. Or, worse, fail. Laundry hung overhead on ropes, festooned like festival lanterns. Thinking about how it had felt to brush his cheek, I tapped gently at a sock. It flew off the line and over a nearby building, hitting a chimney and tumbling out of sight.

"Did you see that?!" I shouted. Adults and children and animals went about their lives up and down the street, carrying burdens and conversations, unaware of my amazing sock trick. Only a bird turned her head at my shout. But this was good. I could touch things other than Illoe. That reminded me of touching Illoe, which I definitely wanted to do again.

Illoe tugged his tunic hem and knew he stood out on Angletide in a completely different way than he did on Temple Mount. He was a beacon of cleanliness, costly dye, and bare legs. Most women and all men on the street wore worker's slacks.

Inspired, I pushed a gust of wind up his leg, flipping the hem to his great embarrassment. A woman whistled from her doorstep and laughed, one arm around her dog, as he hurried faster.

That was an actual trick. I had done a trick. I had brought chaos and amusement! It... probably wasn't anything to write down in the legend of the great trickster god, but it was a start.

Though it had never been very wide, Illoe could swear the street had narrowed in his absence. He thought similarly about the minds of the people who lived there. He should have worn leggings. I floated in his wake. I had volume. The wind was a part of me, that was how it worked. Illoe counted the doorposts as dried leaves scattered in front of us both. The address number had been painted anew over his mother's gate. The darkened courtyard behind smelled of boiled cabbage and sour milk. A flock of clay ducks huddled in the western corner, against the steps. I hit them with leaves. Illoe hit the chimes. After a while, the downstairs neighbor shuffled forward on her swollen feet. "Can I help you, young man?"

"It's me, Illoe, Hela. I'm here to visit my mother."

The elderly woman squinted. "Illoe? Blessed Mother, it is you! Oh, just a minute..." she fumbled with the iron gate latch. "Look at you!" She marveled, hands clasped to her chest. "Oh, after that horrible fire it's a miracle every minute. Come in, come in and give your old Aunt Hela a hug."

She was his mother's landlady, not an aunt, and her arms smelled of stale sweat, but he gave the obligatory hug in return. She, too, had shrunken in his absence. He looked down at the dander on her scalp, and she felt fragile under her thin tunic, like dried wheat. "Is my mother home?"

"Oh, dear, I don't know. She and your father went to the docks this morning. Why don't you head on upstairs and check? And can you ask her for a cup of rice flour for me? My son-in-law hasn't come with the groceries yet this week and I'm starting to panic."

She was about to enter into a long tale of woe, and Illoe seemed to sense it as clearly as I did. "I'll ask her." He extricated himself from her grasp to jump over the bottom stairs.

"Be careful!" the old woman shouted after him.

His hem fluttered high enough to expose the sweet, firm curve at the top of his thigh as he climbed, unaware of how marvelous it was, that each stone step pressed back against his sandals without the need to think them into being.

The door at the top of the stairs was marked with a dried knot of grass, a symbol of Revestre, probably put there by his father. Illoe hoped he wasn't home. He knocked.

His father answered the door with a blank expression that deepened immediately into anger. "Illoehenderen! What in the name of all the gods are you doing here? Does your mistress know you're here?"

Illoe wished his body could collapse into a single point. Could his father have said "mistress" any louder? "Hello, Father. Is Mom home? We need to talk."

His father's fingers dug tightly into his arm. "Get in here before the neighbors see you."

"Hela wants a cup of rice flour," Illoe said, as his father closed and locked the door behind him. "And it's nice to see you, too."

His father shook Illoe's arm, his fingernails separating the meat of Illoe's bicep with burning points. "You're not supposed to come here. Not unannounced. Have you angered the priest?"

"You're hurting me. No. Hitra knows I'm here. When's Mom coming back?"

There was a familiar bang: his mother closing her kiln. "Uja? Is someone here?"

His father let go of him. "If you upset your mother, I will not forgive you."

Illoe rubbed the finger-sized red marks on his arm and turned his full attention on the door that led to his mother's workshop.

She emerged, picking dried clay from her fingers. "Illoe! Baby!" She reached out her hands.

Illoe stepped forward and let his mother hug him. "Hi, Mom," he said. Her shoulder shook against him. She was crying. "Mom," he said, slowly, and caught his father's glare from across the room. He pressed his cheek against her curly hair, which smelled wonderfully of her, of clay and paint. He felt sick and weak with hate and helplessness in the face of his father, and his mother's fussing made blood rush to his cheeks.

"We were so worried! Oh, you're hurt!" She brushed the blooming bruises on his arm and took hold of his hand, examining the scraped skin like his life might expire from it. "Was it the fire?"

The scraped skin was from me, of course, and I was momentarily glad not to be visible.

Illoe's mother continued, breathlessly breaking off her own sentences, "...I know they said no one was hurt and not to call...oh I should have talked to you! But you know your father..."

Illoe tracked the movements of his father, a large man in a small

40

room. Uja had crossed the space in two loping steps and was extracting the broom from its nook with motions sharpened by anger and a desire to be seen. He wanted everyone in the room to see he was getting the broom, once again, to clean up the thoughtless mess his wife had made, once again.

Loata Middlemount leaned back and brushed under her eyes with her sleeve. "It's just so good to see you. Oh, you look so, so..." She held him out at arm's length like a work of art.

Illoe could see his father, bent over the dustpan, thinking of a few descriptive words for his son: Tarted up. Spoiled. Illoe tugged his hem down again. How sticky the world of a family was, full of complications and tangled ghosts of old arguments. Was that how it was between me and Wenne? Was I the only one who had forgotten?

"I've just got a few minutes, Mom." Her eyebrows canted away from each other. He hurriedly added, "Can I see what you've been working on?"

Her face brightened, and he knew he'd made the right move. He followed her through the narrow passage originally meant as a dining area for the apartment; it was now filled with rough drying racks that left only enough room for one person at a time to enter the apartment's fire pantry, which was also his mother's workroom.

She led him to the washboard, which was slick with mud. "I just got the greatest order from a Sanadaru trader. They have a celebration of their own coming up soon, and they need drinking vessels." She held up two oddly shaped cups and rotated them. "Aren't they cute? *Karranga*, they call them, or something like that. They have to be made so they can't stand on their own."

They both heard a slam, the closing of the dustbin. "That's really great, Mom. I'm glad you have work." He closed his eyes before speaking. "Mom, why did you write it into my contract that I have to get married before I'm free?"

He opened his eyes again and saw his mother hadn't moved. She still had the peculiar, conical clay cups in her hands. She looked at the washboard, as though searching for something. Mostly Loata was looking for an excuse not to answer.

"Mom, I want the contract changed. Now, before it's stuck like this."

"Your father and I think the contract is best left alone."

"But I don't."

She set the clay cups down. I gave them the gentlest poke. They rolled toward the slip and she had to pick them up again to set on their lips. Another trick!

"I don't think... I mean... We should trust the priest."

"Hitra is not prepared to arrange a marriage for me. Even if she were, I've already been a woman's property for the past four years. I'd like a chance to be my own for a little while."

"Marriage is not like that. It's not...what you're afraid of."

His mother looked abruptly behind him, her eyes tracking to her husband's position as he silently demanded details on what they were talking about. Illoe closed his eyes again. He knew, as usual, that he could not compete with his father. "This is my life we're talking about."

His mother refocused her eyes on him. "You'll be happier married. And the priest can find you a much better wife than we could."

"It's your job to represent me in this contract. I don't want this clause in. Represent me!"

His voice had raised, and he instantly regretted it. His mother looked helplessly at the washboard, her face wrinkled. Her hands were shaking. "Mom..."

She crouched down and pretended to be checking the fire in the kiln. "We'll see you at Harvest Home this year? Won't that be nice? It's so much nicer to get together at the holidays. People have something to distract them."

"Yeah," Illoe said. "We'll do that." He backed out of the fire pantry.

Illoe's father was standing like an icon in the center of the front room, his broom planted like a spear at his side. "You upset your mother."

Thanks for eavesdropping, Illoe thought. "Would it kill you to support me in this? It isn't going to affect your precious stipend, just my life. All Mom has to do is talk to Hitra. It would take five minutes."

"Your mother sacrificed her own good name to secure your future happiness, and you come here, parading our shame in front of the neighbors."

"I'm supposed to feel guilty because I remind people you sold me?"

His father felt his anger trip over to a new, higher level. "Get out of my house."

"Have I ever failed in my duty as a son? Ever?"

"Out."

Illoe balled his fist. He could sense his mother, not moving in the room behind him, and he knew he couldn't win. He couldn't win because in his father's world, everything was exactly right. He nodded and walked past his father without another word.

As he set his hand on the banister, his mother sent him a weak *It's for the best, it really is. Your father is right. It's safer...*

This time, he got to be the one who refused to answer. His mother believed he was better off, protected from the common faults of young men, locked into a future that had no choice but to lead to marriage, but Illoe couldn't see her mind like I could—he believed she was a coward, too afraid of her own husband to act. The truth was, she didn't fear Uja; she was grateful for his anger and bluster because she could hide behind it and not be held responsible for getting what she wanted.

Hela stood at the base of the steps, her little hands before her chest, grasping air. "No flour," Illoe said, and strode through the gate before he could be stopped.

☽O☾

When Illoe got back to the temple complex, Hitra's chambers were empty. The gathering had cleared out, leaving a wake of overturned cushions, crumbs, and half-empty teacups. He pulled back the tapestries to let the sun in once again. His arms looked lovely with light picking out the curves of muscle, however long shadows stretched out from the mess, making it look worse. A scrap of parchment lay on the dining table, splattered with wax: *Gone to Council. Sched. mtng w/ Jante & Gauta 3 tomorrow. Where is appointment book?*

He scraped the wax with his fingernail and balled the parchment up to toss in the fire. This, he thought, was the woman his mother was

43

too timid to negotiate with: one who couldn't plan her day without him.

) O (

The Council of Temple Adepts met in earnest, in the squat, round room that served as their chamber. Almost everyone didn't want to be there, but I went because I was supposed to be interested in intrigue and influencing people, and anyway, even a god likes to hear others talk about her.

Hitra found the junior priest of Nolumbre had also shown up early, and so moved quickly to bend her ear. She hoped for some solidarity of station at least, for though there was no high priest of Revestre to stand over her, Hitra was also officially a "junior." Nolumbre was God of the East, of Waterfalls, Messengers, and Motion. Her priests tended to be young, eager, and open to dramatic action.

"Stata! Just the woman I wanted to see. How's your congregation holding up?"

Stata smiled. "It's a storm waiting to break. I hope Reha has something better to say today."

Exactly the impatience Hitra was hoping for. "Do you think she'll outline a course of action?"

"We had better pray she does! It wouldn't take a column of fire for some of us to hear the gods. You don't get any more blatant than that."

Hitra scented a possible conflict in that certainty. "Blatant? In what way?"

"The gods want change. Between you and me, it's time Reha let someone who cares about tradition take over as Ritual Celebrant."

Hitra kept smiling, though an automatic tightening happened at the back of her throat. "Yes, well, I think what we really need is for Reha to be active." The last thing they needed was to get caught up in a change of leadership. Hitra scanned the room for other priests to talk to. The elderly Daughter of Hinna was there, and the male priests of Darian. Good, moderate people.

"It was a mistake to make a reformist Celebrant in the first place," Stata continued.

Hitra was, herself, a reformist, and wondered briefly if there was some failing in her that everyone didn't know that. "If we speak as one voice, the Rit—"

"Of course, the very idea that anyone would try to use this for political gain just sickens me. We can't afford to think of ourselves as reformists, conservatives, moderates; we are one church and should stand as one church. But you know Reha, she'll keep spouting her reform party line without a thought."

"Excuse me, won't you? I need to talk to the Sons of Darian. Don't know when I'll catch them again."

Stata, along with several other minds I touched, was prepared for a battle, clinging to certainties against whatever anyone else might say. There was nothing I could work with to create mischief, much less the consensus Hitra was hoping for.

Hitra wove through the wooden benches. Some priests had dropped their outer robes to mark their places. She noted the colors and symbols. Seating was not assigned and so could be a sign of shifting alliances.

Boss? Illoe's voice whispered in her ear.

Busy. She touched her heart reverentially as she approached the elderly male priest of Darian, who returned the gesture. He was a sweet old man.

Just wanted you to know your date book is on your desk. And you had a note on today, something about thorns?

Thanks. She closed the connection. The priest before her hadn't noticed her absence of mind. She smiled in relief and greeting.

Reha arrived late to call the meeting to order. The council room had begun to stink of sweat and perfume. There were no windows into the chamber, an ancient conceit of secrecy, which Hitra hated, but I rather liked: all these people encapsulated together, pretending these walls contained them, while their outreaching minds pierced the boundary without pause. I should do something to show the hypocrisy. A glamorous work of public art. I looked for someone tractable. My dumb high priest was there. Now, what could I force her to do? She was annoyingly attentive to the Ritual Celebrant.

Reha began with a speech about the importance of their role in the community. It was mostly words Reha had spoken before. There was an old joke in the mind of more than one attendee that Reha had only three speeches: The Importance of Our Role in the Community, What Makes a Ritual Sacred, and The Meaning of Faith. Sometimes she would mix them, but in the end, the morals were always the same.

"Remember the first time you ever saw a priest. The wonder, the majesty, the higher moral code — whatever it was that first made you wonder, 'could I be like her?', that is what you must be to the public. That is why we hold off judgment until we can be as certain in our words as we are in the power of the gods themselves."

Reha was working through her favorite material. She leaned on the podium, her head tilted to the side in an affectation of informality. "You are my sisters, and brothers," she added, nodding to the male priests, who were together against the back wall, and hoping they didn't notice the pause. "I value the opinions of each and every one of you. Let us talk openly, and frankly. Get it all out, so that when we leave this room, we present a united face of faith to the nation, and the people, of Casu. Now," she smiled and leaned back. "Talk to me."

There was a vacuum of thought. If I could have been sure to be heard, even I didn't know what to say.

Hitra was irritated. She found Reha's separation of the nation and the people subtly bigoted.

This felt like the sort of thing a trickster god could work with. In secular politics, Reha was a member of the Reform party, the same as Hitra, and so Hitra viewed Reha as a sometimes-ally, when church and secular policies met. Inside the party, however, Hitra was Liberal and Reha was Moderate, so they could sometimes be enemies. If I could figure out a way to make them attack one other... well, then what?

Quite frankly, there was a tedious array of political parties, religious sects, sub-sects, and movements. Hitra swam through this quagmire, at home in her environment and her role. I wish I felt the same.

Not a single priest recalled the protest that was so monumental to Arel and his friends. They were wholly uninterested in finding events in the past to explain the fire column. Discussion centered on how to use the sign and disruption to further their pet causes.

I concentrated on moving tips of sleeves and the robes around their feet. Not very dignified, I know, but I was gaining control, and it gave me something to do while I was thinking.

I managed to get a few priests to think the person next to them had poked or pinched them, and I knocked over a stylus-case which got the High Priest of Dioneltar convinced the Junior Priest of Nolumbre was out to get her. So that was something.

I wondered what Illoe was doing.

At seventh hour a call came that the priests were dining in council. There was barely enough time to pack a meal for Hitra, but Illoe did a remarkably good job, if he did say so himself. He tucked in a note with her current schedule changes, some fresh fruit, and her favorite sachet. He could only imagine how the council chamber smelled; one of the orders, he forgot which one, did not require their priests to bathe daily.

He worried he'd taken too long, but when he got to the corridor outside the council chamber, the doors were still locked. Servants sat cross-legged along the walls, baskets, bowls, and trays of food near them or in their laps.

"Hey," he said to the skinny girl who served the Priest of Telumene, because he recognized her, and because she was blocking his path.

She rolled her head against the wall. "Why does the owned boy get to show up late to the great wait?"

"Good to see you too." Illoe stepped over her outstretched legs. He'd stand next to the guys. They were at least subtle about showing their dislike for him. His best friend, Oke, wasn't there. Of course. He was still in the kitchens, cleaning the pots that had steamed the buns and roasted the meat pies each servant had in his or her basket.

Illoe nodded to the freckled kid who served Reha. He was a nobleman's son and sort of in the opposite situation: hated for being too high for his position rather than too low. Eiti was his name, and he returned the nod, albeit with fear.

Don't worry; I won't try to make conversation. Illoe set his foot against the wall and waited for the council chamber doors to open.

Someone muttered, "I'd better get paid overtime for this."

I slid a finger down the fullest point of Illoe's left calf. I felt him feel it. The muscle twitched. Illoe assumed it was the girl sitting on the floor next to him and resolved to ignore it.

I considered the girl. Should I pinch her and make her mad at Il-loe or could I make her think he was propositioning her, and which would be more chaotic?

The doors opened. The priests poured out as servants shook their tired legs and straightened trays.

Hitra was one of the last out, to Illoe's unsurprise and disgruntle-ment. She contacted him with her mind before they were in arm's reach. *Everyone has had just enough time to research a personal theory. If two people in that room have the same one, I haven't noticed.*

Illoe held up his basket, and she took it. All around there was a susurrus of items changing hands, quick questions, and agreements. *"I cleared the appointments you made. Just let me know when you're coming home."*

She unfolded the napkin around the meat pie, but it flopped back in her way as she tried to take a bite. *As soon as I know. It could be days. I wanted Reha to declare the fire not a miracle, plain and simple. Now I just hope I can get the church to officially say we don't know. I think I have Ecthetar's contingent on my side, but if it's put to a vote, they'll play the party line, I just know it.* Illoe took the pie from her, refolded the napkin around it with one side exposed, and handed it back. She dug into it. Illoe tried not to smile at the picture she made, a priest of the temple, leaning against a wall and scarfing her lunch like a student. *The re-formers and the old guard are both speaking in carefully couched bi-partisan nothings. No one wants to be caught with an opinion. So we argue texts and translations while personal theories are treated like they arose in a political vacuum.*

She was gesturing as she thought, a habit more common among the non-adept than a high-level priest, and an herb dangled from her lips. Illoe gave her his best smirk and scratched the same spot on his face until her eyes widened and she wiped the offending leaf away.

He took the crumb-filled napkin from her. *Boss, not only are you not supposed to tell me details like that, I really couldn't care less.*

He unscrewed the cap from the bottle he'd brought and she took it from him. Her head jerked. *Blessed Mother, they're calling us back al-ready!*

He repositioned himself to be squarely between her and the door to the council chamber. "Take the rest in with you and chew more slowly."

She slumped into a smile. "Thank you. For still being you."

Stop. I'm the mean man who makes you take care of yourself. Now get back in there and overwhelm those priestly minds.

She nodded and stepped around him, drawn in with the tide of robes and headdresses. He hung against the wall until the corridor was mostly clear. Some of the priests stayed out to hunch over their boxed lunches. He imagined Hitra ate hers standing, flitting from one knot of discussion to the other. *That was exactly what I saw her doing, albeit not with the frenzied energy Illoe pictured.*

Illoe was the last servant to leave the corridor, but then, unlike the others, he didn't have another life to go home to.

☽○☾

Hitra finally came home at tenth hour. Illoe woke when she bumped the end of the couch he had fallen asleep on. He smeared his hand over the small drool spot he'd left on the upholstery. "Boss, it's..." he squinted for the clock.

"Late. Shh... go back to sleep. I'm heading to bed myself. Ow!" She hopped on one foot, trying to take her sandal off without stopping to sit, and fell onto the couch.

The flint striker had been lying next to his belly. Illoe fumbled for it and lit the oil lamp on the low table. Hitra bent to untwist her trailing sleeve from the table legs. She had it free by the time he'd lit the rest of the lamps. "Boss, you should use the guide light."

"It went out." She looked up at him pathetically through mussed hair. "Oh gods, I could kill Reha for keeping us there all day. At the end, people were agreeing just so she would let us go." She massaged the sandal-strap impressions in her feet. "It's a coward's tactic."

Illoe re-lit the guide light in its niche by the door. "You have no one but yourself to blame if you're tired, because I know you fought every second." He stood a moment, holding the flint striker in front of him like a blessing staff. "You should be wearing one of those big hats, you know. You do more than some High Priests."

She looked down, and Illoe imagined her shadowed face bore an expression too sad to see. This wasn't true; she was smiling at the

49

compliment. Illoe was turning into a handsome man, and that was exactly why she knew she had to tell him she was developing feelings a priest should not have for her servant. Thinking this, she got up and moved as quickly as she could away from him. She grabbed hold of her sleeves and shrugged out of her over-robe. "Two days of this. My schedule's ruined into next week."

"Beyond that. Next week starts the build up to Harvest Home. Don't forget, you'll be bringing out the sheaves." Illoe picked up the guide candle from its niche by the door and followed her. "Let's get you to bed."

Illoe lit the hallway lantern and the candle on Hitra's desk while she meekly crawled into bed. He went back to the front room for her robe, and by the time he returned to her bedroom she had the covers pulled up and thoughts of his youthful body thoroughly banished from her mind. Mostly.

Hitra lifted and rearranged her pillow. "Your mother called."

Illoe draped the heavy robe on Hitra's clothing trunk. "She did?" The relief was such that he almost couldn't stand. He sat down on the foot of the bed. "What did she say?"

"She wanted to know if you really did have my permission to go visit her today."

"Oh. You... you didn't say 'yes'?"

Hitra waved one hand in a weary imitation of a scolding. "I will have to perform three rituals of contrition tomorrow, young man. You made a consecrated priest lie for you, and in a telepathic link, no less."

"Great." Illoe tapped the flint-striker against his palm. "That's all?" He wanted to bring up the contract, he knew he should, but he felt put-upon that he had to, that his mother hadn't done it for him.

"You're lucky I have the power to do it." She pressed her chin against her chest. "Would you take that look off your face? I told her of course I knew you went to see her, that you had my express permission. She thanked me and closed the connection." She turned her head to press her cheek against the pillow. "Revestre will forgive me. If you ever want to visit your mother, all you have to do is tell me. I'm not going to say 'no'."

"Did she say anything else?"

"Hrm? No. I don't think your mother likes talking to me. Asked her question, thanked me, left." Hitra yawned and spoke into the fabric. "Snuff the lights for me?"

He pulled the top sheet over her shoulder with weary resignation. "I'll schedule time for your acts of contrition tomorrow before breakfast."

"You're a cruel man," she muttered into her pillow, and fell asleep.

☽○☾

Night is never as calm as it looks. Insomniacs stare at walls; deliverymen go about finishing the day's work or getting a start on the next. My sisters wandered the sky, passing through dreams and prayers and fears. They were getting more distinct now, but still wavering, like figures seen through sheets of ice. I was waiting to approach them until I had some solid knowledge, some advantage to use. They would be expecting tricks from me.

Looking out on the deserted High Street Circle, beyond Penitence Gate, which was closed, separating the Temple from the City for the night, a man stood with a placard about his neck and crystal lanterns at his feet. The candles cast small circles of warmth and color in an area made large and grey by night. The placard said "The God Has Had Enough! Sinners Make Peace." The last three words were cramped, 'peace' especially being near illegible, squeezed into the last bit of space. The effect was of an idea fizzling out. He had been surrounded by others all day, other placards, other candles and signs. He was proud to have lasted into the night. He was also cold, tired, alone, and wondering if he was wrong

In the Middle-City Hospital, an old man screamed, certain he was dying. The night nurse was more certain he was not. The trouble in his stomach was understood, but though a hospital full of telepaths would rather give him the teas that cause sleep and ease pain, the decision had been made that such were too dangerous for this patient. The night nurse had explained it to him many times, and given him a bag of soothing salts to smell and an extra blanket. Still he howled as much as breath allowed, pausing now and again as a child would, regaining strength, annoyance his only weapon against the cruel and uncaring nurse.

So much misery, and no one doing anything about it. It took just a pinch of my will, compressing the airway inside his throat, to halt him, and his body settled down into sweat-stained pillows. He should have had a soul, a mind freed from his suffering, floating out and away, but somehow, I missed it.

Chapter Four

Visitation

Somehow, I missed it.

In the watery predawn light, Hitra stumbled out of the bathroom. She closed the door and then turned to put her hand on it, as though surprised it was solid.

Illoe came into the bedroom, stopped, and turned his head aside. Then looked again, just long enough to verify that his mistress was, indeed, naked. His blood rushed to his skin and parts of him swelled and he felt flushed full of sensation, the hyper awareness of her nearness, of the air on her skin, and the horror that his body was reacting and she would see.

All of this swirling inside him, while she stared at her hand on the wood of the door, wondering at the ordinariness of both.

The time at which it was appropriate to say something passed. Illoe cleared his throat and Hitra, for the first time, noticed he was there. "I heard voices," he said. She pointed at the door. He reached for it.

"No!" she cried, but he opened it. She was startled by the steamy view of ceramic-coated brick, the recessed tub in the floor with the water mirror-still. The room was empty.

He peered into each ordinary corner, then returned with a towel. He held it toward her. His emotions were squirming around in his mind with thoughts about propriety and where to set his eyes and how he could pretend not to notice the wet, bare flesh in front of him. It helped pull his thoughts away from her body that she was so obviously distressed. He finally set his eyes on hers, which were darting around, frightened. His eyebrows, pretty and dark, crinkled together.

"Are you all right?"

Her thoughts were too disordered for me to pick apart. "What did you see?"

For an anxious second, he thought she meant what he saw of her body, but then his mind caught up. He turned his head. "In the bathroom? Was it a spider? A snake? I didn't see it."

Hitra sat down at her desk. Her hands shook. She took out a fresh parchment and overturned the stylus jar. Illoe went into the bathroom again. She heard him drain the tub and run a brief spate of water. The sound was exactly normal: a groan of metal, a high-pitched squeak, and the silver-cold sound of water.

She fumbled with the stylus, trying to fit it into the cleaner. It clattered to the desk, playing out a series of nulls and sets like footprints as it rolled. She grasped her hands together to stop them from shaking and looked down. "I'm naked."

"I noticed," Illoe said. The bathroom door squeaked on its hinge. He tossed her robe to her. It fluttered open and sailed briefly, then caught against some unseen thickness of air (not me) and fell into a curve of white on the patterned carpet. Illoe rubbed his nose, feeling helpless even to hand a robe properly. "I'll, uh, I'll go wait in the anteroom."

"No!"

Illoe was hopelessly confused. Hitra was too upset for it to be some random bug or pest sneaking into the bath, and there had been nothing out of place that he could see. "Hitra, really, what's wrong?"

"Just...don't leave me alone right now." She crossed a hand over her breasts and bent to pick up the robe. "I'm sorry. I'm sorry, I don't know what..." She shrugged into the robe and stared at the bathroom door. It was open. Inside, the same ordinary light reflected condensation on the brass fittings and glass tile. She tied the robe shut in front of her.

"I'll get you some tea," Illoe said, "and tell Maede you can't make it to breakfast."

"No!"

"Hitra," he crossed the space between them and retied her robe sash so that the knot was properly formed, not on its side. "The fire pantry is right there. I'll be in earshot the entire time. You need tea."

Her waist was constricted under the sash. He had tied it tighter than she would have. She touched the satin bow, flattened it to her stomach. "Yes, good idea. Thank you, Illoe. I'll..." A single droplet of moisture ran down the bathroom wall, over the tub, collecting smaller droplets as it fell. The wall was unquestionably solid. She expected it to tear at any moment like a film. Why did she think that? She turned her head to the left and saw the red brick of the fire pantry, likewise solid. Hitra sighed. "I'll get dressed."

She watched Illoe test the fullness of the tea kettle, then, with a perverse feeling like she wasn't controlling her own actions, she walked into the bathroom. She touched the wall. It was cold. She pressed her fingers until they turned white and then pink under the nails.

She went to her chest of clothes and dressed by habit, but she felt they were the clothes of a stranger. She watched her feet on the patterned carpet of her room and the mosaic tile of the anteroom.

This was maddening. I was supposed to know everything and I couldn't know what happened if she didn't think about it!

Illoe arranged a breakfast for her on the dining table. He set her calendar next to the tea, a neat line through her first appointment. "Maede sends her regrets." He drew the chair out for Hitra. "Insincere, of course. She thinks I'm holding you hostage. You owe me for making me talk to that woman so early on a weekday."

Illoe, she realized, was playing at being Illoe. Cheerful, joking. She felt an odd sort of companionship in that, and took a long sip of tea. "I..." The tea burned her palms through the cup, but she held it tightly, for the reality of it. "I saw my god. I saw Revestre in the bathroom."

"What? Was she using the..." he stopped on the cusp of an off-color joke when she looked up at him. His smile lingered despite the emotion behind it fading into confusion. He did not have an interpretation for her words, joke or otherwise. He moved the pot of honey closer to her. "Maybe you shouldn't go in to the office today."

"No. Maybe. Yes." Tea sloshed onto her hand as she set the cup down. She pressed the scalded back of her thumb to her lips. "What are my appointments?"

Illoe pointed at the paper beside her plate. "You have that meeting scheduled in the low chapel at third hour; I had to put it right after the ritual. Then you have reform committee meeting, choir, orthodox committee meeting, residential board meeting, and dinner with your mother. It's all on the calendar."

She stood. "Cancel everything. I'm going to see Reha."

"Hitra, maybe you should wait..." He followed her to the door, but she didn't look back.

He leaned against the closed door a moment, letting the cool morning chill bleed through to his forehead and hands, repeating a silent mantra: *She's my boss. She's my boss. She's my boss.*

It didn't matter if she went mad, or if her dark nipples and heavy breasts swung in front of his face, he had to keep her working.

☽○☾

In Hitra's memory, at last I see it: a fan of light, as of a blind being raised, and then a penetrating warmth, the sponge turning cold against her arm, the water rippling on the surface of the tub, a reflection forming in the water. Hitra raised her head.

The memory stopped. Hitra flinched away from what came next. It started again. I watched it four times while she hurried through the morning chill into the center of the temple complex.

☽○☾

Illoe finished Hitra's untouched tea. He'd spent a long time going over the bathroom for spiders, other freakishly ugly insects, or loose tiles, to no avail.

Hitra forgot appointments, stayed late at charitable events, made him keep track of the names of hundreds of people she thought were important, but she wasn't a nut. Illoe concluded, correctly, that something had happened to her, and it would be some time before he understood what, exactly. Perhaps a form of hallucination brought on by overwork or some cruel prank by a fellow adept. He incorrectly assumed whatever it was would be forgotten by the weekend, along with the mysterious fire, which he expected to survive only as the sort of unexplained phenomena people tell each other about simply because it is unbelievable. He had no idea how huge the column of fire was already in the minds around him. I suspected he was exactly as wrong about Hitra's event.

In the kitchens and laundry, all was noise and steam, the servants of the temple filling orders that had been delayed by the previous days' confusion. Even Oke, who was a renowned shirker, didn't have time for more than a shrug and a smile when Illoe stopped by his station. The only topic of discussion was the column of fire.

"We're going to mark our days from it," a delivery boy said. "The fire. I don't know about you, but I feel different about everything."

The boy who said this lifted a basket of bread onto the same shelf he'd lifted one onto the day before and the day before that, and would lift it again tomorrow. Illoe leaned toward Oke. "I can't believe people are still going on about that."

"You're joking. It's the only news," Oke said. "Hold this a second." He handed Illoe a steel pot that was bigger, almost, than he was.

Illoe struggled to keep the huge, heavy thing steady while Oke ducked inside with a scrub brush. "Can't you set this on the floor?"

"No. It'd mark up the tile. Tilt it higher. There." Oke's voice echoed and was followed by vigorous brushing sounds. Oke had a thick, strong back, and Illoe suspected he was seeing why.

"Since the line of fire," another kitchen worker said, "I've attended Sunrise Ritual every morning. It's changed life."

Two days, wow what a new life, Illoe thought. "You know what I want to talk about?" Illoe yearned for an opening to bring up Hitra's odd behavior.

Oke looked over the edge of the pot at Illoe. A smudge of black soot was on his sweaty brow. "Not really. We got work to do."

It was too loud and too crowded, and Oke was in no mood to gossip. Illoe stayed to wash two more pots, to be polite, before claiming some urgent work of his own needed to be done. Except when he got home, he had nothing to do and all day to do it.

Just like me.

He thought he should be feeling great. The front room was in perfect order, and he had the fresh memory of it in disarray to congratulate himself with. Illoe stood inside the door and scanned the scene before him for imperfections. The windows looked a little dull, but not yet truly dusty. He itched for something to take his mind off the unshakable feeling that he was falling outside of Hitra's priorities, that he'd never get to talk to her about the contract. He had the day before Harvest Home marked on the calendar, of course, a red circle of deadline staring at him, not getting any further away.

He knew if he started on the windows, he'd want to do them outside as well, which meant talking to the lecherous groundskeeper to borrow a ladder, and then there would be the draperies to wash. Illoe's mind spun with an endless cycle of maintenance chores, fully convinced that no job could be done by half-measures. The thought of a day spent ironing curtains did nothing to quiet his anxiety. He paced. He wanted a way out of his life, out of his skin.

Did I have a way out?

☽○☾

Hitra paced back and forth in front of the brass doors to Reha's office. Her head swam with questions and queries: *Priest, the ceremony's started without you. Hitra, did you really mean to cancel choir practice again? Are you coming to the social hour afterward? Hitra, I demand to know why the cancellation. Honey, are you okay? Hi. You were supposed to call me? Your boy said...*

Her side of these multi-threaded conversations was something like this: *No. Cancel it. Cancel that, too. I'm meeting with the Ritual Celebrant. Yes, now. I don't know when I can. Call Illoe. Everyone, just call Illoe.*

She didn't want to think about schedules. She didn't want to think about anything, and she burned with the belief that Reha would make it better. She clung desperately to the hope that Reha, herself another flawed mortal, could dispel her doubts and fears with words.

Her mind masochistically assaulted itself with memory, looping endlessly those moments in the bath. At last she pushed the recollection forward. If I had breath, I'd hold it.

The simple uniformity of a grid was lost, the tiles wobbled, seemed to turn liquid—no, the wall was liquid and once rigid lines of grout danced with the ease of waves. Slowly, a bright light worked its way outward from the center, the tiles sinking into the light like ice falling into water, like spring thaw, and the light was white, but began to deepen to gold, and at that point Hitra had slapped herself, once, twice, three times, her jaw warm with the impact of it, her skin warm, the thin layer of water on her skin making the slap loud and metallic. A face formed in the light.

Revestre. I knew her even in someone else's memory, but I didn't recall ever seeing her before. She looked serene yet joyful. I knew her.

How dare she appear so significant, so alarming!

☽ ○ ☾

Illoe did Hitra's shopping for her in the High Street market, surrounded by other servants with baskets and bags. He had first planned to go to the Glory Street market, a few blocks down the mountain and much cheaper, but Oke had said other markets in the city were disrupted by the fire-panic, sold out of grain and cheese.

Illoe scowled. "Why is it always cheese?"

"Because it keeps," Oke said, and laughed, because cheese itself was a joke in the kitchens. Illoe could never figure out if this was some euphemism he didn't know, or just one of those things that becomes funny through repetition.

The market was exactly as it had been the day before, and the week before that. High Street was never practical enough to be bothered with current events. The wealthy didn't shop so much as sit on the edges of the market and indulge in fruit drinks with shopping available nearby.

Illoe hated the High Street market, and he hated the mesh bags Hitra made him use. They were decidedly feminine and cheap, but Hitra insisted, something about one of Revestre's chosen prophets being a net-maker and not squandering church funds. He kept them balled up in his fist until he had to make a purchase. Without them, he didn't look like a servant. Most servants wore the same drab clothes their parents had, but Hitra kept Illoe outfitted with the latest styles. He hated shopping with the cheap, unattractive grocery bags and his perfectly fashionable clothes because the combination made him owned. Being young, male, and owned no doubt sparked areas of imagination he'd rather not feel sparked in the fat-folded eyes of the rich. Being owned made him an unfortunate, a byproduct of parents too poor or too trapped to find any other way out of debt. Simultaneously, it made him decadent, a living extravagance of the nobility held over from a bygone age.

There was another reason to hate the market: Maede came there, when she didn't have someone else's business to be in. Her home was two blocks over, one of many near-uniform confections of alabaster that lined High Street all the way to Penitence, the avenue that led into the temple complex.

Maede sat at a tiny table, looking like a swaddled bird, the breeze blowing her long sleeves behind her like wings. She was blinking into the wind and arguing loudly and animatedly with a server — probably demanding that he turn off the wind, or move the entire restaurant so it sheltered her.

Illoe would have to walk past. He lingered at a jeweler's stall. Symbols of the gods, of good fortune and happiness shone in the sun. The shopkeeper gave him a dirty look. "Can I help you?"

Illoe set the grocery bags near his feet and picked up a trinket. "I'm looking for a gift for my mother," he lied. He already had a small gift for her for Harvest Home, and no other reason to shop for one, but it seemed the sort of thing a person would be doing at this shop.

"How much can you spend?"

That was rude. Discussing price first was not something people on High Street did. Illoe dropped the overpriced trinket like it was dirty. "She's my mother. I don't think cost should be an issue, do you?"

The shopkeeper smiled, then, and started laying out interesting pieces in front of him. Illoe picked one that looked like his mother's taste — minimalist, abstract, but still religious. He handed over the asking price, half his shopping stipend, without blinking and walked away wondering why he felt like he had to do that.

He'd also forgotten about Maede, who saw him and whistled.

Whistled. Like you would to summon a dog. He kept walking.

"Hey!"

He turned and tried to appear startled. "Oh, Lady Faydehale." He raised the ugly grocery bags to show. "Just doing some shopping." He turned to continue on his way, hoping if he did so fast enough, she'd have to let him go.

"Come here," she shouted. "It's rude to shout."

The never-ending intricacy of noble manners. Illoe bit the inside of his lip and approached the spidery little table. Now, if he were watching, the shopkeeper would know Illoe was a mere servant, coming when disrespectfully called. (And how he hated that he cared what a random shopkeeper thought!) "Yes, Lady?"

"How dare you cancel my breakfast with your mistress this morning."

Illoe set his grocery bags down. "I'm sorry, Lady Faydehale, but as I said in my message, Hitra had an emergency appointment with…"

"What did you say to her? What have you been telling her about me?"

He picked the bags back up. Perhaps this wasn't going to take long. "She had an emergency meeting with the Ritual Celebrant that had nothing to do with you. I'll tell Hitra to call you as soon as she can."

Maede leaned back in her chair. Her eyes tightened to hard little points, her loose-fleshed face fairly quivering with something akin to a thought. *Are you having sex with her?*

He was seized with a horrible fantasy—that Maede, with her adept powers, knew about the naked morning. (He was wrong, of course. Even I couldn't see memories un-replayed, and Maede was laughably far from my level.)

He trembled and his voice came out an airless squeak, "What?"

"You heard me."

Illoe shook his head and started walking away.

Is that a yes?

He didn't look back. Face red, he spoke curtly to the shopkeepers as he concluded the last few pieces of necessary shopping as quickly as possible.

☽○☾

No, I didn't rush off to watch Illoe shop because I was upset, and I didn't return to Hitra because I had calmed down. I am a god and my attention wanders.

Hitra bowed before Reha's massive desk. "Eminence, thank you for seeing me on such short notice."

The Ritual Celebrant nodded, distractedly, still marking a parchment with her stylus. "I'm supposed to be meeting those special investigators the Assembly sent over. Not that I'm thanking you." She set the stylus in its jar and raised her eyebrows.

Hitra sat down carefully on one of the enormous chairs in the Ritual Celebrant's office. They seemed to be made to make the sitter feel insignificant. "Have they found anything?"

"Heh. No. I doubt they could find the ground if you kicked their feet out from under them. But each one is eager to blather on to me about his or her special theory. That's the secular government for you. Many voices, none with authority. So, what was so earth-shatteringly important? Make it quick; I have a thousand things to get done in the next hundred heartbeats."

$$\mathcal{D} O \mathcal{C}$$

More memory: Closing her eyes gave only a moment's false restoration of normality, the pressure of her bones on the bottom of the tub, the clamminess of skin, the rapidly dissipating heat on her upper body, and then her eyelids were penetrated, and the face was before her, more beautiful than any mortal woman, and the golden light filled Hitra's veins and swelled her heart.

$$\mathcal{D} O \mathcal{C}$$

"I saw my god," Hitra said.

Reha uncrossed her arms. "Well, that's not one I expected to be coming from you."

The anger was good, it grounded Hitra in reality. "I'm not some awe-struck layman who saw a face in a water stain. I have always had the deepest faith in..." She pressed her sleeve to her eyes, utterly unsure how she meant to end that sentence. "I feel like I'm going insane. Help me, Eminence. How do you know, when something unnatural happens, that it happened, that it wasn't imagined?"

"Usually because someone else sees it. Three quarters of the city saw the fire column, Hitra. It happened. It was real."

"Not that, damn it!" Hitra winced at the force of her words. Reha herself was nonplussed. Hitra set her hand on her chair arm. "I saw Revestre. Or it was something that said it was her. It felt like...like nothing I have ever experienced before. Light and warmth and hope."

Reha said, "And this happened in a public place?"

"In my bathroom, while I was bathing."

"Alone, then, I take it."

"Of course I was alone. My servant was just outside the door, though. He heard it. He told me he heard voices. What is this? Why do I have to prove this to you?"

"This is about the three-hundredth time someone has told me they saw a deity. First time for Revestre, I think, but you already know she isn't that popular. People usually see Our Sacred Mother or Darian, or, of course, their patron god. Monks, nuns, junior priests, there's one every year who has a dream and then takes it as a sign. I blame all those confessional books they read in seminary."

"This wasn't a dream. I was in my bathroom. I was wet. I could feel how I was wet. I could feel my ass going numb from sitting too long on the hard tile bottom of the bath. I just..." Hitra pressed both hands to the sides of her head, an act that made her voluminous sleeves bell out like a neophyte's veil. "Believe me or don't believe me. Tell me what to do to get my mind back, my clarity. This is affecting my ability to do my job. Fix it."

Reha leaned back and chuckled. "Oh, Hitra. I did have you pegged right. All right, calm down, calm down. There's really only one way through this, child. Come on, come with me."

Reha walked to the side door of her office. "Come on."

A spark of hope burned bright and beautiful in Hitra's breast as she followed Reha into her private chambers. "Close the door," Reha said, and the spark fluttered with an anticipation of dark and holy secrets.

Reha opened a pearl-inlaid cabinet and from its velvet-lined depths drew a decanter of amber liquid, and then two glasses, which she filled. She pressed one into Hitra's hand. "Sit," she commanded, "and drink."

Hitra's emotions sank with her body, bereft of hope and the will to stand, disillusioned. "Eminence, are you ordering me to drink hard spirits during the work day?"

Reha raised her glass to the light that filtered through tall, jewel-toned windows. "Definitely. No more talking until half this decanter is empty. That's an order. And call me Reha. There's no ceremony in here."

The Celebrant had never mentioned a penchant for liquor. The richly colored liquid coated the sides of the glass when splashed and burned Hitra's senses. She coughed. "Eminence, I don't think getting drunk is a responsible or even rational course of action."

"Sometimes kicking what's broke fixes it. You've had a head-jarring experience. Let's jar you back to reality."

The alcohol, little enough as she had ingested — breathed would be more appropriate, it evaporated as soon as it hit her tongue — must have started its magic. Hitra's head echoed with emptiness. She set the glass down. "People are scared. People are scared because things are happening that no one can explain, and all you do is sit in your private room and get drunk. Don't you even care about your station?"

"I am not getting drunk." Reha continued to hold her glass of alcohol like a sacred relic. "Are you finished?"

"No. What am I doing here? What are *you* doing here? We are in a religious crisis! Reha, gods do not appear to people in bathrooms. Columns of flame do not just happen! And if they did, they wouldn't burn continuously for an hour and then vanish without a trace. It's too perfect."

Reha sipped her drink, then set her glass next to Hitra's on the table. "There it is," she said. She wasn't as confident as she sounded. Reha knew she had to tread delicately to get this particular priest through this particular crisis. She pressed her fingertips together and waited until Hitra returned her even gaze. "Do you want to be relieved of your post?"

"No!"

"Do you want a leave of absence to figure this out? You could go to the plains and help the brothers of Revestre's monastery with their harvest. It could give you some healthy perspective, not to mention peace."

Hitra bristled inside at the idea of all that slow, open, dusty land.

She shook her head. "I'm not running from this, nor from my post."

Reha nodded. "Then I suggest you take some time for yourself to meditate. Cut down your commitments. The youth program can survive without you for a few weeks. Let your acolytes take a more active role. Sit, and think, and when you have a course of action, bring it to me."

"Eminence, with all due respect—"

"I know what you're going through," Reha said.

"You do NOT know what I'm going through."

Reha looked stonily at her, letting the ringing silence answer for her, unaware that Hitra was correct. Reha didn't suspect for a second the deeply unimpeachable nature of Hitra's experience, too familiar with lesser, invented touches with the divine. Reha picked up her glass and raised it toward Hitra. "We've all had a crisis of faith. The world has changed, irrevocably, in your eyes, but it hasn't changed at all—you have only seen another piece of it. Getting through this is more about accepting it than analyzing it. And when you are through it, you'll be awfully glad I kept you from doing anything rash."

Hitra stood, her fury turned to the cold realization Reha had nothing to offer her. "Thank you, Celebrant."

Reha shrugged. She continued to sip as Hitra left. There was no sense wasting good spirits, and she hoped a little muzziness would make her meeting with the secular government smoother.

)O(

I was considering whether to follow Hitra or stay with Reha, when strange thoughts intruded into my mind. Words not of my own making, insistent, loud, and unignorable. *Who do you think you are?*

It wasn't addressed to me. *I think I'm the one who knows who she is.* That also wasn't me, and not directed at me. *I am the Ocean's Daughter.*

Then go home to her. The words were coming faster and stronger. Before I knew what I was doing, I was pulled up, mingled with the chimney-smoke of the city. Dioneltar and Telumene were there. They had determined each other's names but could not agree on anything else. *Stone,* one said. *No, I'm stone. Buildings-stone. Mountain-stone.*

Ocean floor…

"Ladies," I said, "you both have stone as a domain. Get over it. I have this thing I'm trying to watch that might hold answers but definitely involves guilt and drunkenness and you're distracting me."

Their confusion was as indistinct as their personalities. I could hardly tell where one let off and the other began, all commingled as they were and pulling bits of themselves aside, inventorying their parts.

"Who cares which of you is Queen of Mountains? I'm God of Magic and Mischief. Let me go."

Let her go? You let her go. I'm not holding anyone.

This was Wenne's job. She was the Queen of the Gods, after all. I tried to feel her in the mish-mash over the city, the commingled and separate vaguenesses that were my sisters. Dioneltar and Telumene had pulled me to them, accidentally. Surely, I could pull another god on purpose? What was Wenne? A face of flame. A rude gesture. I held her in my mind. "Wenne, get over here and lecture these two about the timeless pact…thing. That timeless pact of the gods? How we don't fight with each other anymore?"

Wenne was…a patch of warmth. She was there, I guess, and not there, and as irritated as I was. She started to speak and be ignored. Dioneltar and Telumene did not care that there was an ancient agreement to always let Wenne decide quarrels. Wenne wasn't surprised. She'd been running into that a lot.

We weren't making words anymore. These feelings were passed as impressions. We didn't have forms. I had no form. I didn't know who I was or what I was in charge of. Some part of me ruled the mountains and some ruled water and some ruled the gods. It was all muddled. I separated myself, closed myself off and willed my form into a solid, person-sized thing. I planned to drop like doom or rain into the alabaster rooms of the temple. The other gods tugged at me, pulled bits of me. "Don't you want to know why things don't work the way they should?" I asked, but that just made them want to follow, clinging, pulling at my boundaries to let them in, pull me back into that horrible muddle.

I concentrated on Hitra alone, on being with just one other mind. I'd grown used to her; I could hook onto her easily. I felt myself tear away from the others, like ripping a clump of hair out of a tangle.

Hitra stood on the gravel path that led to the shrine of Revestre and inhaled damp air, rich with the smell of the temple gardens. She was angry, too, and trying not to be. It felt good to be outdoors, though the wind was strong and the ponderous sleeves of her autumn robe tangled behind her. She tried to empty her head, just hear the crunch of the gravel, smell the juniper bushes, and see the small shrine, a white arch against the rough-hewn north wall of the garden. It was cool inside, where the living rock of the mountain surrounded her. Even in summertime, this little niche was cool. Hitra touched the cold face of the icon. A rounder, softer Revestre, indistinct with wear. It was wet with condensation, as it was most mornings in Spring or Fall. Flowerpots were arranged at the icon's feet. Hitra knelt and moved them to the front of the niche. The acolytes should have done that at dawn. She pressed her hands in the soil. They hadn't been watered, either.

Hitra sat back on her heels and looked out on the well-manicured lawn of the temple. She paused with a frown, and I thought she saw me. She turned back toward the icon. "Revestre," she said, "would want me to do my job."

Revestre wasn't here. Revestre, near as I could tell, hadn't given Hitra a second thought after disrupting her entire life. I was here. I was the one she should be trying to talk to. Not that she knew that.

Hitra swept away the dried remains of yesterday's offering. It comforted her to do things she knew how to do. She fetched the watering can and freshened the flowers, the bitter root, the wheat, the sweet rose, and the thorn, and said the prayers appropriate to each, thought on the simplicity of their symbolism. She was a priest. She rolled the word in her palm with the ceremonial chalk as she drew a few extra devotions on the pots, which chimed so pleasantly, a resonance shared with the brittle clay. She had always liked that, and the slight rime the chalk left on the edges of the path, where inevitable rains would wash it.

Feeling Hitra calm herself calmed me. I thought about possessing her. It was a sudden idea, picked up from some random mind I'd touched, a superstition, that gods and spirits could slip inside a person like putting on a coat. How lovely it would be, to be one with

Hitra, not those monstrous others. To have a past and competence and plans.

Hitra stood, watering can in hand, comforted by the rough, real feel of it. She walked toward the temple. I concentrated on lining myself up with her physical space. I was where she was, over her, around her... but I might as well have been a cloud. She passed through me.

A man who had been peering at her for some time, between bouts of pretending to be interested in one of the garden's tortuously trained fruit trees, took hold of his courage and took a step closer to Hitra as she walked past. "Excuse me?"

Hitra hadn't noticed him as I had. She jumped. The watering can hit the gravel. Hitra grabbed a handful of robe and bent to pick it back up. "Sorry, you startled me."

It was Forthright Jeje, who had interrupted Maede and Illoe two days ago. "No...no...I should be sorry," he bowed low. He worried his hat in his hands. "Your...um...Holiness, am I...would it be...can I talk to you?"

Hitra turned her full attention on the peasant man before her. This, too, was her job. "Of course. Will you walk with me? I have to return this to the tool shed." She hefted the watering can. I tried to feel the weight of it. Some muscles in her arm contracted, others did not. I touched something and her fingers tightened. She thought this meant she was more nervous than she realized.

Forthright Jeje bowed several times, and looked down at his hat twice, then mashed it into a pocket in his trousers. "I stopped by your place. I know I shouldn't. Anyway, I hope you don't mind. It wasn't right, that day, that fire was going on and I was so scared I wouldn't get a chance to speak to you again if I didn't right away."

"I will always have time for my congregation," Hitra said. I touched a muscle in her cheek. She worried Jeje saw her twitch. Too tired. Not enough salt in her diet.

"N-no, ma'am, I'm not in your congregation. That's sort of what I was afraid of. Strange things start happening, and someone like you might not, well they might not want to be seen with someone like me."

Hitra turned to the man, and noticed for the first time the pale color of his eyes, marking him as not a member of the uniformly dark-eyed Casu. His skin, too, though sun-darkened, was not the richer color of Hitra's. "You're a Sanadaru?"

"Anichu-Sanadaru. Is that a problem?"

Hitra flinched at the thought that she might be perceived as bigoted. "Well, no, no of course not, but I'm surprised you'd come to speak with me here." I tried to hold her legs still, but there were so many muscles! So many nerves. Hitra continued walking toward the tool shed, struggling internally, feeling like she was stumbling through small, invisible obstacles, thin as wires despite all this work I was doing. She was smiling too much to cover her distress and Jeje was getting worried.

"It's about my daughter. She's in your program. The singing program? Her mother is Casu, you see. Bala thinks the world of you, Holiness."

Illoe's thought-voice imposed itself in Hitra's ear. *Boss? Are you done with Reha? Listen, we have got to talk...*

Not now! Hitra pushed Illoe out of her mind. Her anger hurt her, a pressure against the inside of her forehead. Muscles contracted under her scalp for no discernable reason. She wondered if her earlier calm was a lie, if she was heading for an emotional breakdown.

"...and that's why I hoped to talk to you. Before it's too late. I want to know that my daughter will remember her heritage."

Hitra, and I, had missed his whole argument. She set the watering can on its worn iron hook and lifted her sleeves to keep them from getting caught as she closed the door to the tool shed. "Citizen...?"

"Forthright Jeje."

"Citizen Jeje, I'm not sure what you're asking." Heart quickening, vessels dilating. Everything so fragile and necessary. I could stop her life, but could I do something more interesting than that? Hitra touched her chest, tried to slow her breathing. "I can't take a parent's place in the spiritual life of their child."

"I'm not asking that." Jeje's face wrinkled up. She'd just completely ignored him. Because he was Anichu? "I'm asking for one hour to see my daughter once a week. Look, just let her down easy, if you can. I don't want her hurt."

Illoe's words came again. I felt them vibrate her ear. *Boss? Can you give me an idea when you'll be done?*

Hitra pressed a hand against her eyes. She tried to listen to the wind whistling over the walls of the garden, tried to clear her mind. "Jeje, your daughter chose to be a part of the temple youth program. Have you considered that she wishes to follow a Casu path?"

"She's six years old, Holiness, she can't know what she wants, and her mother won't let me see her. This other singing program meets at almost the same time. Please, help a poor father out. I'm not asking you to lie to the girl, just drop her from the program. You must drop people all the time."

Boss?

Hitra looked back toward the small shrine. It was so tidy. She'd done that. Think on that. Fluids slowed, muscles loosened.

The Sanadaru man kept talking. "Bala should be able to choose which religion she believes in at a later age, when she can really understand..."

I really, really need to talk to you about this before I lose my nerve.

"You've always represented a tolerant view, Holiness, everyone says so. Could you really want one less Anichu child in the world?"

Almost there. I held onto nerves, formed my idea of myself inside her. We shivered, both of us. I felt it. Hitra felt a strange heaviness and she also felt Illoe, still in contact with her mind. She closed her eyes and pushed out. I felt myself flung. I hovered over Hitra, seeing her from outside again. "No," she said. "Citizen Jeje, if your daughter has any sense she'll stay with the Casu program and follow a god that exists."

Hitra didn't quite believe it as she said it. You never said that the Sanadaru gods didn't exist. It was rude. She opened her eyes and saw his confused expression, but anger was growing underneath it. Hurt. Her head hurt.

Jeje hurt, his week of finding another singing program, one for his particular sect, that would let him come and watch, days of running all over the city, to arrange one little hour he could see Bala singing, loud and off-key and proud as only a child can be...it was all crumbling to nothing in a glare from a dark-skinned priest.

"Revestre is real. I've seen her."

Hitra walked away without looking at Jeje again.

Chapter Five

Tests

Flung off like mud, rejected. Me. A god.

At least I hadn't been alone. In the laundry room of the temple residences, someone pushed Illoe onto his side. He was on the stone floor, confused how he'd gotten there, the overturned washtub dug into his upper arm.

"Illoe? Hey, buddy, what happened?"

He blinked away the memory of the red moment, the force filling his senses, wavered, but found himself again, climbing to his knees. The other resident servants were cleaning up his spilled wash water. He righted the tub. Hitra's green under-robe clung to the floor like seaweed. He dragged it up and wrung it out.

Oke grasped his shoulder. "You get hit?"

Illoe frowned. "I was talking with Hitra and she…I guess…didn't want to talk."

His friend winced. "Oo. You got hit."

"That's what it feels like?" Illoe balked at his memory of the sensation, dissipating along his nerves. He had always assumed the pain-giving powers of the adept were exaggerated by his contemporaries, wanting to appear both tougher and more pathetic than they were.

Oke patted his shoulder. "Congratulations. You almost made it to majority without pissing off an adept."

Illoe knelt by the tub. It needed refilling. He had Hitra's robe clutched to his chest, soaking his own tunic, but he couldn't quite move, yet, trying to resolve in his mind this feeling of violence with Hitra. She would never do that. For a man sold by his own parents, Illoe had little understanding of betrayal.

Then he thought: The push had delivered an undercurrent of defense. Fright. Panic. Someone drove Hitra to do that. He could accept that. It wasn't her. It was this other person who made her afraid, made her attack.

It looked, from his point of view, as if I had forced Hitra to hurt him. I...no. That wasn't my fault. I remembered the thoughts, the moment, the exact shape of Hitra's thoughts... she hadn't wanted to hurt anyone, just to get what was in her out.

To get me out. I...I left him.

)O(

Wenne was not in the temple. I stopped myself from searching farther. Was I any smarter than Hitra, rushing to my boss? Reha had been no help, but she felt smarter than Wenne.

Reha folded her hands over the glass blessing-staff with practiced elegance. She always added a twist with her thumbs to bring the sleeves of her robe up.

I wondered how to make my presence known. Something...not violent. Respectful.

"Go forth with good will," she said, and the penitents bowed and stood. They were awkward. Not regulars, they didn't know whether to back away from the shrine or turn and go, and tried to hide their indecision in curving steps and glances at each other. Reha smiled down at them, gestured that they could turn, and waited for them to leave the chapel before she moved to place the staff in its holder and wash her hands at the sacred font.

Yes, I was hesitating. I didn't want to ruin her first impression of me.

Reha's secretary was waiting in the equipment room just off the blessing chapel. "Eminence, an arbiter to speak with you."

Reha dried her hands and looked over at the woman her secretary indicated, standing in the entrance to the sacristy, her short purple tunic and pants cut in the spare, form-fitting manner of the civil service were jarring in the religious surroundings. "We don't commonly let secular officials back here," Reha said.

Sorry, her aide instantly sent to her.

Reha handed him her towel with a dismissive wave. *Not your fault. Pushy arbiters.*

The arbiter raised her eyebrows. "I will ask you not to indulge in private conversations in my presence. As an eighth circle adept, I can hear them and I am charged to share anything I find here with my superiors should it be necessary in an arbitration."

This was more power than I had seen in mortals, and the arbiter, Nerte, was completely confident in it, even in the face of the Ritual Celebrant herself.

Reha was undeterred. "I don't commonly think what I'm not proud to say and have heard. You pushed your way in here by intimidating my staff. Isn't that correct? Let's head to my office so you can tell me whatever it is you've come to tell."

Nerte had learned to snatch vibrations in transit, like a copper wire touches a vibrating wire and vibrates itself. It would be easy to talk to her. So I did.

Hey. Can I ask you something?

She...ignored me. Nerte thought I sounded loud, shrill, and low-class, and she didn't even attempt to trace where my voice had come from. "Ritual Celebrant, I would prefer to speak it here and now. My colleagues have secured the area."

Reha glanced back toward the shrine, and its small, now empty audience chamber. "Fourteen private citizens just left here."

"I am aware of that. They have not been disturbed."

Nerte's four assistants had worked fast, checking each mind, recording their radius of hearing and thought, and encouraging each to move out of that range. Because they moved so silently and competently, their efforts were invisible enough to impress the Ritual Celebrant, and Nerte accepted that as their due.

Hey. I pushed my words right into her smug little ear. *I am not some random zealot. I'm a god.*

Sure you are. Nerte's opinion of me, if possible, got lower. "Ritual Celebrant, the Council has determined there is no evidence of a physical fire on the temple grounds that could have caused a display such as was seen on Wenne's Day. Furthermore, we have found no combustibles of sufficient amount to have been procured within the city for the past month."

"Well, congratulations. It wasn't a fire." Both women tried not to project their irritation at the other. Their minds were full of the familiarity of power, of being powerful. I didn't think either one would fear me even if they knew what I was, and that was all the more irritating.

You're going to be so mad when you realize who you're ignoring.

Nerte mentally compared me to a certain unfortunate cousin and coolly kept her regard on Reha. "We believe the column must have been illusory."

Reha started unbuttoning her ritual robe. "I don't sense any humor in you, but I assume that is a joke."

Nerte thought, correctly, priests only saw what they expected to see and didn't know how much they didn't know. "Illusion is the only logical explanation."

"Logical." Reha pulled back her cuffs to undo the buttons at her wrists. "Logic has escaped the crown's attention completely. Illusions! No one has ever been able to make one, even with the considerable amounts of time and alcohol students consume toward that end."

"High level adepts can create emotions in others, even physical sensations. It is not unreasonable that one could make a person think she saw something that wasn't there."

That...could have been what Wenne did. Was there really a fire that did no damage, or had she made everyone think there was, including me? If so, it was more impressive than I thought, which I didn't want to be true.

"Ah, so four thousand adepts we have never seen before came into the city and tricked the other forty thousand inhabitants into thinking we saw something? And then, what? Vanished into the ether before we could catch them? The scoundrels!"

Nerte's opinion of the Ritual Celebrant was as bad as her opinion of me. She thought how a much lower-ranked arbiter could have met with Reha, and felt honored by it instead of annoyed. Yeah, I knew how that felt. *Hey. Nerte. I know who did it. The fire. She confessed to me.*

Finally, I had her full attention. Nerte could sense my honesty. Her forehead creased despite her attempt to appear unaffected. She dispatched quick, coded words to her underlings, who commenced an intense sweep of the area to locate my body. My turn to feel smug as Nerte searched the shadows of the sacristy, eyes narrowed. *Who are you? Who sent you?*

The cheek. *No one sent me.*

Reha lifted her outer robe from her shoulders. "Are we done here, arbiter? I assume you came for more than to waste my time." Reha's aide rushed to help her with the robe, relieved to have something to do other than stand back and hope no one noticed he was hearing this conversation.

"One moment, Celebrant," Nerte said, uncaring how rude she was being. *What do you want? I can help you.* She didn't know I could see past her façade of non-judgmental helpfulness to the eager preparations to trap me. A rogue adept, she thought.

I want nothing, you worm. I am Senne, the moon at zenith.

The arbiter felt a flash of irritation and tried to keep it buried lest the person she thought I was felt it. *Tell me more. I never spoke to a god before.* She nudged her underlings, annoyed at their lack of progress locating my incorporeal form. Her fingers twitched, wanting to push more energy toward them. She had her hands clasped behind her back, and tightened the grip, annoyed at herself and this old habit.

It was ridiculous. I could feel her lack of belief, her confidence that I was a mad adept, hiding behind a pillar. *Wenne sent the fire column. She did it because of some stupid prophecy about announcing where she's going to show up.*

Reha suspected that Nerte's mental conversation with someone else was merely a power play or delaying tactic, perhaps faked. "If that is all, arbiter, I have a church to lead."

Nerte put her thoughts of me and what I could really be on hold and did a good job of looking conciliatory toward Reha. She even projected an emotional wave of pleading. "One more thing. The Crown requests your assistance. You are the most powerful adept in the city."

Reha smirked. "I didn't do it, if that's what you're asking."

Nerte found that ironic, given what I'd said. "We need every trustworthy adept to search the minds around them for anything unusual and report back to the crown. Can we rely on you?"

Reha let her own incredulity speak for itself — the arbiter could feel it well enough. Reha considered searching minds a shameful breech of privacy, and her position as head of the church would make it doubly sinful. She looked for her aide and gestured, making her own power play. "Where is my schedule? How much time do we have before the reform committee meets?"

Nerte spoke before the aide could, through clenched teeth. "Ritual Celebrant, we face the very real possibility of rogue adepts within the city."

Within the room, actually, I sent to her, warming up to this new way of tormenting someone. It worked. Nerte was boiling inside.

Reha put a reassuring hand on the shoulder of Eiti, her aide, who was trying to slide behind the robe hangers. "We face that possibility all the time. Are there rogue adepts? One might as well ask if there are stars in the sky. They are about as harmful. Untrained, unaffiliated, they can no more create illusions than you or I can call down the gods."

The old cliché was robbed of its certainty by recent events. I sent Nerte a wordless nudge, like clearing my throat.

The arbiter was the only one of us unmoved by the ominous pause, she was too busy struggling to balance a need to capture me with a need to obtain the agreement her unreasonable superiors had demanded. She was like a string too tight to vibrate. "Because something has not happened in the past, there is no reason to assume it cannot be happening now. A group of rogue adepts, working in concert, is the most likely explanation for the temple mount illusion. It is paramount to discover them before their next demonstration of power."

"I don't know if I can fit scanning all the minds of the city in my schedule."

Nerte ignored Reha's sarcasm. "Do what you can. Because your government requires it of you."

"Did it occur to you that there might be a theological explanation? Are irrational events not the purview of the church?"

You two deserve each other, Nerte aimed at me with a wordless invitation to bring my threats and demands to Reha. "I am not authorized to debate the Crown's reasoning. You have received the Crown's message. She will expect a response."

In other words, say "yes" or "no" so I can leave. Nerte wondered why she had to spell this out, since the Celebrant was so clearly eager to see her go.

"So that's how it is." Reha flicked the collar of her under-robe so it would stand properly on its own while her aide fussed with the cords and pleats. "Her Highness has gone about this in entirely the wrong fashion. You tell her that. I am not a bureaucrat to be assigned at her whim. The church has enjoyed its sovereignty since before her family sat the throne."

Nerte's boss was not going to like that response. "Then it would be wise for you to comply, rather than reduce yourself to the indignity of receiving a public summons."

"When the queen asks me herself," Reha said. "Now get out of my church."

Nerte bowed politely and strode out the door. She'd done all she could, and now, at least, she could concentrate on locating this rogue adept.

While it was delightful watching the arbiters set up a tight cordon, knowing their careful enumeration of exits was going to lead to exactly nothing, I was definitely not going to get anywhere with Nerte. I supposed I should have talked to Reha all along, but looking at her, I felt unsure. What would she say differently to me?

Reha nudged Eiti toward the niche. *She's talking rubbish. It will be all right.* His shoulders did not relax. She tickled the back of his elbow until he released his breath and laughed.

"It will be," she repeated out loud, and this time he nodded. Eiti was a young man, given to blushing, and Reha knew some people objected to her keeping him around, but she felt that the occasional boyish blush, like the occasional glass of spirits, was an indulgence necessary to life.

Yes, I could imagine the conversation:

Me: I am Senne, and Wenne caused that fire column.

Reha: Prove it.

Me: Check out my ability to make a sock fly!

☽○☾

This was all actually Hitra's fault. She was the one who had pushed me out of her, who had hurt Illoe and sent me looking for answers when I wasn't ready to.

Hitra was feeling awful. Good. She had retreated to her apartment. It was dark, empty, quiet. She hoped it would calm her down.

I was deciding what sort of scary noise to make when she heard something that terrified her all on its own – the back door opening. She knew it had to be Illoe and she was afraid to face him, knowing she'd lashed out and unsure how badly he'd been hurt.

All the rooms of the apartment were in a row with each other, except for the bathroom, which was off the bedroom. It was the only place she could hope to hide from him. She rushed to get there before she ended up in his way. She didn't want a confrontation. Because of this, she inevitably got in his way, the two of them entering the narrow fire pantry from opposite ends. Illoe had a full basket of laundry.

"I'm going to my room," Hitra said. Illoe, instead of stepping aside, dropped the basket at his feet, blocking her passage.

Sullen silence. Illoe couldn't decide on a retort bitter enough.

Hitra tried to soften her tone. "This isn't like you. Interrupting me at work," she knew she'd hit him, and he was justifiably angry, but she hoped she could somehow convince him she hadn't meant it, or that it wasn't worth being angry about. "... and you know, my mind is on other people and I can't..."

He wasn't budging so she turned sideways and stepped over the edge of the basket, nearly tumbling in the effort. Illoe exhaled and kicked the basket forward. Kick, slide, kick, slide, he punished the laundry into the front room.

Hitra continued into her room, unbuttoning the heavy autumn robe. She glanced at the open door to the bathroom. The white tile reminded her of seeing Revestre, and being alone suddenly wasn't better than facing a sullen Illoe. She turned to go back into the front room. Illoe was standing in her way, a scroll case cocked in his hand like a crossbow. "Have you found me a wife yet?" he asked.

She refastened the button in her hands. "What?"

"I have six days, Hitra. Six days left before this contract cannot be altered. So I thought I'd take a look at it. Did you even read this thing when you signed it?"

"Did you say 'wife'?"

Illoe jabbed the scroll case at her. "My half-adept bastard of a father hid a clause in here that says you have to find me a wife before you release me from service."

She shook her head slowly. "Why are you yelling at me?"

Illoe tossed the scroll case on the bed and left the room.

Hitra sat on the bed. The scroll case rolled toward her with the depression of the coverlet. She was looking, however, at the bathroom door, and wondering why the world wouldn't stop for one day and let her catch her breath.

She went back into the front room. Illoe was folding linens over the sitting-couch. She leaned against the brick wall that held the fire-nook. "What happens if I can't? Find you a...well, a wife."

He smoothed a napkin against his forearm and said, "You get to keep me. At the present rate of compensation, plus ten percent." He threw the folded napkin onto a stack. "Until you marry me off. That's it. I go from undatable to married without a break, or even a say in the matter. Or I'm stuck in this job forever."

The only sound for a while was the gentle puff of fabric folding and falling. The sinking sun shone across the room, painting the linen peach and gilding the small hairs on his arms. Hitra scratched her elbow. "I forgot your birthday."

"Sorry I snapped." Illoe raised a sheet up against the light and with a flick of his hands the fabric cracked like a flag. "But I've been trying to talk to you about this for a week. You need to talk to my mother, renegotiate, and have the clause stricken. Unless," he pressed the sheet against his chest with his chin, "you have a beautiful, rich, single woman I don't know about hidden in the closet."

"We'll strike it. No one makes clauses like that anymore. It's not civilized."

"And here I thought you'd met my father." He dropped the folded sheet on top of the stack and twisted around to pick another from the laundry basket. He didn't know that twisting like that showed off the beauty of his body. He didn't know that Hitra ever thought about his body. That she was horrified at the prospect of more time together because of how she thought about his body. She had meant to talk to him about releasing him from service, but it always seemed easier to wait another year. Now there was this.

Illoe was thinking how he should be happy that he'd finally gotten this off his chest, but all he wanted was for Hitra to apologize for hitting him, and for her to do so without his prompting.

Hitra thought that it was good he'd asked her for something, that she'd agreed to renegotiate the contract. It was something she could do for him, and it was as good, she thought, as an apology.

It wasn't, and it wasn't like I could ask her for one, myself.

So I spilled her inkwell all over her desk papers and, when that didn't feel satisfying enough, I emptied her sugar bowl into the trash. Senne, god of minor pranks.

☽ ○ ☾

I thought it would pick up my spirits to tail the arbiters searching for me , but they were not very emotional. They felt I would show up eventually, they only had to wait. Nerte had gone home and her replacement in charge of the operation was thinking more about a novel she'd left off reading than what I could be like.

The only stir was when one arbiter broke off to check on a disturbance in the Ritual Celebrant's expected pattern of movement.

Reha informed her staff that she required private meditation time — yes, again — and secured herself in the old router tower behind the men's dormitories. She left her guards and aide at the base of the tower and climbed the steps alone, herself.

Her retinue was exceptional: competent people skilled at blending into the background until needed. Most of the time, she forgot they were there, but still, closing the door behind her was something of a shock. She tried to remember when she had last been alone.

It was dark, and darkness has a way of making marble glow. She sat on the dusty floor of the tower — its chair had been removed — and let herself relax, admiring the weathered stone, the carved spindles between windows open to the chill mountain night; the shutters had been removed as well.

She felt silly. She had the power to do this from anywhere, in any lesser adept's company, but she came here, like a pilgrim, kneeling on cold stone.

"Well, here we go," she said. "Senne, it's your hour. I should be asleep, but it's appropriate to conduct this sort of business under your auspices. I call your name without fear, and without protection. Shall we return the favor and not be a complete bitch?"

I wasn't offended. I had a feeling she was about to do something great. I imagined myself sitting cross-legged in front of her, the ready acolyte.

She chuckled to herself at the hubris of calling a goddess a bitch and closed her eyes. Feeling out over the city, over the network of routers, ignoring them, she selected the mind she was looking for as easily as I could. Arel, in his own bed.

Ah, Arelandus. There you are. How are you, child?

She felt him startle, then recognize her and grow angry, then carefully close off his feelings. He stared at the slack face of his sleeping wife. He sent no words to Reha in response, but neither did he refuse the connection. He thought that would be too much like speaking.

Easy. I'm not trying to insult you. Be as silent as you wish. There's no sin, even to a Husher, in listening. You know how I feel about your decision to leave the church, and I know your reasoning behind it, so let's skip that conversation and go straight to the meat of the matter, shall we? The royals are getting involved, love. They'd rather believe in rogue adepts than the will of the gods, and they want someone to blame. Someone like you. Get out of the city, just for a short while.

She waited against hope for a response. Of course he wouldn't. Arel was a man who kept his oaths, and picked the toughest oath he could take. *Please, just think about your safety.*

Reha waited, counting her breaths. She thought she might have made things worse. He would be the sort to stay just because he was advised not to. With a sigh she moved her tired body, her aging knees to the spiraling stairs. She kept her mind's eye on Arel until she reached the ground level again, but he didn't lower his shield, didn't let her see how he had reacted.

Arel crawled out of bed. His hands shook. Without lighting a candle, he sat in the dark front room of his house, crying hot, bitter tears. There was power in him, and anger, and I waited for him to do something with it.

He prayed, to Wenne.

No, I didn't seek her out. What kind of god seeks someone else out to explain things to her? I would look within myself, my memories, my thoughts.

My self. Amorphous, without volume, even. My memories…went back less than a week. My thoughts…were now just thinking about thinking.

Introspection felt weird. I went to watch Illoe.

Illoe awoke early the next day and let Hitra sleep in. Somehow, he doubted she'd insist on her usual predawn bath. Mist clung to the grass outside, and the air was sharp, the first feeling of autumn cold. The priests' chambers were all dark, and he squinted up at the moon, wondering how early it was, if he should have checked the clock.

The door to the communal kitchen spilled buttery light out onto the grey world. He stepped into the warmth and steam. Oke was stoking the fires. The sides of the copper pots sweated.

"Hey," Illoe said.

Oke laced his fingers and pressed his palms toward the ceiling. "Out late or up early?"

"Couldn't sleep."

"Aw, poor baby," Oke said, and kicked a coal that had fallen on the edge of the fire pit. "You're here when I leave. You come in as soon as I arrive. Who do you bother when I'm not around?"

Illoe pulled the broom out from behind the door. "I often engage in civilized discourse with gentle folk." He went to work on erasing the black streaks of dropped coal Oke had left all over the floor. "Not that you know what that's like."

Oke waved at the broom. "Det'll get that."

"Someone has to do your work, layabout."

"There you go again, flirting." Oke moved crocks off the worktables and onto the floor. "Oh hello, what do we have here?" He waggled a pickle in the air. "I've found true love for you. Enjoy this and stop using me to fill time until your mistress gives in to your wicked charms."

Illoe stopped sweeping. "Don't even joke about that."

Oke raised both eyebrows and leaned back against the racks. "Or you could give in to her charms. Is it more against the law that way?"

"A skrok of a noble accused me of sleeping with Hitra within hours of…none of your business." Illoe pushed his friend aside so he could reach into the jar of pickles.

"It's gotten into 'none of my business' territory, then? You and the holy hottie?"

"Shush. You make one more joke about Hitra and me and I'll… I'll…"

"Oh? You'll?" Oke grinned, bits of pickle among his widely spaced teeth. "Oh, mistress!" Oke fell back in mock faint against the butcher block. "Oh, you are so gorgeous and unobtainable! Teach me what it means to be a man!"

There was a clatter, and both boys turned, Illoe with his hands around Oke's neck, Oke bent back in the midst of theatrical flailing. Eiti, Reha's servant, picked up the discarded broom. "I'll come back," he said.

Oke wished fervently he could see exactly how they looked from Eiti's point of view. He hoped it was just shy of pornographic. He should have lifted his leg. Oke liked Eiti's eyes, and he had nice thick thighs with soft hair that Oke suspected would feel marvelous against him.

Illoe fervently wished he could get through this conversation without further embarrassment. He straightened and tugged his tunic hem down. A move that could be called "the Illoe."

Oke stretched his arms luxuriously. "You're both uptight morons."

Emboldened by insult, Eiti strangled the broomstick. "The Celebrant needs her food early today. She's eating before dawn blessing."

Oke gave Illoe a playful jab and rolled off the butcher block. "Sorry your Lordlet-ness, but what we got is what you see, and ain't nothing getting done before dawn."

"I'll get some biscuits," Illoe said.

Thank you! I'm so glad YOU are here.

Illoe winced at the simpering tone of Eiti's thoughts. He knew, without any such bond with his non-gifted friend, that Oke thought Illoe was being an impossible goody-two-shoes. The biscuits were easy to find, though, lined up like soldiers on the cooling racks.

Oke had some pickles and cheese wrapped in a napkin by the

time Illoe retrieved the biscuits. Eiti accepted these offerings petulantly, curling the bundle to his chest. "Reha's on a special investigation for the queen," he blurted.

Illoe took the broom from him. "Eiti," he said, folding his hand
over the wealthy boy's, "You really are a skrok."

Illoe and Oke laughed together as he turned red and left.

"I'm proud," Oke said, and fished another pickle out of the jar.
"Superb timing. Get him hard and slap him down."

Illoe sat on the edge of the butcher block. He felt guilty about
insulting Eiti; he had wanted to build on their almost-friendship, but
Oke brought it out in him, the desire to push others and insult because
it made them a them. Illoe shook the thought off, he wanted to get
back to the easy camaraderie. "Yeah. What was with that? Like we
care what his boss does."

Oke shrugged. "He's probably been waiting all week to blurt that
little beauty. It would make his sheltered heart stop if he ever got a
whiff of half the gossip I get." He shook his head and bit solemnly into
his pickle.

Illoe could tell Oke wanted to tell him something. "What gossip?"

"Yes, there are improvements in that area since your last inquiry.
Word is your very fine looking mistress went holy war yesterday.
Hauled off on a Sanadaru. Told him she saw her god." Oke nudged
Illoe's arm. "What's the inside scoop? I'm the temple's news source.
You don't think they pay me just to boil water?"

Illoe was grateful then that Oke had no telepathic gift to overhear
an errant sending. "I... don't know anything about it." He still had the
broom in his hands, so he quickly went back to sweeping.

Oke went back to sorting the stores for morning, but didn't stop
talking. "Old Kala saw it, while she was trimming rose vines. Hitra
went apocalyptic; that's how Kala put it. The Sanadaru was in literal
tears. Not very Reform, was it?"

There was a piece of straw on the floor that resolutely refused to
be swept. The broom went over it like it wasn't there. Illoe kicked it.
"You talk to Kala? Why? She's awful."

"I was telling her how you finally got hit." Oke set down the pot
he was carrying and slid into Illoe's personal space, shoulder first, like

he was going to lean against him. "And, incidentally, you still haven't told me what you did. Was it awful? Tussle-with-a-sacred-virgin awful? It's always the quiet ones."

"I didn't do anything!"

The door from the dining hall banged, heralding the arrival of Determined Re, an elderly Sanadaru who managed the pots and keeping the kitchen clean. Illoe raised a hand in greeting, which was returned with a grunt as Det made his way slowly toward the storage lockers.

Oke instantly assumed a more business-like demeanor, not wanting to get a scolding from the older man. "What's the word, Det?"

Det's response was not a word though it bore a similarity to a curse. He was secretly fond of the boys, but didn't want them to know that.

As soon as Det was busily banging about the closets, Oke tugged on Illoe's sleeve. "Come on! You had to have done something to rattle her gorgeousness. She's ice on rice, usually. You can tell me…you finally did it, didn't you? Told her you wanted out?"

Illoe didn't know how to answer, because he had told her, but that wasn't why she hit him, and suddenly Oke's casual cheer was all too much. "I'll see you at lunch." Illoe backed out of the kitchen.

☽〇☾

Hitra was standing at the entrance to his room when Illoe came in from the back door. She was in her sleeping robe, clutching it tight in front of her. "I'd like it if you stayed in my room while I take my bath."

"That's a little weird, isn't it?"

"Just stay there. I'll have the door open. We won't see each other, but if something happens, you can come in quickly."

"I'll do it," he said, "but you owe me."

Relieved, Hitra led the way to the bathroom. She stopped at the doorway and looked back at him as though afraid he'd go somewhere. Illoe took out the accounting records and settled down at Hitra's desk to pay the bills. The first was always the bill for him, for his indenture, that went to his mother. In name only — his father would likely spend it all. Illoe ran a finger over the embossed number and considered that he could easily forgo a payment on Hitra's behalf, just for spite, but he would be the one to suffer when his father made a fuss to collect.

"I read the contract over again," Hitra said. Her voice echoed from the tile and water. He heard a few soft splashes as she got into the tub. "I don't think there's really a problem. It just says I have to keep you until you find a wife, not that you have to get married right away. I mean, that was sort of what I thought would happen anyway. You can stay here as long as you like."

"I'd rather go." Illoe hoped he said it politely.

There were a few splashes, and then the sonorous wave of a body moving completely in a tub, then silence. Illoe stopped writing, so that there was no noise to distract him. There were gentle sounds from the bathroom, choked sounds. She was crying.

"Hitra?" Silence. "Boss?"

"I love this soap. You know that? I really love this soap. I don't even know where it comes from."

Illoe fiddled with the stylus. "The soap's spicebush. Happy Sun spicebush soap. They're on High Street."

"It doesn't smell like spicebush."

"I know; that's why I like it. I don't know what else Happy Sun puts in their soap, but it's different, that's why I started buying it." He waited for her to say something. He began to worry what it would be. "You knew the contract was going to end after four years. You know this isn't how I plan to spend my whole life."

Hitra almost didn't say it. She couldn't say it out loud. Her feelings were raw. She tried to send the words without emotion. *Don't leave me. I just can't bear it right now. Not now.*

Illoe contacted the bank and, using a ritual of phrases and responses, transferred the appropriate funds for Hitra's debts. Then he marked them carefully in the ledger. When Hitra spoke to him again, he didn't answer, and when she cried, he pretended not to hear it.

Chapter Six

Annunciation

Guilt. Illoe flushed hot when he got close to thinking about Hitra crying.

Two days ago, when I ended a man's life, the nurse had felt that same hot discomfort. I didn't like remembering the feeling, seeing it reflected in Illoe. It was a repulsive emotion.

That I caused. And I found myself returning to the hospital, but of course he was gone. The man didn't exist anymore. He'd been someone and now he wasn't. So fragile. Like Illoe's palms on the concrete walk. Like the delicate flutter of his blood squeezing through the tiny passages in his fingertips. I returned to Illoe , half to make sure he hadn't disappeared when I wasn't looking, like water boiling away.

A flash of warmth. "You found something?" Wenne had snuck in next to me. She was confined, person-sized, alone. Rude.

"Was I talking to you?"

She rolled her golden, slightly glowing eyes. "Your thoughts are so loud. 'I'm so close to finding something out'."

I hated that she put it like that. I was closing in on a disturbing new thought. I wasn't sure I wanted to be.

She pressed, "Is it about our memories? None of our sisters can recall past a week ago."

That…was welcome news. I wasn't the only one who couldn't remember. "I'm working on it."

"It looks like you're watching a young man doing accounting."

He was done with the accounts, actually. He was checking over Hitra's schedule and making calls on her behalf to confirm meetings. He would rather have been doing the accounts still.

"I'm studying their thoughts and emotions." I could feel Wenne question the usefulness of that, so I explained, "They've helped me master talking and touching."

Illoe glanced over his shoulder. He'd heard my voice but not my words.

"Show me," Wenne said.

Like I was going to perform for her!

Hitra came out of the bathroom with a cloud of steam. Her gaze focused on the edge of the desk, her tears washed away but her eyes still red. "Clear my schedule for the morning. I'm going to the archive."

"But I just…" Illoe ran his hand over his face. "You have an opening at third hour. Go then."

His insolence gave her enough courage to glare at him. "Just do it." Then she felt guilt, raw and cold and sinking. She hurried to her clothes chest and threw it open.

Wenne was waiting. I didn't explain myself. She could see it was a delicate situation.

Illoe went into the bath to drain the tub. The warmth and steam soaked into his clothes, leaving him clammy. The energy that had pulled him early from bed had all been used up. He turned off the oil burner under the bath and splashed some cold water from the pump onto his face. He heard Hitra pulling tomes off her shelf. Again. Probably the same ones she'd pulled the day before. They fell with nice expensive-sounding thumps and something glass crashed (an incense tray) and Hitra cursed.

"Explain to me how this teaches us anything," Wenne demanded.

Illoe didn't react to her voice. Wenne hadn't vibrated the air, only transmitting thought directly to me through the medium that formed us and nothing else. Here was another new thought. It was easy to communicate so only Wenne could hear. "You're not thinking about it the right way. I wasn't, either, for a long time. Really look at them, the way their thoughts change into actions and words."

Illoe squinted at the mirror and set his hair to rights, unaware of us, but aware of every permutation his hair could hold and the subtle messages it would send to others.

Illoe put the soap and the skin scraper away and watched the last water drain from the tub. There wasn't anything else he could think of to occupy himself and make Hitra wait. He sighed noisily and made a tromping display of walking around Hitra and her books to check the calendar.

Wenne started to pull away. I had to restrain her. A metaphor of hand against chest, urging her to wait and see.

Illoe tapped today's date on the calendar page. Four more days until the eve of Harvest Home. Third wholemonth, Darian's Day. Like the calendar day before and after it, the paper was full of crossing-outs and little curving arrows pointing to crossed-out things pointing to cramped notes. He knew that already, but wanted Hitra to see him looking. "You have a full day today. There's no clearing it. Not after we cleared all of yesterday and the day before."

She flapped her outer robe, trying to get her arms in the sleeves. A stack of books waited on top of her sleeping robe. "I just need an hour."

"It's the men's committee, Hitra. You've put them off three times now."

"One hour," she said again, pleadingly. "It has to be."

"You don't know how hard it was for me to move your schedule as it is."

Wenne imagined hurling me through the window. "What is the point of this?"

I couldn't quite explain it. The way they were thinking and feeling and trying to be understood.

Hitra picked up her books. "Just send an apology, or send Jante."

"They don't want Jante." Illoe put down the calendar and followed her to the front room. She pressed her hand to the little window over the guide-light. It was freezing. She shook her fingers and went to pull her cloak from its peg.

"Hitra! I'm serious, you can't skip this meeting. It's Overfalls and Southmarsh again. They want to know why no men are heading committees for Harvest Home."

Fastening the cloak, Hitra gave Illoe a smirk that only solidified his anger at her.

"This is serious, boss."

Did Wenne see the beauty of that communication? History, opinion, amusement, dismissal - all in a glance.

Maybe. She smirked at me.

"Send Jante," Hitra said. She grabbed her scroll case and the two volumes and without a moment's pause, she was out the door, leaving it open in her wake.

Illoe shuddered at the sudden cold. His thoughts flew after Hitra as he closed the door. *They won't listen to Jante and you know it.*

They have no choice. The committee heads were decided months ago!

"Yeah," he said, throwing his hands up. "And then a miracle occurred, and now everyone wants to be important." He sighed and waved his exasperation at the closed door.

Wenne thought firmly how she'd given watching Illoe all the chance to make sense she could. "You're thinking like you're one of them, Senne. You're not. You're a god. Start acting like one."

Wenne vanished with a rude gesture.

The worst thing was Wenne was right. I shouldn't be wallowing in…whatever this was. I should be finding answers. Why couldn't I remember? Why couldn't Wenne? Why did I have to learn how to interact with the world I helped create?

Hitra wondered why Revestre had appeared, and then not re-appeared. Why the gods were acting now and hadn't before. She thought the archives would help her.

Our questions were the same, really, or at least, inverse sides to a central question we didn't know to ask, yet.

☽○☾

Hitra was not so stalwart as she'd made herself appear to Illoe. She approached the priestly archives with much the feeling of one who approaches a precipice with intent to fling themselves over. She could not bear a pause because she knew her nerve would go.

The priests' archives were at the very back of the temple complex, nestled inside the stone of the mountain itself. The front entrance was carved for the convenience of giants, should any appear, and had the desired impact of making one feel small.

Inside it was worse, the ceiling many stories up, painted with a marvelous mural of the great achievements of civilization, starting at the eastern end with Wenne giving wisdom to primitive humanity, who tottered off to a procession of ships discovering the northern lands, with peaceful Sanadaru greeting their conquerors, then a panoramic founding of the city, and culminating on the western end with the building of the archive itself.

I was conspicuously absent. You'd think Senne giving humankind the gift of mental speech would be worth a few squares of inlaid glass. But then, there weren't many religious milestones up there. No depiction of the sisters who founded the tribes of humanity, no first temple, no Revestre teaching humanity to plant grain. For a priestly archive, its decoration was strongly concerned with the mundane.

Great mortals of history stood on false pediments along the walls. All those important women in their trailing robes, pointing gravely with long, bare, strong arms made Hitra seriously doubt she would ever be thus depicted, alongside the inventor of the water wheel, the creator of glass, and the legendary man who invented silk—one of the few men up there, his bare legs shown to great advantage as he reclined over the arch of a tall window, his weaving across his lap and dangling down the wall as a realistically rendered curtain.

The windows were almost opaque, having been made decades ago of unimproved glass. This made everything diffuse, glowing, and otherworldly, down to the frail old antiquarians who welcomed Hitra and led her, helpless and unwilling, to a comfortable chair by the silk-weaver's window.

"No, it's no trouble, Holiness, we'll fetch whatever text you need," said Efa, the chief librarian, smiling with watery eyes.

"I want the oldest written mentions of Revestre," Hitra said, "and any accounts of a priest being directly visited by a god."

I followed Efa into tightly-packed shelves, hidden from view of the patrons in the grand room. Dangling tags carried a coded language only librarians understood, sorting the texts by subject and age.

Could all my answers be here? I pulled a scroll from the shelf. It fell, heavy, and the librarian glanced back, thinking she'd pick whatever it was up when a patron wasn't waiting. Scrolls and tomes had a habit of falling, randomly, and (ironically) this was attributed to Senne's mischievous servants. (Which was another question: where were my servants, my talking mice and birds to steal coins and untie sandals?)

I unrolled the thick parchment, proud of my manipulation. I didn't damage a thing. The bleached animal skin was marked in the faintest red lines. It was ancient, older than the city. Here were the secrets of forgotten days. I could just make out the symbols. Wool. Mountain. Two tens and five. River. Seven and eight pieces? I skimmed ahead, noting the pattern, and then I reached the map.

It was a catalog of prices, for parcels of land.

☽O☾

Illoe brought breakfast for Hitra, but she hardly looked up and asked him to take it back. He lit up with rage only I could see.

I wasn't getting anywhere with the scrolls (other than causing librarians to curse and laugh and theorize about squirrels). All I'd found written about the gods was vague nonsense. So, I followed Illoe back to Hitra's rooms. He refolded the wax cloth that protected the biscuits, muttering about how easy Hitra thought his job was. Oh, just reschedule! Yes, how simple!

He returned to the fire pantry and found a soggy, half-eaten biscuit on the counter and threw it into the basket he used to collect indoor wastes. It bounced out again, bringing a curl of parchment with it and some dried wax drops.

He stopped himself short of making a worse mess by kicking the full basket.

"If she had to do my job for one day..." He squatted and carefully gathered the trash back into the basket.

There was a cart by the necessary where refuse was collected by the groundskeepers and taken to the incinerator. Illoe had to carry the wastebasket through his own room, which in his current state of anger he now considered a great insult, though it was just a consequence of having the rear door next to his bed.

That door opened onto a cinder path that connected the backs of all the priest's residences, a nice little courtyard, with the necessary on one end and an archway that led out into the gardens on the other.

The groundskeeper, Kala, was raking the cinder path.

Illoe looked up at the skies, and in an uncharacteristic moment for an atheist, asked the gods why they must constantly try him this way?

Would I have put Kala in his path? I hadn't spared a thought for her. She was a gnarled woman, old before her time from hard work, and she was worrying about how to hide a gambling debt from her husband.

Illoe started across the grass rather than the path, to avoid her, but of course as his shadow fell in her vision, Kala leaned against her rake and said, "Hey darlin'!" She thanked the gods for sending the pretty boy her way just when she needed cheering.

These people really had a habit of assuming we were doing stuff.

"I don't want to talk." Illoe continued his stiff march to the waste-cart.

"Oh ho!" Kala raked the cinders near her a little more, getting them off the grass and back onto the path, and then she trotted to catch up with him. "I didn't ask anything, sugar."

Illoe tossed the trash into the cart with more vehemence than was strictly necessary, and a fruit rind rolled over the far side.

Kala put her hand on his arm. "Baby, you can tell your old pal Kala all about whatever's bothering you."

Illoe wondered how Kala could not notice how much he hated her touching him. He said, "I'm fine, thank you," and turned on his heel.

"Aw, sweetie." Kala hurried to match step with him. She draped her boney arm over his shoulders and he flicked it off. "Your old girl's under a lot of stress, isn't she?"

"Hitra's fine." He tried to get past Kala to his own door, but she was leaning against it now, her rake hugged to her side like a confidant. Illoe thought the woman was like a human choke-vine.

I felt better about myself, seeing Kala's naked desire. "Is it the fire? I know a lot of these priests, they spend all their time thinking about the ineffable, and when it happens, well, they're just as unprepared as us 'effable' folks, eh?"

"It's not the fire," Illoe said. "Hitra's stronger than that."

Despite Illoe's unsubtle body language and tone, which was set to imply that he found Kala loathsome, and would rather she left him alone, Kala was convinced that she was well on her way to wearing down his icy resolve with her compassion and understanding. She pressed on. "Is it drink? C'mon, you can tell me. Trouble with her family?"

"Why do you care?"

Kala set one narrow hand against her chest. "I care," she said. "I feel like you're my family, honey, you and all the residents."

"Oke says you already know what's going on."

Kala's eyes got bright with excitement and she leaned forward. "She said she saw Revestre. You think it's for real?"

"She believes it. Look, I have a lot of work to do, and so do you."

He pulled the door open despite Kala's slight weight, sending the skinny groundskeeper staggering.

"Rumors can be brutal, baby. Just let me know if I can help," she called as Illoe shut the door on her.

Kala even took his shoving past her as a good sign! You wouldn't catch me so blind I hurt the boy I was trying to seduce.

Um. I went to see if Hitra had learned anything.

☽○☾

Casu, living on the western side of the country, had first worshiped a god of grain called Reave in the distant days before the unification of the five tribes of Cassia. This was likely the birth of Revestre, who was included in the main pantheon with the building of the first temple at the unified capital, which was at Narrow's Rise, along the Green River. The name change probably came from conflating Reave with the northern Casu harvest-god figure Arastre, who may have only been a demi-god, the daughter of Senne, who was god of the sky in many old pantheons, and a human man who represented the earth, possibly an early version of Darian.

Yeah, I had children. Maybe. In another legend Arastre was the daughter of the sea god and a defunct male god of the home.

This is just a sampling of the utterly useless information Hitra gathered as she spent not one but three hours in the library, getting increasingly desperate and less careful as she skimmed.

It was hard to ignore the way all these stories made more sense as fiction. I skimmed the minds nearby. Four were researching the column of fire, specifically. Three of these were endlessly distracted with their own pet theories, searching for any text that backed it up. The fourth was making a list of potential source myths, hoping she would be applauded for this tedious work when other scholars realized she'd saved them time.

In one corner, a male student re-read a passage he'd found which he was sure proved that men could be priests of all gods, not just Darian, and he wondered how everyone else had missed it.

How could they not? Dozens of library patrons scanned for passages that agreed with their preconceptions, and discarded the rest.

When Hitra noticed the archive staff lighting the lamps she stood with a gasp, remembering that she did, indeed, have other duties to attend to. She gathered up her scrolls and reached out for Jante with her mind.

☽O☾

Hitra burst in the front door like a storm gust, but Illoe was at that point in his nap that a minor earthquake wouldn't wake him.

Not seeing him on the other side of the sofa, Hitra dropped her scroll case on his stomach.

He gasped, she screamed, and then they were both standing, the couch between them, clutching their chests.

Hitra was half laughing as she asked, "What were you doing on the couch?"

He didn't catch her playful irony, instead thinking seriously that he had every right to a nap. "Could you look before you crush a guy?" He snatched the scroll case off the floor.

Illoe dropped her case on the counter of the fire pantry and got out the striker to light the lamps. "I had to listen to Southmarsh make his argument five times before he gave up. And I had to tear out three pages in the calendar book and start fresh."

"I'm sorry." Hitra sat down to unlace her sandals, feeling considerably less than sorry.

"So, was it worth it?"

She looked up to see him standing, arms crossed, like a professor awaiting recitation.

She lay back and looked out the dining nook window. "Revestre supposedly appeared to Queen Shalana the First, when she prayed to find out how to end a great drought."

"So are you going to pray for an end to stupidity?"

"I wish I could talk to Queen Shalana the First."

In happier times, Illoe would have cut in with a quip about how he wished she could talk to the men's committee, but he was still too angry. "I'll grab dinner from the kitchens." He walked out the front door without looking back or asking her if she had any preferences.

Hitra hugged her knees to her chest and felt after his mind. *I need meditative peace, I think. That's mentioned a lot in accounts of contact between man and gods.*

No response but tired irritation. A gnat bit Illoe on the back of one hand and he scratched, breaking its little body and flicking it away.

Hitra watched her toes clench and unclench against the soft upholstery and wondered if she'd ever achieve meditative peace again.

But then Illoe came with food, and took her cloak and hung it, and brought her night-robe and soothing tea, and she thought less and less, unaware of how lucky she was.

And it was night, and it was morning, and I had wasted another day.

$$\mathrm{)O(}$$

Hitra stood before the congregation. The harvest season was a special one for Revestre, and a few worshipers came who might not otherwise, to see her carry the gilt sheaves of wheat from their storeroom to the altar, where they would be on display throughout harvest season. There were few farmers in the city, one of the reasons the position at the temple had been easy for her to nab. Revestre was worshiped in the countryside, by nuns and monks who valued their simplicity and didn't scramble like acolytes of Wenne would for a position at the temple.

Which was all to say the crowd was much larger than expected on this day, one week before Harvest Home. The chapel was packed and more stood outside the columns, in the gardened cloisters that flanked the chapel. Hitra felt their eyes on her. She had never sweated so much preparing a ritual. The day had dawned warm again, almost summer-like, but the shadows gave away the season even if the temperatures did not, making the day feel feverish.

The sheaves were small, weighed nothing, but they slipped in her grasp and her feet slid back and forth in her sweaty sandals. She should have worn slippers.

These were motions she knew, but just that: motions. How had she gotten into this? When had she become a priest? She remembered making clay pots at winter camp, singing in the choir, the absolute peace her pastor seemed to carry. But had it been necessary? Could she have simply enjoyed these things, not mentioned them to her mother, gone to the Academy instead of the Seminary? She looked out on the faces of people who believed, and wished she could remember what it was like to be one of them. How could they stare at her, bow their heads as she passed, when she was just going through the motions? Didn't they see?

☽ ○ ☾

A cold shock, like falling upward, into water, and then Hitra was diminished and yet stronger, an externally confident little toy priest. I hadn't realized how close I'd gotten.

A presence, yellow and warm and bodiless—Wenne—said, "I'm calling for a council of the gods."

She shimmered into solidity. Damn. She'd been practicing. Her semblance was better than I'd obtained yet, diaphanous fabric blowing around a well-turned calf and draping between pert little breasts. "Now. I'm calling the sisters together. We need to talk."

I felt the horror and fear of that weird mingling that had happened the last time we'd gotten together. "I'll pass. Let me know if anything interesting happens."

"Senne, you are second among the gods. You must attend."

"And yet, I foresee myself not going."

She contemplated force—balling me up like a discarded robe and carrying me to her meeting. We measured our strengths against each other. There was a chance she would succeed. Had I been wasting away in my passivity? No, I'd fight her to the end. If I didn't, she'd never stop ordering me about.

She shifted slightly in color. "Maybe you're right, that observing the mortals closely holds the answer, but they'll still be there later. I need you now."

I had a half-formed witty retort, about how she didn't need me, the god of chaos and mischief, since she was doing such a phenomenal job spreading both. I didn't get to compose it just as I'd have liked, since she heard it in process and reacted.

"The scriptures *dictate* I would send a column of fire to announce my return to dealing in mortal affairs. It's in four different books. Why are they struggling to understand something they wrote?"

"Maybe you should try sending a letter instead of an enigmatic symbol? Or, here's a novel idea—talk to them?"

Flicker of embarrassment. Had she tried and failed? I wanted to see details. Wenne closed her mind from my probing. "This is the way things are supposed to be done! Why won't any of you obey me? The ancient covenant says you all listen to me!"

"We're not going to find out standing around asking each other."

Illoe's legs itched, below, from the jagged ends of the mown grass. His shoulders pricked from the sun. Sweat trickled down his side between his skin and his tunic, while at the same time his rear felt positively cold from the soil underneath him, and yet he was sitting, precisely where he didn't want to be. Hitra hadn't even asked him to come, or made her usual statements about putting up appearances.

Wenne groaned. "Of course. Senne is distracted by a man. Don't you remember Darian?"

I didn't remember Darian. Did she? Maybe Wenne and the others were just fine, remembering everything. Maybe I was the butt of an elaborate joke.

Sarcastically, Wenne continued, "Son of Cassia? Transformed by YOU? Elevated to godhood? THAT Darian?" No. Her thoughts had no depth of memory. She was recalling scripture. Mere words. Stories.

"Of course, I remember him," I said, just to piss her off. "Sexy boy. Don't understand what he saw in you." He was supposed to be the man who was my undoing. What had he looked like? Something like Illoe, I guessed, young and dark with downy hair on his arms and petulant, expressive eyebrows. "Come to think of it, shouldn't Darian be…somewhere? I'd go to your silly meeting if there were a chance of seeing him there. Where are all the male gods, anyway?"

Wenne was getting impatient. I could feel her getting pulled and tugged in other directions. I wasn't the only one she was trying to talk to at once.

"That's rude," I said.

She solidified a little more, some portion of herself returning to the whole, perhaps more than one portion, and I didn't know whether to be honored or annoyed. "This is serious. The people are getting out of hand." She showed me a shop in the lower city, the windows broken in and religious slurs painted on the stone. "They're violent, afraid…we have to do something."

"So do something. You're a god." Below, Hitra had forgotten a part of the ritual—a word or a gesture or something, she wasn't sure what but it was gone, a blank space in her mind and she was telling the acolytes to start the song so she could have time to remember.

Wenne's mind was being tugged. Dioneltar and Telumene were at it again, bickering over stones. Resignation, acceptance flowed through her like falling leaves. "You won't help, but I seriously doubt you'll harm. Farewell, sister."

"Oh, I can cause all sorts of harm," I said, but I wasn't feeling the villain role. I went back to Illoe. Microcosmic Illoe, who would rather be miserable unbidden than to obey.

I guess that made two of us.

He could see the ceremony finishing—they were through the song and into the affirmations. This opened the harvest, a holy week that ended with the Harvest Home celebration, the largest holiday on Revestre's calendar. It had never seemed to come so quickly. He moved further into the shade. He rested his forehead on his knees and opened his mind. *Location code 62, please. I want to speak to the router.*

Location code 62, how may I…Illoe? This isn't funny.

Will you come talk with me, Ele? Please? When you're done with work. I'll buy you dinner.

Silence. Illoe shook his head. He should have known better. He just felt so entirely alone.

Unexpected, his brother's voice came back, softer. *I can be up there half past seventh hour. Where do you want to meet?*

Ele felt the loneliness in his younger brother. It made him feel overcome with protectiveness. How I would love to feel something like that directed toward me! I suspected, though, that Illoe would be offended if he felt his brother's reaction.

Hitra pulled the congregation along with her as she left the chapel. Two acolytes flanked her, pushing people away, patting arms and hands with blessings. Here's how close I'd been; I hadn't noticed the anger in the congregation. It was trembling under their outward piety. Hitra was lying. Hitra had made them come out for this dull ceremony and hadn't given what they were owed.

Just as Hitra feared, in the absence of official statements, an unofficial canon was being written. The fire column had appeared outside Hitra's rooms. Hitra had seen Revestre. Ergo, the fire column had been sent by Revestre. A pious man near the front of the throng had a following of his own, believing this was the dawn of an age of the plants. Another was certain it meant that Revestre was an aspect of Wenne all along. It didn't matter how divergent their opinions were when they were united in wanting something from Hitra. They didn't know what, but they were prepared to do violence to get it.

Not that everyone was so passionate. There was the girl by the wall who was only there so her mother would let her go to the market on her own next week. She picked a scab on her elbow and thought how grown up she would look carrying the market basket and ordering the boys at the fruit stalls around.

The frightening thing was how Hitra didn't notice either the impious girl or the zealots. They were a blur named Congregation in her mind and she was insensible to the chaos tightening like a coil inside them.

Illoe stood as Hitra approached. His legs awoke in a flare of prickles. He stamped his feet and set his face in an expression that dared Hitra to bring up the subject of his not having been formally at the ritual.

She didn't notice. She grabbed his arm in passing and pulled him alongside her without a word. She pulled me along, too, and an invisible storm front of violent emotion only half-perceived.

Chapter Seven

Rites

That night it rained. The air chilled and the columned halls of the temple complex echoed with many tiny impacts. Illoe swept the front room while Hitra went into her bedroom alone.

As the water-clock filled to the sixth hour, Hitra came out, dressed in her best robes. "Where is the gift for my mother?"

"The hall cupboard. I'll get it."

"No, that's all right."

Illoe returned to the dining nook and stood in the cold light of falling rain. He heard Hitra open the cupboard and search around. "It's on the left," he said. "Second shelf."

The cupboard closed. Illoe heard the temple chimes ring out sixth hour. The water clock was a little fast. He probably overfilled it that morning. Hitra walked to the door without looking at him. There was a brief struggle with the knob, a blast of rain-smell, and the slam of the door closing. She was gone.

Illoe put away the broom. With a feeling of eminent domain he took the fine table linens from the cupboard and smoothed a hand over them. A quick query to the kitchen told him dinner was on its way. He surveyed the front room with a new eye for its inadequacies. The border mosaics were dull with years of accumulated scratches. There was a spot on the carpet where a candle had spilled years ago and he had never gotten the wax all the way out of it. He moved an incense burner over it. He tugged the tablecloth until it lay perfectly centered and tried not to worry. He would light the lanterns, and set teacakes to fry. That would fill the apartment with the sweet smell of baking and warm light. Yes. He just had to think of it as another dinner engagement.

☽○☾

Ele winced as the door opened in front of him. He hadn't expected to meet Illoe's eyes near a level with his own. His little brother was suddenly taller than him.

"Give me your cloak, I'll hang it up," Illoe said.

Ele stepped into the antechamber, awed by the rich glitter of the mosaics. From Ele's point of view it was a lavish apartment, draped in floral tapestries and lit with stained glass lanterns that cast irregular squares of color over fine furnishings. "So this is it: The squalor of servitude."

"I'll show you my room; you'll be less impressed."

Ele looked down at his rain-soaked shoes on the glass-inlaid floor. It was clean enough to eat off of. He put his hand on a column and pried the wet leather off his feet. Illoe took each shoe as soon as he removed it. "I'll put these next to the fire. They'll dry by the time you leave."

Ele stood awkwardly, one wet foot still up in the air. "You're not my servant."

"I'm your host. Go on into the dining area; it's straight ahead, up those steps." Illoe walked to the brick-walled fire pantry with the wet shoes dangling from one hand. Ele couldn't help comparing the filthy shoes to his brother's perfect cleanliness. Illoe's tunic was cut in the latest fashion, out of a fine but unadorned linen. The wide collar exposed his shoulders. His hair shone with health like a freshly shelled inknut. At some point in the past four years, Ele's brother had become a handsome young man. Ele felt a new unease he hadn't expected, that Illoe was alone most of the time with powerful women.

Illoe set the shoes down where fire colored the tiles. He straightened and noticed Ele staring. "What?"

Ele shifted his gaze. He'd left a handprint on the wall. "So," he said. The center of the room was covered in a thick fleece carpet. He knew it would feel wonderful on his wrinkled toes, but he kept to the glass tile knowing it would be easier to clean his wet footprints off of it. He reached the three wide steps that bowed out into the room, and found them to be covered in fleece as well. He peered into the curtained space above.

"So?" Illoe leaned in front of him. "Will you sit down? You look like you're walking through briars!"

Ele took a few steps back. "Does she know? That I'm here. Your priest."

Illoe's face curled into a sneer and he was a boy again. "She isn't my priest. And no, she doesn't know. So?"

"Aren't you going to get into trouble, then, having a guest? This isn't your home, Illoe. That's not your food on the fire. That's not even your tunic you're wearing." Ele tightened a fist, mad at himself for saying more than intended.

Illoe rolled his eyes.

Ele folded his arms to hide his fist. "I'm not going to stay if it gets you in trouble."

Illoe turned his back on him. "Sit down. The food is ready."

"What does she do to you? She can do whatever she wants, can't she?"

Illoe went to the fire pantry. He spoke to the oven as he ladled soup into bowls. "Oh, hot coals, pokers, prayer vigils on bare stone. And that's when she's happy." A metal lid rang against its pot. "It may surprise you to learn that Hitra is a kind and decent human being. She even lets me eat."

Illoe put a special emphasis on the word 'eat.' He carried a tray into the room and looked at Ele like a disappointed parent.

Ele rested against the brass stair rail. "Why did you invite me here?"

Illoe walked past his brother. "To torture you. Why did you accept?"

Ele couldn't tell him he had felt panicked and protective. His brother was old enough to take offense at that.

In the ensuing silence, Illoe started setting bowls and plates out. "If Hitra doesn't renegotiate my contract before Harvest Home, I won't be freed next year. She said she would, but she hasn't. I don't think she wants to let me go. And I tried talking to Mom..."

Understanding dawned for Ele. "Father told me you visited, but not why. He was manic. I'm avoiding home until he calms down."

Illoe set the last bowl in its place and stood over the table, deprived of busy work. "I'm sorry."

Ele could no longer think of a compelling reason not to, so he climbed the three steps to the dining room. The carpet did feel good. A thick, meaty broth steamed from glass bowls. Ele's stomach rolled with hunger. "It's not your fault," he said, though he felt unconvinced. He sat down. Illoe sat and fussed with the tableware. There was a lull as both realized they were not eating. Ele picked up his fork. "None of it's your fault, is it?"

Illoe raised his hands over his head and let them fall. "I feel like I've been accused of something every time we talk. Didn't we used to get along?"

"You got along." Ele stabbed his stew, separating out the chunks of meat. "I got to watch every friend I made gravitate to you. And then I got to watch you leave without a fight, and hear every day about how good a brother I had, that gave up so much so that I could get my unworthy self into the Adept Academy."

"That's not my fault."

"I know," Ele said. "That makes it worse."

For a while, at least, the silence between them was excusable by the slurps and scrapes of a meal in progress.

The door chime was struck. Ele froze, his fork halfway to his mouth.

"It's all right," Illoe said. He folded his napkin beside his bowl. Ele watched him walk to the antechamber. His brother walked like he expected to be watched.

Ele could not see around the columned archway that separated off the entrance to the apartment, but he heard the door open and his brother's soft, businesslike greeting.

A woman's raspy voice replied at nearly double the volume, "When will she be back?"

Illoe's response was unintelligible. The woman shrieked, "You have no idea how…how serious this is! Let me past at once. How dare you? How…what? Are you hiding something? A woman? You have a woman in your mistress's home, don't you? Oh, Sweet Revestre!"

Ele set his fork down and leaned back as far as he could in his chair. He caught just a slice of a woman's black tunic, a wildly gesturing arm—and his brother was pushed back, and Maede was suddenly looking directly at Ele.

Her face hung slack with surprise. Illoe bowed theatrically. "Lady Faydehale, if you please, my…"

She raised a shaking finger toward Ele and shrieked. "A man. Not even a woman. Holy Mother of Us All! Lust! Lust with no interest in marriage, in a priestess's house!"

Ele stood. "Excuse me?"

"May I introduce Lady Faydehale." Illoe threw himself between them. "My elder brother, Eleteralenil Middlemount, an Adept of the Second Order."

The lady arched one thin eyebrow and Ele felt her mind touch his, as an adept, an all-out probe that was as graceless as it was powerful. He stopped her at the perimeter, pushed his credentials across with a delicate under-seam of annoyance. Doubt flickered in her, and she closed the connection.

Ele kept his eyes on her, but sent to his brother, *Don't introduce me like that.* Ever since he had passed his tests, the very day, he was no longer referred to as a person, only an adept, or at most, "a male adept," which was worse.

"Lady Faydehale," Illoe said, "Hitra will not be back until very late. There's no point in waiting for her."

Maede folded her small hands in front of her and walked deliberately to sit on the couch.

I'm sorry, Ele. This woman is a complete nutcase. Hitra only lets her come around because she gives obscene amounts of money to the church.

"Well," Ele said, "I'd better go. Thanks for dinner. We'll have to do it again."

Don't! Don't leave me with this she-skrok. We'll go back to my room.

Oh, that will be better, yes. Hide in your room together. Illoe, I shouldn't even be here.

Talk to father?

Three words that struck fear in Ele's heart. He could feel his brother follow him to the door. He turned around, realizing that he wasn't going anywhere without his shoes and cloak, and Illoe had them in hand. Ele recoiled as Illoe tried to help him put his shoe on and kneed his brother in the shoulder. Everywhere he tried to move, there was his brother, in the way.

The door chimes sounded.

Could this get any better? Ele took over fighting with his soaked shoes while Illoe got the door.

Illoe frowned at the crowd of rain-soaked figures cowering under the portico. "I'm sorry," he said, "but Her Holiness is not here."

An anxious woman standing near the front—Illoe reasoned correctly that she was the one who had struck the chimes—said, "We don't intend to waste the chosen one's time. If we could just be permitted a brief audience, you will be rewarded."

Illoe was still mouthing "chosen one?" when Maede shouldered her way into the antechamber to shout, "Who are you?"

The woman was alarmed, but nodded a polite greeting to Maede. "We are faithful followers of Revestre, come to hear the prophet's words." Inside the politeness she was gearing up to fight. She'd negotiated hard to get this role, to be the leader, though two men near the back of their group had done most of the organizing, and she blamed them for not mentioning this other person who might be in the priest's quarters.

"Prophet?" Illoe looked at his brother.

Ele leaned against the pillar behind him. *Does this sort of thing happen often?*

Maede pushed past Illoe. "The chosen one deserves her privacy. How dare you come to her home like this? Have you no respect?"

Illoe found the words "chosen one" even more ridiculous on Maede's lips. In truth, even the ardent faithful outside the door were a little embarrassed by the terminology, but they were getting used to it.

"Is it true?" A man raised himself on tiptoe to look over the heads of the women before him.

Maede flapped her sleeve like she was shooing a pest. "Of course it is true! But that doesn't give you the right to barge into a priest's home! Out, away with all of you, or I'll have you arrested!"

Illoe and Ele found themselves standing together while Maede argued with the people. More were arriving. Latecomers from the organized group and a few passers-by drifting in like moths to the flame.

Illoe frowned as an unfamiliar voice entered his head. *You're her servant, aren't you? Tell us what she saw. Were you there? Did you hear The God?*

The God. Thought with capital letters, like she was the only one. Other voices joined in, overlapping, confusing. He covered his ears. "Ele. Help me...I can't shut them out."

Maede turned sharply and suddenly the voices were gone. The silence rang.

"Hey," Ele stepped forward. "You can't just enter my brother's mind like that!"

Ele and Maede stared at each other. Even the petitioners outside were silent.

Illoe had gone deaf. Soundlessly, Ele mouthed words to Maede. I was so focused on Illoe that I'd missed what transpired. The petitioners had been poised, half-ecstatic with the promise of adept violence, which was not something they got to see every day, but whatever Ele said crushed their hopes. They cleared a path for Ele to walk out into the night.

Maede pushed Illoe back and slammed the doors. He heard that.

"Just because," she said, with emphasis, as though those two words represented a lifetime of ideology, "Just because a commoner attains the second rank that does *not* make him the equal of a noble." She nodded in agreement with herself and stomped her way to the couch, where she let out an exaggerated sigh. "Fetch me tea."

Illoe set his hand against the closed door. The crowd on the other side milled around, debating striking the chimes again. Illoe's head ached. "My brother and I haven't seen each other in years. Thank you, Lady Faydehale, for showing him the nobility of your station."

Maede glared at him, one of her typical, depthless glares—she didn't understand his sarcasm—but this time, fresh from a firsthand experience of what the adept were capable of, Illoe withered under the force of it. This did not pass Maede unnoticed, and even she was aware enough to be pleased.

Illoe started toward the fire pantry, walking closer to the wall than was necessary, and tried to cover his fear with a tired and quiet, "Now get out of my house."

Maede's will hit the back of his skull like concrete. He found himself on the floor, white specks dancing on the edges of his vision. Yes, this he could believe.

The tea. The words sounded in his ear like a scream, but Maede was still and calm on the couch, her chin tilted up, exposing her stick-like throat like a particularly smug stork, though inside she was almost pained by the strain it took to deliver a mental blow. He didn't know that. And, yes, she knew it was wrong to use power in that way, but she defied him to object; he had all but told her to do it.

Illoe pushed himself to his feet. He just began forming the rudiments of a snide remark when another thought hit him: He needed Maede's protection from the crowd outside. Nausea hit him as he straightened, an aftershock. He gasped, and the gasp sounded embarrassingly like a cry. He pressed against the wall and nodded.

The teacup chipped against the saucer as he set it down. He almost dropped the iron kettle and was filled with an icy stab of fear. The handle dug into his clenched fist. How could he be afraid of her? Of Maede, of all people!

But he was afraid, and there was nothing he could do about it but calm himself and serve tea. They were both increasingly aware of the power imbalance between them, and both waiting for the other to do something about it with eagerness and fear that were so equally intense as to be almost the same emotion.

I wanted to do something, but I couldn't stand being there.

)O(

This was Revestre's fault, obviously. Her stupid face. How was she, minor secondary god that she was, the only one of us to successfully communicate with a mortal? What was she even trying to achieve?

She was easy to spot because she was incandescent with frustration. She was following Hitra.

Hitra was nearing the end of her miserable pilgrimage down High Street. Hitra's hair was heavy with rain, and no matter how she wiped her brow, water poured in rivulets in her eyes, so she was frustrated too, but a more defeated version of the emotion. Her parents' home hung over her like a cliff, the ornamental eaves doing nothing to shield her from the downpour.

"This is not what I wanted," Revestre said, in exactly the wrong way for Hitra to hear her.

The ponderous door groaned open, and before Hitra could form a smile and apology for her appearance, strong hands took her and all but lifted her over the threshold.

"Holiness! You should not be out in the rain alone!"

A servant glanced out, seeing me, but not Revestre. To him I looked like a vaguer version of Hitra. He took me for a penitent and slammed the door.

I wasn't offended. Revestre wailed that no one had felt her presence, not since Hitra in the bath. Had it been Hitra's doing, not hers? I thought about that push outward. Could Hitra have made Revestre appear because she wanted her to?

Revestre was deeply offended at my thoughts. It hadn't been about Hitra wanting her to appear, it had been simply that Hitra had all the information, how to appear, what light was, what sound was, and she'd had it all on the surface of her mind, brought up by meditating on ripples on the water, so it was ripe for Revestre's plucking.

The daft god hadn't studied what she was doing and couldn't remember how without Hitra actively guiding her. In the house, someone unclasped Hitra's rain cloak while another set of hands rubbed her head briskly with a towel. She sputtered and flailed. Someone was unlacing her shoes. She was led to a chair. A warm blanket was wrapped around her and a hot cup pressed into her hands.

When the towel lifted away she saw herself surrounded by a gaggle of her mother's servants, holding towels, slippers, tea things, and each expressing concern or sympathy. This was not her usual welcome.

"Where's Mother? Has something happened to my mother?"

She didn't look like the sort of chosen one who could command a god. I gestured at her. "Revestre, you idiot. It's light and sound and vibrations. I could explain it to you, but I won't."

I hoped I wouldn't. My thoughts were so transparent to my sisters.

Revestre thought I was being too simple. Too secular, in my suppositions. That it couldn't come down to stimulating delicate nerve fibers and pushing air around. And anyway, I was evil. I tangled men's hair and spoiled fruit and tarnished silver.

"You're thinking of air," I said, and even showed her how I said it, how only she heard me.

Hitra's mother's voice echoed from above. "Get away from her, all of you. Can't you see you're overwhelming her?" Lady Hautridge stood at the top of the staircase, both hands on the marble banister. "Cayja, clear this room immediately. All of you back to your duties. Hitra, come up to my office at once."

"Is something wrong?" Hitra fumbled for her pocket and the holy pendant Illoe had purchased as a gift.

Her mother's mind was opaque of emotion. *Come upstairs, Hitra. These are not times for us to be talking where servants may hear.*

Hitra forgot the present and took to her feet as quickly and humbly as a summoned neophyte on Ascension Day. Cold little streams of water continued to escape from her hair, down her neck, making her miserable. I picked apart the water molecules, drying them from her scalp before they gathered to fall.

Revestre shouted, "She's not your priest."

That felt like winning.

In her mother's office, Hitra felt nineteen again. Lady Hautridge stood regal behind her desk, fully willing to encourage that feeling. "First things first, Hitra: are you sure? Are you absolutely sure you weren't dreaming?"

Hitra supposed her mother would not be consoled by knowing the Celebrant herself had asked that. "How did you find out?"

"Everyone knows, Hitra. It's being posted in broadsheets. Your father was all but attacked at his club meeting and I was a virtual prisoner in my office all day. How could you do this to us?"

"I didn't exactly choose this."

"Yes, she did," Revestre snapped petulantly.

Hitra's mother knocked on the smooth desk surface. "You may very well have thrown your career away. Do you realize that?" Hitra kept her eyes focused on a neutral point on the opposite wall. Her mother began to pace. "Visionaries and hedge-prophets, Hitra, are not the sort of people who are appointed to the High Priesthood. You'll never make it into the inner council unless you renounce these allegations quickly. With luck, in a few years, all people will remember is that your name is familiar."

Revestre was horrified. Was she so awful to have been seen? My fellow god felt as chastened, as cowed by Lady Hautridge, as Hitra herself.

"I don't think being visited by a god is something you should lie about, or try to cover up. I saw her. I did." Hitra's voice sounded thin and breathless even to herself.

Her mother turned and pressed her hands on the desk again. "Are you sure?" Hitra nodded, shaking. Lady Hautridge lowered her head, regarding her hands. "I don't know how to handle this."

"Maybe we shouldn't 'handle' it at all."

"No, we'll find a way. Before you leave here tonight, we will find a way to make you come out of this smelling like incense."

"You can't fix this for me, Mother."

"Oh, baby," her mother came around the desk to hold her shoulders. "You are confused and scared. It's my fault for letting you become a priest. But the church is no different than politics. I've already spoken with Panla Faydehale about this. The Ritual Celebrant is very unpopular in the noble's congress. We could make this out as her doing, have you flee the church, a persecuted saint. Panla practically owns the High Street Temple..."

Hitra pressed herself against the hard ladder of the chair. "Please, Mother, by all the gods, don't help."

Her mother's hands fell. "Don't you trust me? I have you situated to be the youngest High Priest in Casu history. I got your good-for-nothing brother married to a baroness! This is nothing, child."

"It isn't 'nothing' to me."

She backed up a step, hands raised. "All right. You're an adult. You want to do this on your own. I understand. Here's how you'll do it..."

Hitra gave up, sank into herself and let her mother outline plans. None of which had anything to do with helping me. Revestre didn't leave so much as fade into a cloud of despondency.

☽○☾

It was up to me, alone.

Maede drank two cups of tea in silence, and stared sourly at the chip in the saucer, so Illoe could see she wasn't complaining. After that, though, even she was bored with exercising her superiority through denial of conversation. She held out the saucer. He left his post by the wall and obediently took it. "Are you sleeping with her?" she asked.

He glared at her, so she said, "Don't think I won't discipline you, young man. You are perfectly capable of answering a question."

Maede liked mental violence, it was much better, much more civilized than striking with hands; she saw it as the natural superiority of any act done by an adept over its mundane counterpart.

How to stop her?

"You can't keep doing that!" He fought to keep his voice steady. "I am going to tell Hitra what you've done."

"You prey on her kind nature," Maede said, and was proud of having figured it out. "She ought to have disciplined you more. Now answer the question. I can't have the public asking questions about the Holy Prophet I can't answer."

"No," he bit the word out, "I'm not sleeping with Hitra."

She brushed an imaginary crumb off her lap. It was the sort of delicate gesture ladies were supposed to make. She wanted to look delicate and prim as she imagined his naked body. "Well, you must be sleeping with somebody. A handsome boy like you all alone, surrounded by women from the seminary all the time, and those girls in the youth group too. They haven't taken any vows, have they?"

"Not that it is any of your business, but I haven't. Is it required by law, now?" He turned his back on her, daring her to do her worst.

Maede rearranged the hem of her gown. "I won't even acknowledge such insolence. It's beneath me and I've had enough of your back talk." This was to cover up that she didn't have the strength to hit him so strongly again.

Maede was frustratingly artless. She didn't even see him—not as he was. She saw the strong line of his thigh beneath his tunic and thought that encompassed every aspect of him.

I could try possessing her. Sure, it hadn't gone well the first time, but there would never be anyone simpler, sturdier, to try it on. Hadn't I just proved to Revestre that I understood the physical world?

I slipped into Maede's eyes first, and it worked. My vision narrowed, grayed, fuzzed. I saw what she saw: the room was different from this angle, both larger and smaller. She was following Illoe's movements as he put away the dinner things. I let myself relax further into her mind, her body, felt her pulse, the heat of the heavy gown she had to wear because a noblewoman must dress to her station. We turned our head; it was harder than I thought it would be: so many muscles, so many impulses in so small an act. Fear tickled! I relished in it, and my savor became hers, and we looked at Illoe. It was wonderful, raw, animal; the chemical emotion of living lust.

Maede quaked, and as through thick mud she moved herself. Her teacup fell off her lap. We were both surprised by its crash. She thought of holy tremors and afflictions of the soul, terrible sicknesses of the mind cured by even more terrible surgeries. Her heart thumped painfully, extra hard, extra slow thumps. She moved her hand again. I wasn't trying to control it anymore, and it flitted feverishly over the front of her skirt. How much easier it was for her! But she didn't have to think about every single muscle, she didn't have to think at all, really.

I was learning a lot.

Illoe set something on the counter beside him. I couldn't see what it was. I didn't know what it was because Maede didn't know what it was. I was limited. Could I be trapped, even killed, like this?

Illoe knelt beside us and gathered up the cup. He had a warm, wet rag and we felt it through the side of our shoe as he wiped up the tea. Touch. I tried to move her hand again, to feel purposeful touch, even just the unpleasant fabric of her dress. I thought about the way it felt when she moved, the thoughtless parts that triggered. I moved our hand to Illoe's head. His hair was slippery, almost soft. She squealed, a choked little scream, and started babbling, "Holy mothers, something is wrong. Oh Wenne, Wenne Revestre Darian gods protect me..."

Illoe backed away toward the kitchen, his eyes wide. Maede's heart was stuttering. I left her before it could stop.

☽○☾

Hitra wasn't far. She relaxed as the smell of the temple grounds permeated her nostrils. Earthy, incensed: it was very different from the sterile world of Nobles Hill and High Street.

The rain had abated, and the air was moist and calm. The moon laced each grass blade with silver. I hovered close, but not too close, to Hitra's thoughts. Her mother had a point, albeit a misguided one. There was a deeper truth to everything, a greater truth than fact. She had to be careful how and when to act. Her pocket swelled with scrawled notes from her mother, mostly names and addresses she already knew, which she would bury in the wastepaper basket. She would do none of what her mother suggested—planting rumors, shaking hands. But even a skewed view was a welcome perspective. Be informed, she told herself. Look at this from all sides, and then, when you are calm, you will know how to act.

And when she knew, I would know.

She stopped.

Strange piles of rags lay huddled along the covered walkway that she shared with three other priest's quarters. She reached out with her mind for Illoe and found him, about where she expected. He was awake, but exhausted. *Is everything all right?*

Strangely, he didn't answer, though she could feel his awareness. He was afraid. So afraid he hadn't heard her, his hands busy washing dishes. She felt Maede in her front room, but did not contact her, or connect her to Illoe's fear. She felt for the Arbiter's station in the central complex. One of the rag lumps moved. She squeaked from fear. The others moved, shambled, stood, and formed themselves into rain-soaked people holding cloaks and blankets around themselves.

Hitra gathered her courage and her cloak to her and strode down the center of the walkway. "I am an adept of the fifth level," she said, "and I do not wish to be disturbed."

One of the crouching people leapt at her. Clammy fingers wrapped around her calf. "Chosen one!"

Hitra staggered out of the hold and ran to her door, feeling other hands reaching for her, minds pressing to her. Someone tugged her sleeve off her shoulder as she wrestled the door open against hands thudding into the wood.

Chapter Eight

Petitions

Arel was thinking about me. About tests and temptations and dark, incomprehensible power. He squinted at the morning sky, found the sun, and knelt to face it. The back stoop had a scoop missing from the center, a frozen remembrance of when it had been the soft silt of a streambed rather than rock. He'd never noticed it before. It hurt his left knee. Hand shaking, he unrolled the leather pouch of chalk. It was powdery and coated his fingers—not very fine chalk at all, and weakened by age. He drew a line. Wenne, he thought, and tried to remember the words he'd learned as a boy, and once considered as essential a part of his life as walking.

☽○☾

Something familiar, at first, the feeling of a boundary. Does it turn toward him or does he turn toward it? Excitement, burning in him from throat to groin, and that loses the connection. He has to hold a breath, release it, and reach again. A boundary—same as a mind, in the heavens. He is right and pure and ready.

☽○☾

Arel raised his head. He could feel a shadow fall against his back. "Arel," his wife said, "what are you doing?"

He dragged the unfamiliar chalk over the rough stone of their back stoop. "I'm praying. In the name of Wenne, first among the gods." The chalk slipped a little, making a slight wiggle at the end of the line. He picked it up and started drawing a perpendicular line along his side. "In the name of…" He faltered, more afraid of the name 'Senne' than he expected to be.

Well, good.

His wife snatched his hand. The chalk broke. Her thin fingers dug between his, clawed to take the chalk. His hand and hers were marked with white. Arel sighed and let go. She threw the powdered stone into the bushes.

"Chalk is expensive," Arel said.

"It's blasphemous. I can't believe you, praying like they do. Are we Ritualists? Are we like them?"

"Maybe we should be," Arel said. He covered his eyes with his hand, and felt the grit against his skin. All he could see was darkness.

☽○☾

A pushing, at first, against a skin, distant and silent, a rising flare of hope, joy, and then the membrane parts, and there is nothing inside it. Nothing inside him. He pushes and pushes and cries out all the names of the gods, but nothing responds. The membrane is no longer there, nothing is. Terrible, perfect void. A mind unthinking. He cries and he is back in the square, back on the cobbles, in the dirt, his throat sore. Someone touches his back, and that is when he realizes it is over.

☽○☾

Debha tried to be patient. "Is this about that priest up on the mount?"

"The gods didn't come to us, Debha. They chose to go to her."

"She lied. Gods restrain me. You have got to stop this. You have got to get over that stupid demonstration."

"Reha believes. Her mind…"

Debha gasped, and her husband trailed off, leaving the unsaid between them. He'd talked to Reha. The Celebrant's name was a curse in Debha's mind, making her feel petty and unimportant. She ground her hand against her hip to wipe the chalk dust off. "Right. I'm not an adept. I can't possibly know what you went through. Get over it, Arel.

Or so help me, I will leave you."

He started to cry, and it made her angry, because men aren't supposed to cry. "Why?" he asked. "Why was there nothing for us, but something for her?"

"I don't know. You will have to ask *her*." Debha slammed the kitchen door.

☾○☽

Hitra remembered little of falling into bed, and only after she was tucked in did she wonder why it was Maede who helped her under the coverlet and kissed her cheek. Some time later, Illoe had come into the room, his blanket tight around his shoulders. "Hitra?"

"I'm awake," she said, because she was.

Illoe knelt down by the bed so their eyes were on a level. "I don't want Maede to come back here while you're not around."

Something about how he'd said it made her wrap her arms around him.

In the morning, it seemed like a dream. Illoe set out her bathrobe without mentioning it.

Without mentioning it, he sat down at her desk to write while she bathed. She watched him, studiously turned away, and was grateful, though she wasn't afraid of gods in the bathroom. Not this morning. She was more afraid of men, and he was becoming one. Was one. The line of his cheek was longer than it had been, leaner, and the dark eye that flicked between his lashes had seen things that she didn't know about.

He was still there when she came out of the bath, though she had sat longer than intended, staring at the staid pattern of tiles on the wall. So solid, as though they had never had any intention of moving.

He tapped a stylus against the edge of the desk. "Have you talked to her yet?"

"Maede?"

"My mother. About the contract."

Hitra looked over the clothes he had laid out for her on the bed. He'd already tucked the blankets and pillows neatly back into place.

"No," she said. "I'm sorry. I'll do it today. First thing. Right before…
before…"

"Your staff meeting."

"We'll get it done today, I promise."

He nodded and put the stylus back in its holder. "I'll get your
breakfast."

"No, no. I'll grab something quick in the cafeteria. I should start
early."

She fumbled with her under-tunic and decided abruptly to wear a
prayer-band for the day, something she had not done since Seminary.
She opened the clothing chest and dug along the sides for it. Illoe left
the room quietly. When he came back he had a basket for her with a
clay jar of tea and some biscuits. "You probably shouldn't go to the
public cafeteria. There are still people out front."

"Ah, me." She ran to the window and peered tentatively between
the curtain and the glass.

"I sent for an arbiter to escort you to your office."

"Right." She reached into the front opening of her robe and tightened the prayer band. It had already loosened with her breath.

Illoe set the basket on the desk. They stared at each other for a
while.

"I did see her," she said, in answer to an unspoken question.

It wasn't what he had wanted to ask. Still, he said, "You thought
you did."

"Please, Illoe. Not you—I can't take this from you, too."

He nodded. She took a breath and the basket.

☽○☾

In the Chapel of the Dawn, on the eastern edge of the temple, carved
through the cusp of the mountain to let the first rays enter a chamber
of brilliant orange and yellow mosaics, Reha lit a series of small lanterns and ignored the Chief Arbiter of Chagrin City.

He was a shockingly handsome man with a hint of copper in his
close-cropped curls and skin a touch paler than normal, which lent
him an exotic air. There were rumors that he'd slept his way to the
top. He hadn't. He didn't think it was as easy to do that as people as-

sumed. He had friends who had slept with superiors and their careers had suffered for it.

He followed Reha through her preparations persistently, repeating the same demands. "Ritual Celebrant, it is your duty as the highest official of the Casu Church to put an end to these rumors and allegations which disturb the public peace."

Reha had run out of lanterns and had to finally acknowledge him. She did so with a gesture of dismissal. "Thank you, I shall certainly take that under advisement."

"Eminence!"

"Young man, if you are going to yell at me about how I am doing my job, you'd best get in line."

The Chief Arbiter was forty-three years old, only a decade younger than the Celebrant herself, and congratulated himself on not pointing it out. Again. "The public peace—"

"Just might need a little shaking up." Reha picked up her non-holiday morning ritual cap, her least favorite garment. It was covered with mirrors, all itchy knots and stitching on the inside. She carefully unfolded it and set it firmly on her head. "Did it ever occur to you that just maybe the gods are speaking to us?"

"Eminence, I would hardly think that a woman of your station—"

"What?" She smiled, a weapon she knew he wouldn't expect. "That the head of the church would actually believe the holy scriptures? Out of my way, lad, I've got to bless the sunrise. If your superiors in the government care to continue this conversation, tell them to send a lady of the court, or someone of higher rank. If I had business with the queen, I would not send an acolyte to her. You are dismissed."

The Chief Arbiter wasn't an underling. His department was wholly autonomous, reporting only to the Council of Arbitration itself. Civilians didn't seem to get that until they were arrested. "It is the will of the council—"

She stopped him simply by looking at him. There were few powers rank and natural gift had given her that Reha found half as useful nor as satisfying as the power of personal charisma. It was the power, she often explained to her priests, to say 'no.'

The Chief Arbiter turned and left the chapel.

Alone, Reha sighed. She felt for her assistant, but he was off on an errand. There were only the concerned, still minds of her personal guard. Reha was alone, without anyone to confide in that she genuinely did not know what to do. No one besides a god who had no better idea herself.

$$\text{)O(}$$

Illoe gathered up the dirty clothes to take to the laundry. As he stepped outside, he tripped over an arrangement of flowerpots someone had left on the front step. The laundry nearly went flying. A stranger ran to take the basket from him, and another started righting the ritual plants. Illoe had to wrest Hitra's dirty underwear from the mob and toss the basket untidily into the front room.

He threw one of the pots clear across to the low wall that separated the priest's private gardens from the park. Pottery shards and dirt sprayed. A wide-eyed man winced and looked likely to cry. Illoe didn't go outside after that.

Every hour or so, he would hear a knock at the door. He'd pause what he was doing, wait, hear the second knock, wait, hear a third knock, then go back to his room to be as far from the apartment door as possible.

Mental connections came more often than knocks. *Is Her Holiness gone? Has she left the temple? Should we harvest the wheat early this year? What news of Revestre?*

Illoe didn't respond. Let them stew. He didn't recognize the voices.

He sat down with one of Hitra's books — an ancient romantic tome, the gods at war with each other, the most beautiful woman and man in the world forced into each other's embrace. It was his favorite of her books, full of violence, melodrama, and metal point illustrations. It was only barely religious, made it into the canon on a technicality and some hasty moralizing at the end, but even it couldn't hold his attention. Another knock. He'd reread the introduction of the young hero three times while knocks jarred him loose from the narrative.

Another knock. *Have you lived a virtuous life, servant? If Revestre has awakened to speak with us, Senne is alive too!*

Illoe flipped ahead to the sex scene in chapter eight. The ribaldry, oblique as it was, did not draw him in as it used to. His eyes slid over the page, unable to sink in. There were more admonishments coming in, to be virtuous and repent. *Go away, Zealot.*

We'll pray for your redemption, child!

He cringed, waiting for the next onslaught from the voice, made more frightening by being ageless, sexless, directionless. (Illoe's power was too limited to detect the subtle sense of self.) But nothing more came. I had seen how Maede artlessly shut down thought-sendings. A blast of gibberish vibrations that held them still. I did one better. If you matched the vibrations with their exact opposites, they canceled out, lost like patterns in the rain.

Slowly, the ice in Illoe's joints melted to slush, and he repositioned himself more comfortably on the couch with a resolution not to be shaken the next time. He reached tactfully with his mind for the Arbitration Office in the residential complex, but did not send any words. He felt safer, like someone had taken his hand.

I did that. I could do more.

)O(

Call Illoe's mother, I whispered in Hitra's mind, carefully and neutrally, so she would think it was her own thought. *Now is the time.*

Hitra did not want to call Illoe's mother. She never knew what their relationship should be, if they had one. And Loata Middlemount was unpredictable and embarrassing in ways that starkly contrasted with Hitra's upper class upbringing, making her feel spoiled and prudish.

But 'before the meeting' had become 'after the meeting' and if she didn't get it out of the way, it would be 'after the counseling session' and then 'after lunch', and then, probably, 'after the contract expired' which would be 'after Illoe stopped talking to her.'

The staff meeting itself had been an exercise in false calm. The acolytes and laymen had said little to nothing while she went down her agenda, but their minds had screamed at her with repressed thoughts and words. Sometimes it was not helpful to be adept.

The youth fall picnic would go on as scheduled, with primary

121

work being done by the staff of the Priests of Guensha, who was a more popular deity in the city associated with autumn and harvest. She wasn't actually a part of the main pantheon, but was rooted to local festivals. Something to do with fish. Her priests, therefore, always took a lead role in Harvest Home with the poor of the city, the common folk, while Revestre's staff catered to purists and those who came to the city from elsewhere.

They confirmed which church would provide decorations, which snacks, who would be the primary contact for games and crafts. They successfully completed the careful dance of making sure each committee and subcommittee and ethnic, social, and political group felt it was being appreciated, useful, and not given a less important or more demanding job than the others.

Then there were the Harvest Home rituals themselves—what had to change at the last moment, what had already happened and happened well. No one discussed the impact of Hitra's visitation, other than to remark on high attendance. That was best.

Now she had time to move on from what was done to what was still undone on her task list. Unfortunately.

A junior priest walked in the outer office, talking to another. Papers rustled. Everything was eerily normal. Except for the arbiter stationed by the cloak rack and the fact that every last acolyte had reported for volunteer service.

Illoe's mother lived just on the edge of Hitra's mental range. If she could, she would make the contact without a router. *Loata Middlemount?*

There was silence, no familiar tug of connection. She pushed into a thicket of unfamiliar minds, like grass, like hairs, all alike from this distance. One would be Loata, a sort of blue mind as Hitra saw her. I found her, and considered helping the connection, but Hitra's forehead began to ache and she gave in and contacted the local router.

The connection was dark, no confirmation or salutation. Not a good sign. *Loata Middlemount? It's Hitra.*

Reluctance and discomfort were very clear under Loata's response. *Good morning, priest. Is something wrong?*

Loata, we need to discuss Illoe's contract immediately. Would you be willing to meet with me?

There was a pull, and Hitra had to keep herself from following it. Loata was communicating with someone else, artlessly, no attempt to hide it. Hitra could easily have listened in on the conversation. As it was, she had to avert her virtual eye.

I don't know if that's such a good idea, Holiness. Um...the contract seems just fine to me.

Hitra had the power to hide her emotions, to smooth the contact to just the words themselves. Which was good: Loata was nervous enough without picking up Hitra's irritation. *It is not fine to Illoe, and therefore it is not fine with me. If you will not meet willingly, I will contact the local board of arbitration.*

There was a brief spike of panic, and then confusion as Loata tried to carry on another conversation, deep and shallow, vocal and mental. Hitra was unwillingly exposed to fluttering parental concerns, fears, hopes, and a touch of unreasonable expectations. They honestly feared their son would never marry unless Hitra arranged it — powerful and influential Hitra, who no doubt could pluck a noblewoman off the street for the honor. She gritted her teeth.

That was when she noticed the acolytes were running back and forth in the outer chamber. Oh gods, not now. She had hoped the zealots would not find out where her office was in the administration building.

Holiness? Illoe's mother sounded hurt, afraid. *Don't you think this might be a bad time, for you? I mean, what with the visitation.*

I told you, Illoe went to see you with my blessing. Hitra stepped back from her desk, toward the wall, out of direct line of sight with the doorway.

No, no, Holiness. I heard a rumor about you, and your god...and, well, wouldn't it be best, all considered, if you didn't bother with the contract right now? Surely you must have more important things to do.

An acolyte leaned in the doorway, stared at the empty desk for a second, turned, and winced in surprise to see Hitra creeping along the back wall of her office, trying to hide. "Holiness, the Celebrant wants to speak with you immediately, she..." The acolyte looked behind her. "Oh, um...Eminence!"

Loata, I'll have to call you back later, Hitra sent, and felt defeated because she knew how hard it would be to pin the woman down again.

But the young acolyte had vanished, leaving Reha, in full ritual costume, filling the doorway like a mosaic idol.

"You missed the sunrise."

Hitra tried to meet Reha's gaze without flinching from the dazzling light of her mirrors. "I hadn't planned on attending. We had a staff meeting."

Reha nodded. She took the shimmering cap from her head and dropped it unceremoniously on Hitra's desk. She scratched her scalp. "So, what did she say?"

"Eminence?"

"What did Revestre say to you? Had to have said something, didn't she?"

Hitra found she was twisting her sleeve-hem between her hands. She let it go, and shook her head.

"Nothing?" Reha shook her head. "The gods are bitches, aren't they?"

Hitra felt her shoulders drop.

Reha sat down on the edge of the desk, next to her deflated hat of mirrors. "We have to talk about your sudden celebrity."

"I don't think this is a good time."

"I don't see a better one coming up."

Hitra looked at the door, and Reha added, "If there's anything you don't want your staff to hear, we can do this silently."

Hitra's hand sweated from being held too long in a fist. "I told no one," she said. "No one."

"I don't care how it got out. I care about what you're going to do next."

"I am not denying it."

Reha's head swooped in an emphatic nod. "Good."

"You don't...?" Hitra wondered why she'd been so sure the Celebrant would ask her to deny the visitation. She rubbed the sweat from her palm on her thigh. "What do you want me to do?"

"Tell the truth."

With all due respect, Eminence, I have been telling the truth so much my throat burns from it!

Reha's eyebrows raised. "I don't recall saying otherwise." She stood. "Go forth, if you have the strength, and tell the truth, personally, painfully, about what you experienced. Tell it to everyone. Hold an open forum. Be precise in what you say. Leave out details if you can, because any deviation from one recount to another will be leapt upon. And then, Hitra, you must give them a message. Since the god was not kind enough to provide one, I suggest you come up with a moral. Brief. One word, if possible. I suggest peace, or tolerance. Revestre knows we need a little of either one about now."

This was exactly what Hitra had been urging Reha to do, since the fire, and packaged almost in exactly the same words. Hitra swallowed a throat full of pride and nodded. "You don't think it wrong, putting words in Revestre's mouth?"

"All we do here is put words in the mouths of gods. It's a homily, Hitra. You're a priest. Write it, or the masses will write it for you." Reha plucked her mirrored hat carefully from the desk and scratched her head one more time before setting it in place. "One more thing I feel I ought to mention: priests make bad celebrities. Someone will find something in your personal life to despoil, even if they have to make it up." She raised a hand as if in blessing, but then dropped it. "You might want to send that handsome young man of yours away for a few days. By all the gods, I hate even suggesting it."

"Illoe? But..."

Reha was halfway through the archway, but turned to raise her eyebrows again. "It's never sat right with the residential priests that you keep an indentured servant, and he is attracting more attention now. The two of you have always been close...Sometimes, we have to make awful choices about our private lives. I've had to myself. There was a young male priest I was fond of, once. We were just good friends, but because we laughed together too loud or long, well, I had to send that good man to the other side of the country."

"No offense, Eminence, but you are more of a target than I am. No one would ever think — "

Reha stopped her with a look. "I have seen priests who no one thought could do wrong expelled from the temple on the force of rumor. The question, Hitra, is how much being a temple priest means to you, and how well you can live under the scrutiny of those who have no understanding of your calling."

"My relationship with Illoe is not going to be an issue."

125

"I hope you're right. But I can't say I haven't heard rumors already, and the gods love to make fools of those that say they know the future." She stepped to the door. "Peace, Hitra, and clarity."

The Ritual Celebrant was through the outer office door, and it had closed firmly behind her, before Hitra came up with her withering reply, and it wasn't that good. She dropped back into her chair and seriously, for five minutes, considered not becoming High Priest of Revestre.

Jante brought her a copper cup of chilled water. "If you want to, well, if you want to do what she suggested, Holiness, I'll help Kirta with the scheduled meetings so you can write something. I mean making a statement. We could show it to the youth choir tomorrow. Start with a friendly audience?"

Hitra took the cup and grimaced into its metallic-smelling depths. She decided not to chastise the acolyte for eavesdropping on the Ritual Celebrant. "Thank you, Jante. We'll do that." Reha was wrong. There was no reason to worry about Illoe. She took a piece of paper and wrote a note to call his mother again after her speech was written.

☽○☾

Arel's supervisor at the fish yard squinted at him and repeated the words "spiritual life" like they were some sort of insult. Arel smiled, bowed, and walked out of the office, not waiting to hear the rest. His wife's job could support them, he reasoned to himself, and though Debha would not be happy about that, in time she would forgive him. She always had.

It was astonishing how he could talk himself into believing such nonsense. His wife was terrified of Arel losing his job because their combined incomes barely kept the household afloat. He left the pier and took the long road up to Temple Mount.

His mind was still on the void, picking it like a scab. It bothered me, too. Where was I when this was going on? I had a feeling, like Arel did, that the gods should have noticed when he had tried to contact them. I did not agree with his idea that we should have leapt to helping and explaining, like some eternal valets. (What was truly ridiculous was how universal his expectation was in mortal minds.

As far as I could tell, there wasn't a single scripture where we were so obliging.)

Arel left the main road at High Street for an alley that wound its way between shops, a path well known to students of the seminary and almost invisible to the more casual visitors of the mount. The stair cut into the terraced wall behind the shops, which was usually deserted, had an arbiter guarding it. Although he knew he was breaking no law, Arel averted his gaze and kept walking, through an increasingly narrow passage lined with refuse and back doors. He ended up climbing a trickle of a path that might have been formed by ruminants or even rain. It dug into the undeveloped surface of the mountain, a sheer outcrop of some rock too hard or too inconvenient to be reshaped to suit the city's needs.

This former priest crawled among roots, pushing soil out of his way and emerging with dirty, sore knees. Peasants and petitioners lurked all around the temple gardens, skulking behind columns whenever a purple tunic walked by — not that hiding from sight would help. Arel thought seriously about evicting the fools from the sacred grounds, but he had as little right to be there as they did, an accident of circumstance that both annoyed and humbled him.

The furtive and lurking civilians easily lead the way to the priest of Revestre's quarters. They circled like carrion-eaters. Arel could hear them assailing Illoe with mental queries. He could also feel the poor boy's exhaustion. He wished he could help. As an adept, he had the power to block the others, but as a Sectarian he had vowed against such uses of the mind.

Yes, I did feel superior. I quietly blocked a few calls. No one noticed; I made them feel like they had connected and just not been answered. I was getting good at this.

Arel walked the gardens, as he had in his seminary days, though not quite the same, conscious of the differences both in himself and the flowering plants. The lodgings of the residential priests were not far from where Arel's had been in the men's dormitory, years ago, when he was an acolyte of Darian. His hands clasped, taking in the serene beauty, the change of the seasons becoming evident, as he meandered the paths to stay clear of the arbiters. When none was present, he went up to the door and knocked. Three times he took his opportunity, in rotation with others. I wished I could block sound as easily as thought. Illoe did not answer.

) O (

When Hitra was ready to head home, an arbiter contacted her mentally, rather than ringing the door chimes. Her escort's mind was dull, smooth: the dutiful mind. He hardly blinked as he turned to walk beside her. This was a long-practiced skill, to be unremarkable. It helped when you were a male arbiter and half your job was being strong enough to restrain grown men when needed and the other half was not intimidating the powerful women who constantly surrounded you. He was good at being beneath notice. Hitra watched him, though, as it kept her from acknowledging the people who crowded her office door. They parted, like autumn leaves before the wind, a few stragglers staying their ground. As afraid and awed as they were of Hitra, they had a more conventional dread of the arbiter, no matter how quiet his face.

Hitra was immensely grateful for the bubble of security he provided her. He could tell, which made the lonely feeling a little better.

But when they turned onto the covered walkway to the priest's residence, there was another crowd of people centered on Hitra's door, and halfway up the path, in front of them, blocking the way, was Arel. He twisted his leather cap in his hands. "Please," he said.

Neither of them knew who Arel was, of course. They just saw a large man, his feet set wide, his expression teetering on desperate. The arbiter stepped smoothly in front of Hitra, and she felt the power rise in him, a gentle push, expanding outward into the consciousness of everyone nearby. A wordless salutation: I am here; I am powerful.

The others—the weeping old woman, her bored child, the foolish teenagers dressed like ascetics—pressed to the edges of the colonnade.

Arel didn't budge. "Please, it will only take a minute. My name is Arel, Arelandus; I was a priest once, here in the temple."

Nausea began to color the underside of the arbiter's presence, a trick to discourage loitering, though the only motion he made was to turn his head slightly toward Hitra, a non-verbal 'what would you like me to do?'

"I want to talk to you personally, if I may," Arel continued, his eyes intent on Hitra alone. "About faith."

Hitra hugged the lunch-basket to her chest and pushed her way past Arel. He tugged on her robe, but she let the cloth tear and continued forward.

Locked in step beside her, the arbiter said, "That was probably best." His thoughts were firmer. It *was* the best outcome. The tension that had been building collapsed down into his preferred mode: ordinary calm. The endless petitions I'd been keeping from Illoe dropped away. No one was brave enough, yet, to risk arrest.

☽ ⦿ ☾

On the downhill, lake-facing side of Sorrow's market there stood a stone archway the same color as the cooking benches, but sharper, having weathered time without the constant use that rounded the lower stones. Carved on it were the ten principal gods, passing the sphere of The World between them, all the hours of the day depicted simultaneously. Wenne, of course, was at the apex, her hair streaming out around her head like the sun's rays, the relief-flattened ball of all creation held to her stomach like pregnancy.

Since there were ten gods, an even number, the five on Wenne's right were cramped together. My depiction was on the western leg of the arch, the one with fewer gods. That allowed it to be large, but it could have been larger, more equal to Wenne's. I had Darian clasped to my side and the ball of the world resting on one hand overhead, like I was going to toss it.

Darian ended his story married to Wenne. I don't know why it was more popular to depict him being abducted by me. I suppose it was nice to be the one depicted with the boy, but it made my story feel half his.

Ele passed this statue each day as he went to and from his lunch in the market and never gave it any thought, beyond a vague appreciation for art in an otherwise industrial scene. Today he looked at the image of me and thought about his brother being like Darian, clasped in the arm of a powerful woman.

He set his hand on the gargantuan calf of Dioneltar to watch a wedding parade pass through the market. The new husband and wife sat together on a bier of fruit branches, holding aloft the glass staves of their office, king and queen of their party, new rulers of the kingdom of their nascent family. The bride supported her forearm with the opposite hand and Ele was certain she was complaining good-naturedly about the weight of those scepters, and hers was the larger of the two. An irritating custom of some sects of Casu, to make the bride's staff larger than the groom's, when her arm was likely less strong. The bride remarked that it was a hazing ritual concocted by husbands. Ele felt both sympathetically indignant for the groom and mildly smug at his family's superior, more orthodox faith.

I copied the bride's pretty dark skin. It helped to have a specific model in front of me as I formed myself. I laid my hand against the statue and was pleased with how like Ele's hand it appeared, fingers flexing against pressure just so. I threw what I hoped was a coquettish smile at Ele. He was watching the procession.

As the crowd moved on, the reflected cheer left Ele's face, though he hadn't known it was there, and he was deflated in its absence. He patted Dioneltar's leg and continued on his way to work.

I flew in front of him, remembering at the last moment to re-form legs and walk. I felt him notice me, a fluttering impression, "woman on your right." He adjusted his course to accommodate mine.

"Do I look like a god to you?" I asked.

He switched to active avoidance, subtle tensing of muscles, composition of a bland expression. I was either going to aggressively flirt with him or ask him for money or both.

I did not look like a god to him.

)O(

Arel felt pangs of hunger, but decided, in convenient hindsight, that he was fasting. It was pious, helped bring clarity, and had the added bonus of being free.

The other penitents thinned out with the dying light. Arel considered writing a note and leaving. He hadn't told Debha where he was going, and she would be worrying about him. He had a moment of rage against a city that refused to invest in non-mental message-sending systems. The Sectarians had set up a nice set of baskets and chalkboards to leave notes for each other. All that was missing was a corps of runners to carry them.

He could have gone home and come back. Instead he spent the night in an alleyway down by the high market, wrapped in some sacks that were waiting to be returned to the grain merchant and re-filled. He woke damp and aching when the sun peeked over the wall at him, hurting his eyes but not offering any warmth.

By the time he'd found a fountain to wash in and made it back up the path he'd taken down, the priest had left her rooms again for the day and wasn't expected to return.

Another hungry day lay before him.

He strode up to the door and tried the lock.

Illoe hadn't refastened it. Arel felt the betrayal of his fellow peti-tioners as he stepped into the priest's home and locked the door be-hind him.

Illoe sat, cross-legged on a couch, a timeworn book in his lap. His mouth hung open. "I'm sorry," Arel said.

A call to the arbitration office shot out of the boy, and Arel instinc-tively snatched it from the ether. He winced at himself, almost dou-bling with apology. "I shouldn't have done that. Gods forgive me; I didn't mean to do that. Just, please, don't call the arbiters. I only want to speak with your employer."

Arel and I could both feel Illoe's fear, but he affected a disdainful tone. "She isn't here. Go to her office. In the temple."

"No, please, I must speak with her immediately. You know where she is, you know how to get in touch with her. It is a matter of the utmost importance."

Illoe shook his head.

"I have to talk to the priest today. Please, I won't hurt you."

Neither of us believed him. "You're an adept," Illoe said.

"Yes."

"So call her yourself!" He raised his book and tried to look like he was reading it.

Arel sat down on the couch opposite Illoe, who did not move, but also did not try to call the arbiters again. He was afraid of what the adept would do if he did. Arel chose to ignore the fear. "After I tested fifth level, do you know what they said to me? 'Arel, don't test again. No one wants a man in the sixth level.' And the only woman who believed in me, who told me to reach as high as I could...well, I ended up having to leave the church to protect her."

Illoe pointed at the door without looking up from his book. "The arbitration office has free counseling. Follow the balustrade until it ends and it's on your right."

Arel appreciated the joke. "I only mention this because I can feel power in you. Here you are—a housekeeper? Yet I feel you could pass the first level test today, untrained. What's keeping you down? Is it your religion? Your family?"

"I'm not answering your questions. I'm calling the arbiters. What is wrong with you?"

Illoe positively oozed information, after his long mental fight to keep others out. Arel sighed. "Ah, I see."

Illoe's book bounced against the couch cushion. "No, you don't see."

"Was it worth it? Do your parents think it was worth it, to sell one son to send the other to the academy? For as high as this society would let a man rise?"

"Get out of my house!"

Arel continued to look at him calmly. "I'm not here to hurt you. I just need you to call her for me. Go ahead. I don't mean you, or her, any harm. I need to talk to her now, for both our sakes."

Arel felt the weak signal, unsure, probing out from Illoe's mind. His eyes unfocused, as was the habit of the untrained.

Illoe's eyes refocused sharply and he straightened. "Hitra doesn't know when she can get away. You'll have to go to her office."

"That's not good enough. You have to try harder. Please." Illoe's eyes shifted left. Arel leaned forward and put a hand on his knee. "Calling the arbiters would ruin my life, son. Don't do that to me. I'm a good man. Don't make me," Arel shook his head, tears rimming his eyes a little. "Don't make me do something I'd rather not."

Carefully, Illoe nodded to the man and sent words to Hitra. *Boss, he's still here, and he says he can't meet you at your office. He's refusing to go.*

Send him away, Illoe, or call for an arbiter.

Arel watched him with steady eyes and seemed to hear every thought. Illoe chose his words carefully. *I would really rather you meet with him. Or just give me a time when you'll be home?*

I don't know, Illoe. I'm sorry, I wish I did. Oh, could you call my mother? Assembly is in session, and you're always better at getting through to her than I am.

Illoe looked directly at the strange man opposite from him. *He's an adept, boss.*

There was a brief pause. Hitra's response had the curt quality of a word squeezed between others. *So?*

Boss, don't pretend you don't know what an adept can do.

Silence. Arel was still watching him, closely, intently. Illoe shook his head, mouthed an apology.

Hitra's thoughts came back staggered, as she was trying to juggle two other conversations. *Just...send him away. No adept...no one's going to hurt you. Honestly.*

Hitra should have known better. What could I do? Make myself known? As myself? As an arbiter? As Hitra? Arel flexed his fingers together. He looked down at the floor. The void, he meditated on the void. Cold, dark...it was undamaged by the filter of his memory; I saw it as clearly as he had, and it was oddly familiar. What he found horrifying to me felt...comfortable. The comfortable void, and then a voice moved over it, and told us...we were an us.

The room grew darker, and all three of our minds were touched with anxiety. It spilled out to the petitioners outside, who stirred, unaware why, but drawing their cloaks tighter about them and putting the walls to their backs.

Illoe tried to reach out to Hitra again. She refused the connection. With the spark of this minor betrayal, and the many indifferences she had shown him, Illoe turned his mind angrily away from her. "She has choir practice tonight. She never misses that. I can tell you where it is."

Chapter Nine

Canticle

Take a quick look in her mind and you'll see Hitra had always planned on leading a choir, before she had even thought of going to the seminary. When her career path led to the Mount, she found the temple already had three choirs: a mixed choir, a women's choir, and a children's choir. All three met in the airy music balcony above the main ritual hall, and all three had an extensive, entrenched and talented staff. But that didn't discourage her: all three featured the wealthy. The children's choir was the worst, populated with precious little lords and ladies in silk jumpers and gold-trimmed play tunics. With a fair amount of prestige, limited spaces, and a long commute to the temple for the poor, it didn't look like that would ever change. So Hitra had written letters and spoken passionately about the church's role in the community. She had caught the ear of Reha, and within a year had a special 'Community Youth' choir filled with awed, trouser-clad children, some with parents in tow, others alone, seeming to hang within themselves with worn hems and wooden shoes.

They were not given the choir loft to practice in, so at first Hitra had let the choir meet in her own chambers — but that was met with a reprimand from the housing department. Then she had let them sing outdoors on the temple's green lawn — and was admonished for unsightliness. They met for a while in the stuffy acolytes' gymnasium, a rooftop room with ancient straw mats and walls lined in wood, but their schedule was constantly changing around ritual practices and sporting clubs. Many wonderful, delicate, at-risk students stopped coming.

It was one of the students, actually, who had scratched her head and said, "Well, my mom says there are all kinds of secret rooms under the mount; can't we meet in one of them?"

A network of tunnels and chapels ran under the temple complex. They were damp, and their construction beautiful only in the eyes of an historian. Here Hitra had gone as a student, to read ancient texts off the walls and replace all the verbs with curses, drink cheap wine, have sex, and engage in all manner of rule breaking with her friends. Candles had painted their gowns the same egg-cream color as the walls, and they were sisters and brothers together, secretly exploring the dark rituals of secular life before the day would come when they would truly be bound together by laws and oaths.

It had seemed a betrayal when, as an ordained acolyte, she learned that the faculty of the seminary not only knew of these sorts of uses for the catacombs, they were fully condoned as a part of an initiate's matriculation.

Getting permission wasn't hard; the space was literally abandoned. If it weren't for her choir, the only voices ever heard down there would be seminary students losing their virginity, or the squeal of rats drinking spilled beer from the floor. Some said it was a fitting choice: filth in the cellar. But in time, controversy muted into commonplace. Now there was a sign-up procedure; the accounting office, the lay board, and others were using the long-abandoned halls. Hitra could marvel in quiet pride at one change she had wrought in her short time in the church.

Tonight, she was grateful to feel the heavy, slightly damp stone around and above her. The catacombs represented her lost innocence, and the new bulletin boards told Hitra she could influence the world around her. It was also a hard place to get to by accident, which offered its own form of protection from her new, rather insistent fans.

Their meeting place was one of the largest and nicest chambers under Temple Mount, and theirs permanently by right of tradition. It was a barrel-shaped chapel consecrated to a forgotten god of music, his symbols dark with ancient soot from the days before glass wicks. The chamber had low risers built into the floor, and the choir members' knees poked up and wavered as they sat on them, talked and fidgeted. A few parents stood along the back wall, moving less but whispering more. Hitra unrolled a music scroll and ran a hand over the comforting embossing. "I thought we'd sing one of our first songs tonight. Does everyone remember 'The Sun Awakens the Day'?" There were some shy smiles. It had been a favorite, easy and pretty. The older students looked bored. Hitra doubted her own plan, but raised her hand and counted out the rhythm. "The sky is a palace..."

The children started slow, raspy, mouthing words without interest, but slowly their voices came together, melded in the rich acoustics of the chamber, and began to ring as true notes do. Even Dara, an older girl who only came to practice because her parents made her, began to lose her perpetual annoyed expression and lean toward the music. Her voice blended with others and was lost; the song became something greater than all of them. It was just as Hitra remembered with her first choir director, and the cold mornings she had shared in the vault of the High Street Temple, unlocking the simple, pure mysteries of notes. Her memory melded with the present, and it almost made me believe, as she did, in the redemptive power of religion.

Arel's memories were wrong, they had to be. We weren't new, we were old. We were part of something beyond description, the vibration of air in the presence of beauty.

The parents at the back of the room watched like carrion birds waiting for a final breath to be expelled. They did not sing along. Neither, though, did they interrupt. Hitra had the choir sing their well-known songs until the magic of familiarity seemed to have reached its limit, and then one hard piece at the end, from the pantheistic New Year ritual. It was a quick, complex round, but the children performed it admirably, laughing and falling over at the end as the pace wrecked and muddied their words. Exhausted, like a dance. Even the parents smiled.

As the children filed out and Hitra rolled her scrolls, the adults came forward, shadows detaching themselves from the wall. The first woman to reach her just nodded. "That was beautiful, Holiness."

"Good practice," another said, but stayed where she was, rather than following the majority out into the catacombs.

Another mother stood at Hitra's elbow, a man behind her. Behind the closing circle of adults, children tugged like fish on the invisible lines of their guardian's presence, straining toward the archway and freedom.

Hitra slid her scrolls into their carrying case. "I think we're well on track to perform three pieces at the Harvest Home closing. Mother Nyla—your daughter sings beautifully. I think we really have a talent in her."

The adults shifted nervously. Hitra kept shucking scrolls into her satchel, as though everything was quite normal. "Citizen Southmarsh, I do hope you bring your youngest next time. I'm thinking of starting a separate boy's choir. Interest is high." She turned and caught the eyes of the woman at her right. "Of course, your son should be in it as well, Mother Eastfall."

The parents shifted uneasily, looking to each other for guidance on how to handle this unexpectedly chipper obstacle. "I must say Cala was breathtaking on 'A Child Like Me', Citizen Southmarsh. I'm thinking of giving her a solo come Spring Awakening."

Citizen Southmarsh held out his palms, as though to push the conversation. "Look, Priest, we just want to know that our children are safe."

Hitra was out of scrolls to pack. She held the satchel to her chest and tried to laugh. "We are in the heart of the temple complex. They are with a fifth level adept. What could possibly happen to them?"

"We just want to know our children won't be exposed to...unorthodox ideas."

They were all looking at her to answer a question they weren't willing to articulate. Hitra shook her head. "We are here to learn music." Her face felt sore from smiling, and her arm quivered against the satchel of scrolls. "The only theology is that presented in the standard songs of the Temple."

One of the women reached out her hand, "Umi means no disrespect, Holiness. We're all concerned about...well, about recent events, and the impact they may have on the children."

"Why would it have any impact!?" That was too loud. The parents slid back from her. She forced herself to take a shuddering breath. She should have finished her speech. "There...there will be a speech, friends, tomorrow. At that time..." She relaxed, strengthened by the standard phrase—*at that time* pulled one word after the other, like sinkers falling into water, and promised similar words to follow. "I hope we can put all these incidents behind us and continue our good work, bringing children up in the light of the gods."

"Behind us?" Southmarsh put an implied threat in his tone.

"Completely. Come to my speech, after the fifth hour ritual, please, and join me in putting an end to rumor." She looked directly at Southmarsh, and let go of her fake smile. The man returned her gaze steadily, and a wall of hostility built between them.

Mother Nyla cleared her throat. Too loudly, she said, "That sounds wonderful. An open forum in the evening. Yes, Bota and I will be there." Everyone stared at the small woman, but already, she, alone, had forced them to return to normality. She wove through the crowd to take her daughter's hand.

Cautiously, slowly, families began to pull away, like rust lifting in flakes from a submerged object. And then, a critical mass having been reached, Southmarsh left with his daughter, and the last stragglers followed in one mass.

Hitra counted to fifty after she lost track of the last footfall. Then she'd let herself cry. But all that came out was a hysterical gasp. She pressed her fist to her mouth and whined, a hard shape at the back of her throat. The scrolls rolled out over the floor. All she could think was how she would never have her choir again. Not the same as before. She hated how small that made her.

A singular anger, purposeful: I felt it before Hitra heard a footstep echo in the carved stone hall, and a shadow grew on the wall. "Priest?"

Hitra scrambled to gather the scrolls and her composure. "Practice is over." The words were wet, shaking.

The dust crunched under his foot, closer to her than she'd realized. She pivoted toward him as she was, crouched on the floor with the spilled scrolls and her carrying bag. Forthright Jeje stood at the doorway, a shaking knife pointed toward her and terror thrumming in his heart. "Where is my daughter?"

Hitra set the bag down, her grief slipping away like a dream on waking. "I...who...?"

"My daughter. Bota. Was she here? Was Bota Jeje here?" He didn't like using physical threat, but what else was there? He just had to get through the next few minutes. For Bota's sake.

Hitra crawled backward. She put together his words like a puzzle and came up with his name, but it was just a word, incongruous with his face, with the scattered impressions she had of him. "Jeje?" Her foot caught in the trailing hems of her robes. She felt for the nearest arbiter with her mind. "Think about what you are doing." Her words sounded odd to herself: calm, bereft of echo.

He took a step toward her. "Don't. Don't use your mind on me. Just tell me where she is."

Soft, leather-soled footsteps echoed rapidly down the corridor outside. They both froze a moment, alike in confusion, then Forthright Jeje lunged toward Hitra, and the adept reacted with the only weapon available to her. His arm froze in mid-swing. The knife fell harmlessly from his twitching fingers, clattering against the tiles.

Illoe leaned against the entryway, gasping for breath. "Boss... coming..."

Forthright Jeje made a strangled sound and followed his knife to the ground. The skin on his face danced as though of its own volition, his shaking fingers probing the air like it was muck. Hitra stared at him, unable to reconcile the horror of him with the effort in her mind. She slowly stood and let off the pressure. In retreat, she saw the ragged tear she had left in him, an outline of fear and panic. It was too detailed, horrible to her now, without the blind emotion that had created it. In shudders and stops, Jeje slumped.

Illoe moved around the archway, his hands never leaving the wall. "What are you doing?"

"He had a knife." As though reminded by this, Hitra quickly bent to pick it up. The Sanadaru man rolled onto his back, his mouth feeling for air.

Illoe knelt by Jeje and slid his arm under his head. "Can you breathe?" He put his other hand on the man's chest where the straining fabric of his peasant's tunic showed clearly that the man was breathing, albeit erratically.

"He threatened me." Hitra backed away, both touched and betrayed by Illoe's gentleness. Reluctantly, she reached into Jeje's mind again to smooth over the evidence — no, the damage — of her entrance. With a steady stream of comfort and calm, she cooled the pain. Illoe shifted to support Jeje's now limp head and shoulders. The man's chest rose steadily with sleep.

Over Jeje's head, Illoe glared at her. "What did you do to him?"

139

Hitra was holding the knife out to Illoe when the arbiter arrived. The purple tunic was almost black in the cavern's light, her expression lost in shadow, like the carved words on the wall behind her. She stopped in the middle of the entrance, facing Hitra directly. Though Hitra could not see her eyes, she knew she was not looking at Illoe or at Forthright Jeje.

Hitra said, "It's not…"

"Put the knife down," the arbiter said.

Hitra quickly set the knife on the floor. "I'm the one who called," she said, touching her chest. "I called for you, for an arbiter."

The arbiter's mind reached to her, wordlessly asking for her name, her rating, her position. Nervously, she answered her. *Hitra Hautridge, fifth level adept, of the priesthood of Revestre…actually, I'm acting as high priest until the vacancy left by the late Onta is filled, but my rank is officially that of a junior priest. Revestre…*

"That's quite enough," the arbiter said, suppressing her own fear at how high level Hitra was. Her job was to be calm.

Illoe watched the arbiter, having not been privy to the conversation, nor even sensed its presence. Hitra wished she could send something to him, but talking privately in an arbiter's presence was beyond stupid. Illoe was angry and disappointed in her, that she'd obviously used her power to hurt someone, again, and this was clear on his face.

The officer, Itha was her name, imagined pain and injury if Hitra turned violent, but her voice was measured and her posture still, as she was taught. "Priest Hitra, everything is alright. You may wish to contact a personal advocate. I must ask all of you to come with me to the office. Once the health of these men has been assured, you will all have an opportunity to bring your case before arbitration."

"I haven't done anything," Hitra said.

"Your statement is noted."

"But I *haven't*. I only picked up the knife."

A slight tremble of emotion escaped into the arbiter's voice. "I am aware that you did not use the knife." She tried to be even more calm and friendly in her next words to make up for it. "Please come with me for questioning. No one has been charged with a crime." Yet, she didn't say. She frantically sent details to her shift commander and was reassured by the approach of backup.

Hitra and Illoe's emotions dissipated into resignation. Hitra tried to get her music scrolls and was waved away from them. She felt a fresh, sharp pang of loss. As they were on their way out, more arbiters arrived with a stretcher for Jeje.

I had expected Arel to come into the scene. I went looking for my little lost Sectarian.

Arelandus had not made it far into the catacombs when he felt the presence of arbiters: numbing, careful, gray. Godless, Arel considered them, and his lips pressed tightly at the thought of them within the holy compound. He sank against a wall, knowing they were looking for him, but unclear how the servant boy could have set them on his trail so easily.

Illoe had of course done nothing of the sort; he had merely relied on young legs and a shortcut not covered in his directions to Arel. He had slipped out the back door and ran cold, expecting even as he started that he would be too late to undo his betrayal. Arel, on the other hand, had been slow and careful. It was Jeje's broadcast fear that had brought the arbiters looking for its source.

Arel wanted to feel for Hitra with his mind, but even if it were not forbidden to a Sectarian, it would draw the arbiters to him like lightning to iron. He crept along the wall, ducking to avoid sight. Voices carried to him, conducted along the ancient stone halls, with footsteps, shuffling, the sound of something heavy being dragged. A figure ran past him, stopped, turned.

Arel straightened as best he could. "Hello," he said.

The arbiter, a stout young woman, squinted. As though shocked by her own words, she said, "Arelandus Nereshore, there is a current warrant for your arrest."

Arel ran. It was all he could think to do. They hit him easily, efficiently. There was no pain, only the sudden nearness of the sandy floor.

)O(

The arbitration office was once a corridor between the public cafeteria and the temple baths. It might have originally been meant for servants' use, in the days many years ago when servants were more common. At some point someone had partitioned it with plain walls of sand brick and made it the inelegant home of security at the temple. Each room led into another, chained like beads, though some of the doors were staggered. It made for awkward furnishing. Elders in the department remembered bitterly a more expansive office in the administration building, now being used by the department of donations, the government's fundraising arm.

Hitra waited. There was indelible yellow sand ground into her outer robe around the knees and hem. She felt dirty, sweaty, and cold. The outer door was kept open despite the descending chill of dusk. She could see a colonnade partitioning the busy traffic of parishioners, pilgrims, and lay people that filled this, the main area of the temple complex. They could see her, as well, if they looked. Occasionally a face would glance out from the crowd, and Hitra would look down at her hands. No one recognized the Chosen Prophet of Revestre sitting in the security office with dirty knees. She would, if arrested, be in a special place, a for-persecuted-saints-only place, and she would definitely not look guilty.

Hitra thought about calling her mother, and decided she would. Eventually. If all other conceivable options vanished, forever, permanently. She was trying not to fidget or even move, trying to be a statue of serenity. Trying to find something interesting to look at. Someone uninspired had sponged a loose mosaic pattern on the walls. If she squinted, it looked like vines. Or snakes.

Illoe was just a few thin walls away, stiff within his skin as the arbiters asked questions. He was afraid of them in a way Hitra could not be; she knew the limits of their power.

"Do you understand the purpose of this arbitration?" the man opposite him asked.

Illoe nodded, then shook his head.

"We would like your account of the alleged...of what happened in the catacombs tonight. You may choose not to speak. We will be monitoring you for consistency and emotion. We acknowledge that a heightened emotional state does not equate to speaking false. You must acknowledge that if we believe your words to be suspect, we will remark on this in our report. Finally, anything you think loud enough to be heard will be considered stated for the record. Do you understand?"

Illoe felt cold. "What happens if Hitra is charged with assault?"

The arbiter, Uelo was this one's name, felt a twitch of uncertainty, a sharp desire to explain the difficulty of this particular situation. He had never seen a priest brought in for assault, and certainly had never interviewed a witness with Illoe's unique legal status. Uelo knew the consequences in this case would be more than the usual reprimand, but he held to the standard procedure. "We are just here to ascertain the truth. No one is being charged with anything. Please follow your conscience."

Illoe looked from Uelo to the silent Truth Arbiter, who sat perfectly still against the wall, her eyes closed, breathing deeply. She could be asleep, but her spine was so straight, her forehead smooth but her hair severely pulled tight to her scalp. Illoe could not feel the power of her, pulsing through the room, wrapped around him, measuring and marking every part of him like water expertly matches the surface of a body, but he knew it was not right, not normal, for a person to sit like that. He bit his bottom lip. "I got there just before the arbiters. Everything was just the way you saw it."

"Describe what you first saw, please."

"I saw this man fall to the ground. He had a knife. Hitra was standing near him...She looked scared." He looked anxiously at the silent woman in the corner. "She was scared."

Uelo shook his head. "Are you sure that's what you saw?"

The communications between Uelo and Nana, his partner, were too subtle and continuous to be described as words; they wove a tapestry of thought between them, a picture of Illoe as he would never see himself. It was not quite how I saw him, either. It was like a reflection in water, moving vagaries with small, sudden, startling clarities.

Illoe straightened his spine and lowered his brow. "I won't say anything to incriminate Hitra."

Uelo sagged inside his stiff arbiter's tunic. Illoe saw it. The Truth Arbiter opened her eyes.

"No," Illoe said. "I didn't say anything. I didn't *think* anything!"

"You did, actually. I'm sorry."

Illoe's fists trembled. "Servants get hit every day in this city, and you don't do a damn thing about it."

Uelo regarded him coldly. "If they wish to report it, there's nothing stopping them."

Illoe sputtered. "I didn't wish to report it!"

"Yes," Uelo said, irritated and frustrated, "but you are here to be questioned, and you did recall a previous assault, which makes this not an isolated incident for this priest." Uelo hated how often victims rushed to their attackers' aid. It made his job, the department's job, so hard, repeating the same interventions when something permanent should have been done.

Nana sent him a soothing, silent thought-touch of support and agreement.

"If you arrest her, you'll have to arrest half of temple mount!"

"Thank you, Illoehenderen. We've finished taking your statement."

"No, I'm not done."

Uelo took a step back as his partner stood. Nana felt protective of her partner, who was almost a decade younger than her. She wanted to push this angry young man back, but Uelo reassured her he wasn't threatened. Together they looked at Illoe, unified and outwardly calm. "You're done."

Hitra stood as Illoe returned to the waiting room. Their eyes met and both held still. Illoe dropped his gaze.

Hitra followed the arbiters back into the questioning room. She looked over her shoulder, but Illoe did not turn. The door closed on her view of him. He was standing as though he carried something heavy. It didn't occur to her to probe his mind, but the arbiters were waiting to stop her if she did.

Uelo turned to face her as the second door closed. "Holiness, I have to tell you that you are being charged with assault. Two counts. You may wish to contact your advocate before speaking to us."

Her hand jerked, unbidden, and she felt tears. She sucked in her breath as though she could hold them with suction under the edges of her eyelids. "I was attacked." She jabbed her fingertips against her sternum. "He attacked me."

Uelo held his hands out as though he might touch her. "Holiness—madam priest—you may wish to contact an advocate of the law and specifically have her tell you about the laws governing mental assault. As an adept—"

"I didn't assault him! It wasn't like that!" The arbiter reached for her arms. Hitra shrugged away from him. She was crying now. She fell against the wall and cried.

Uelo felt the distinct discomfort shared by those whose daily work encompasses other people's personal tragedies. There were exceptions for self-defense, of course there were, but Hitra hadn't simply hurt Jeje, she'd repaired the damage and dropped him unconscious, and now she had a previous record.

Nana nodded to Uelo and draped an arm over the priest's back. "It's going to be all right. Not now, but soon, everything will be right," she said, and believed it herself, that belief bleeding out from her for all who could sense it. Hitra's racking sobs subsided, but she didn't straighten.

Uelo was relieved and a little frightened by his partner's power with emotion. He had another hard job to do, however. He came into the waiting room. He glanced up at the small window by the ceiling; it had become flat with darkness. Illoe sat on the right-hand bench, his head in his hands, his legs spread in his short tunic. Uelo wanted to reprimand him to sit modestly, as he would reprimand any young man in his household, but he held the urge down. He cleared his throat, and Illoe's head jerked up. The places where his palms had dug into his cheeks were red. "Illoehenderen, we can release you now. Do you have someplace to go?"

His forehead wrinkled. "Home?"

"According to our records, you live here, on the temple grounds, in Priest Hitra's chambers. Considering the nature of the charges and your...well, your status, the arbitration office would rather you stayed somewhere else tonight. With a friend or relative."

"Hitra and I have lived together for four years. I'm safe alone with her."

"It's our policy, whenever there's a domestic assault. An arbiter will escort you wherever you like, but not to Hitra's dwelling."

Illoe stood and stared at the door as though an invisible barrier blocked it. "When can I go back?"

"We'll let you know." Uelo shrugged. Even though he shouldn't, he said, "I can almost guarantee it'll be less than a week. Probably just tonight. She...well, those are just my personal opinions. You understand."

Illoe nodded with an expression that said clearly he did not. "I'll call my brother."

Uelo relaxed. "Great. I'll get an escort for you. Shouldn't be a minute."

Hitra was oblivious to the arbiters entering and leaving the room where she sat. She was focused on how she couldn't call her mother. She knew it was the right thing to do; her family had a personal advocate; her mother had ties to the arbitration council. Her mother, likely, wouldn't even blame her. Her mother would consider a mental assault the gods-given right of the adept.

Which was why Hitra could not call her mother. She reached her mind out for Jante, but felt the softness of sleep. Thinking about contacting her fellow priests made her ache. Finally, just scrolling through names in her head, she thought of Maede. It was an idea both awful and appealing. She didn't like Maede as a person, but she also couldn't think of anyone more neutral, anyone more likely to come. And she did not particularly care if Maede saw her in this state.

She swept her consciousness across the complex, reaching for High Street, and came across Maede's brownish mind abruptly, close by.

Maede? Is it too late?

There was a start, a flash of understanding. *Hitra? I'm at the Temple Club. Is something the matter?*

Chapter Ten

Venal Sins

Ele lived on Indefatigable—called Indy Street by all but mapmakers, who took a perverse joy in curving the little letters of its name along the short street. It was an arc circumventing the markets on Penitence and Sorrow, and it boasted a slightly more pedestrian reputation. It was the abode of people who would someday live somewhere else, a street lined with boarding houses, cramped apartments and small, neat gardens. Ele's was a yellow-washed house almost exactly halfway down the street, where its steady turn was sharpest. An ancient tree grew out of the garden wall. Illoe paused uncertainly. The bricks were darkened, flaking near the tree, the wall itself swelling out as though the trunk had burst from it recently. The rusting numbers slanted with the bricks. He pulled back a leafy vine to expose the last digit.

"This is the place." He turned to face the arbiter, just three steps behind him, hands clasped. She didn't take the hint that she could leave now. She looked like she was completely unaffected by her surroundings, like she existed in a parallel arbiters-only world that was all gray walls. (Actually, she was enjoying seeing a new part of the city and daydreaming about the lives lived here.)

Illoe sighed and opened the garden gate. The garden was narrow, plants struggling to grow in the shade of the great tree, bright starflowers hugging the walls. There were four glass doors. Illoe frowned.

One copy of his reflection tipped into darkness and was replaced by Ele. "Hey," Illoe said, while his brother looked directly at the arbiter.

The officer nodded and turned on her heel. Illoe wondered what words had passed between his brother and the arbiter, sharing the elite power of the adept, but actually their communication had been wordless.

Ele retreated into the flickering light of the interior. Illoe took one more glance at the moon-drenched courtyard and followed.

The hall was long, without doors, lit with sconces of sputtering oil. At the end, three doors faced a trapezoidal space that was little more than a swelling of the corridor. Ele slipped into the one on the left. "Illoe, Tara. Tara, Illoe."

Illoe looked down, expecting a pet, but Tara turned out to have hands that reached to take his cloak. She squeezed past him to hang it on a peg, smelling of sweet feminine perfumes. "Ele's told me all about you," she said.

"I can't say the same," Illoe said, returning his brother's glare.

Ele's voice filled his ears. *You are NOT telling Father about Tara.*

Tara crossed the room and fell onto a low couch. Illoe stared at her long bare arms and expressive bare feet. She was stocky with unkempt hair and shockingly pretty.

"You don't have a bag?" Ele was looking behind Illoe as though one might appear of its own accord.

"They wouldn't let me go home to pack one."

"Well, come in. You can use one of my shirts to sleep in."

Ele's apartment was even smaller than the one they'd grown up in. Illoe felt large and claustrophobic. Ele pushed a folded tunic into his arms and shoved him through a door into a windowless closet. The bed filled the space, a square of floor barely large enough to stand in along its short dimension. He watched in surprise as his brother shut the door on him.

He sent his thoughts after his brother. *Ele, where are you going to sleep?*

On the couch. Good night.

Feeling in the dark, Illoe found a lamp set in the wall, but he couldn't find its striker. Sighing loud and hoping Ele could hear him, he felt for the height of the bed's footboard with his shin. Carefully he climbed over it and settled himself over the covers, still in his tunic, Ele's on his chest like a funerary bouquet. He tried to convince himself that because he could not see, it may as well have been his own room, but strangeness permeated the darkness.

After a while he could see the texture of the wall near the door, illuminated by a faint flickering along the frame. He thought uncomfortably about Tara's legs. Ele and Tara spoke in whispers and giggles for a long time. Illoe felt himself unpossessed and therefore possessable. *That gave me ideas.*

☽○☾

The temple arbiters waited patiently while Hitra exchanged clothing and instructions with Maede, making her feel like the involuntary star of a one-act play entitled "I am perfectly fine."

"I couldn't find the book you mentioned, but there was a lovely copy of Telre's *Confessions* on your bookcase, so I packed that."

Maede pressed the gaudiest of Hitra's travel bags into her hands. It was dyed straw, with yellow and pink flowers like starbursts: an old gift, she suspected from Maede herself. Hitra tried not to grimace. "Thank you so much, Maede, really, I don't know how to thank you."

"It's the least I could do. Unlike that disrespectful boy of yours. He wasn't even in your apartment. The gods only know what sort of mischief he's gotten himself into during your hour of need."

Hitra fussed with the opening of the bag. "I don't know where Illoe is right now, but it's hardly his fault. The arbiters sent him to spend the night at a friend's."

"What? That's irresponsible! Sending him out into the city! What do we pay these people for?"

"He'd be just as alone at my place," Hitra said.

Maede patted Hitra's shoulder. "You're too kind to him. I probably shouldn't say this, but he's a lascivious boy. If you knew the things he is thinking behind your back...broadcasting *lust* so hard that it violates the senses!"

Hitra thought fervently, *she doesn't know what she's talking about,* for the arbiter's sake, though she hoped they could tell. "He's just young," she said.

"I have a son, Hitra, and he was never that bad."

Nana turned her eyes their way, her expression clearly expressing that they had become a nuisance. As for believing any of Maede's accusations, the arbiter had already formed an accurate opinion of Maede as a habitual exaggerator, not that she had any inclination to assure Hitra. Anxious people were more likely to think incriminating things.

Hitra nudged Maede toward the door. "Check in on him if you can, for me?"

Maede sputtered, annoyed at Hitra's lack of sympathy.

"If you can," Hitra repeated, and tried to smile.

She gave Maede a prim little hug, since it seemed like the right thing to do, and Maede shook her finger at the arbiters, admonishing them to "Look after her."

After Maede left, the arbiters and Hitra stood like strangers accidentally brought together at a cocktail party, no one able to come up with a conversation topic. Finally, Uelo spoke. "Priest, we have only one room to hold guests."

They were waiting for her to say something. "And so you will be letting me go?"

"No, priest. You see, we already have a man in custody. If it were a woman…"

Hitra's shoulders fell. She almost rolled her eyes. "Are you afraid I'll sleep with him or that I'll hurt him?"

Uelo and Nana glanced briefly at each other. Nana sent a wordless urge to continue. "No, priest. Sorry. It's not normally our procedure…we don't normally hold prisoners. If you like, we can escort you to the High Street station."

"I'll be fine." There was something more, something unspoken in their expressions. "Heavenly Mother, it's not Forthright Jeje, is it?"

Their expressions hardened. "No. Jeje is being held elsewhere."

"You are holding him. Is that good? I mean, you must know, then, how he threatened me first."

Uelo looked at his companion, shrugged, and said, "Madam, there's no way for me to answer that question legally. Since you say you have no problem sharing for the night, we'll show you to the guest room. If you are concerned for your safety, an officer will be within earshot all night."

"Oh." Hitra felt small. "Thank you."

)O(

It was the last of the long chain of rooms, the only one without a second door. In it were two wooden beds, mattresses stuffed with dusty straw, and one high-set window.

Arel sat on his bed already, hands in his lap. He recognized Hitra immediately, even bedraggled and in a dirty under-robe. He'd always had a good eye for faces.

Hitra clutched the brittle straw of Maede's bag to her stomach. Arel was dressed in a rough peasant shirt and slacks. His face was soft, cheeks beginning to sag with age, but for all she knew, he was a murderer.

"Priest," he said, which made her jump. She was wearing only her under-robe now, and it should not have identified her so easily. But then, maybe it did. What were the secular people wearing these days?

Hitra kept her eyes on the wall and crawled onto the wooden-framed bed. The straw crackled and broke under her. She coughed.

"Priest?" he said again. "There's no reason not to talk to me now. We'll both be here a while. Please talk to me."

"I can't help you," she said. The moisture on her cheek felt of dust. "I'm not sure I'm still a priest."

There was a long silence. Slowly, the sound of night birds and the gentle slap of water moving undisturbed in the public baths penetrated the room. Some unnamed insect or toad was trilling endlessly to itself. Hitra had a disturbing sense of lying in hay, in a barn, miles from the city. But then there was a sound of wagon wheels creaking, and the ring of a watch-bell, and the city settled around her again like a familiar cloak. She shifted, thought of insects, and tried to sleep.

"I lost my faith," Arel said. He spoke softly, but after attuning her ears to the gentle sounds beyond the walls, it was a shout.

Please no, she thought to herself. Can't I be off duty now?

Of course, her cellmate could not hear her unsent words and continued speaking. "Ever since I was a boy, I thought I could feel the gods, every day, in little ways. I'd see a green leaf on paving stones and think, 'the gods put that there for me to see.'" He held his hands in front of him, as though he could pick up the imaginary leaf. "I started working as soon as I could, delivering things mostly, just to save up the money for the test, and then, there I was, an adept. It was like the gods had told me, like I knew all along, I was destined to their service."

Hitra held still, though her right side was pinched by straw. She didn't want to talk with this man and hoped he'd think she was asleep. His story was exactly like dozens she'd heard from acolyte applicants.

"Now I think...maybe they weren't there at all. Maybe they never were."

"They're there," Hitra said, before she could stop herself. "Believe me, the gods exist. I wish they didn't." She hadn't realized it until she said it, but it was true. Gods that didn't exist were much more obedient to their church's needs.

Arel had started absently breaking straws from his mattress. "You don't really mean that. It must be a comfort to you, to know."

"Let me sleep!"

He let the broken pieces of straw fall, down his leg and over his bare foot to the floor. "Your title and position come with a great responsibility. You can't let the stress of this situation cause you to lash out at a stranger. For all you know, I have never been near a priest of the mount before, and you will shape my opinion of the whole church."

Hitra stared at the man. His face was calm, earnest — his emotions locked off from casual view. "You sound like the Ritual Celebrant."

"There are some matters on which Reha and I agree."

Few people outside the church would even think to call the Celebrant by her first name. Hitra looked more closely at her cellmate. "Who are you?"

"My name is Arelandus Nereshore. I am a Speaker of the Sectarians."

Hitra groaned and rolled onto her back. "I'm not interested in converting." The tiny, high window reflected water on the tiles of the ceiling. Hitra tried to imagine herself drowning in some inverted pool of night-colored water, but she itched too much from the straw bed.

"I've worked very hard to get to see you, Priest. Do you really believe I'd do so only to proselytize?"

"You..." Hitra looked to the door again, then the window, as though to assure herself of her surroundings. "You planned all this?"

"Getting arrested?" Arel smiled. "No. But perhaps the gods did. I count myself blessed to end up here, with you, the one woman in the world who can answer my questions."

I wished I'd gotten him arrested. The arrogance. I had words at last to say. *Tell him the gods aren't interested in HIM!*

Hitra took my thought for her own conscience. With resignation, Hitra sat up and faced him. "Whatever questions you have, whatever doubts I'm supposed to quell, I can't. There's nothing to tell. No special or secret knowledge was passed to me. Believe it or not, I've felt my faith shaken by all this. I don't think there's a soul in Cassia who hasn't."

He leaned closer. "But...you did see her?"

"I saw a woman, shrouded in golden light. She was more beautiful than the sun, and carried a sheaf of wheat before her. She was exactly as I pictured Revestre. She may even be Revestre...It's hard to explain. She wasn't what I believed in. Believe in."

Arel stood. "But...you saw her. Didn't you? You...don't believe in your own vision?"

"Because I saw it." Hitra shook her head. "What do you think faith is? There's not supposed to be any proof."

Arel took hold of her arms. He didn't mean it as an aggressive action, but Hitra began, just began, to feel for the arbiters, and he shook her, lifted her whole body from the bed and pushed her down again. It was surprisingly easy for him to do, and it didn't feel violent from his point of view. Their eyes met, and she felt something stir under the surface of him. She reached for him with her mind and a cool wall of protection stopped her. He was an adept. High level. She sent a true attack against that wall, but he held. He held her off with his mind and held her still with his strength.

I wanted to intervene, to protect her, but that wasn't what an evil god would do, was it? It was what a confused entity Arel woke to consciousness would do. I was Senne and I should wait and watch and hope for violence if it came to shake answers out.

I didn't feel like me.

"What did the god say? She'd said something. About us. About me? She had to tell you why she came."

"She told me nothing."

Arel stared at her, and Hitra let down her defenses to show him her emotion, her honesty and fear. She shivered. Emotional shields were always in place on an adept, they were like clothing.

He let go of her. She fell onto the mattress and threw her arms before her for protection, but no violence followed. She curled onto her side and saw him resting his head against the wall, his fists together, under the window. He said, "I felt...I may have woken the gods."

"I don't need to hear the details of your..." Hitra quickly edited the word "delusions" out of her sentence, but couldn't come up with a good replacement.

Arel turned to rest his back against the wall. He was weary yet calm, like a day laborer taking a break. "We arranged a protest. Myself, and the other leaders of the Sectarian church in Chagrin. There were twenty of us, all told. Some came from as far as Valleyview and Riversend: all the adepts over third level who have taken a husher's vow."

"Protest what?" Hitra pursed her lips and told herself not to go further, but she did. "You people run around crying favoritism and persecution because others won't do what you do. We let you waste your talents all you want, why can't you return the favor?"

"You worship ceremonies and idols. Isn't that enough to protest? Isn't there favoritism and persecution when one point of view is orthodox and another ignored? If we are right, isn't it a sin to let you be wrong?"

Hitra knew she was right, and that there were arguments that could destroy his claims, really good ones, that she'd heard and repeated before, but all she could think to say was, "How dare you."

"We dare." Arel leaned forward and gestured excitedly. "That's the thing. We dare ask why things are the way they are. We dared to touch the gods."

Again, he remembered it, the most perfect memory. The blue sky, the barking dog, their minds pushing up, outward, and the void. The horrible, oddly familiar void.

Not me. I refused to believe the void was me, was us... I pushed his memory, felt a trail of something. Childhood nights staring at the ceiling, stories told by a long-departed grandmother about the edge of the world. *But what is beyond that, Grandma?*

Arel felt his mind moving without his will. He turned to the wall again and set his fist against it. "Either," he said, and his back shook. It was a while before he could continue. "Either the gods don't exist, or I felt them…" There was another, shuddering pause. "Careless, thoughtless. Not thinking."

Not thinking, yes. That's the thing. Not thinking, but there. We existed before that. How long? Doing what? My memory stopped. I could push back to where it stopped, and then play forward, and the first thing was this sense of a retreating presence, wordlessly begging…come to us…guide us…we need you.

It was ridiculous. It was insulting! We made them, not the other way around.

Arel kept talking. "Either you saw an illusion, or else I awoke the divine host," he shook with emotion, spraying spit on the wall, "and they passed me by without a thought to speak to *you*."

Hitra drew her knees up before her and set her back against the wall. "Arbiter!" she shouted.

The wooden door to the room slid open, and Arel's face fell into the same hanging sadness she'd first seen. He sat down on his bed again, hands between his knees, and without looking at either her or the arbiter said, "I'm sorry. I'll be more quiet."

Neither Hitra nor I believed him, and I had plenty of knowledge to judge with.

The arbiter, very young and very junior on the staff, looked at Hitra. "Are you well?"

"Is there somewhere else I can sleep?"

He had no idea. He'd been hoping it wouldn't come up and hadn't completely listened to Uelo's explanation of what to do if it did. "If you want to move tonight, I'll have to call the section leader back. It'll take a while."

Arel rolled onto his bed and faced the wall. Hitra said, "Please do that."

The arbiter left, and they were alone again. Hitra watched Arel's still form, not quite believing, for some time, that he would stay on his side of the room.

155

A wavering lozenge of reflected moonlight broke and reformed on the changeless ceiling tiles. "I don't believe in the gods anymore," Hitra said, and listened to the echo of her words. It felt good to say them out loud. "I don't. Because I know they are real, I can't believe in them. It's crazy, isn't it?"

Arel did believe. He believed so much it hurt him. It took them both a very long time to fall asleep. I was afraid neither one of them could help me.

$$\mathfrak{D}O\mathfrak{C}$$

Forthright Jeje was not asked any questions, which was how he expected his arrest to go. The Casu arbiters simply took Hitra's account and the account of their own officers. They felt no hypocrisy in treating a Sanadaru man different from a Casu woman in their procedures—it was a known fact that Casu were inherently more honest and trustworthy than Sanadaru. At least, a known fact to the Casu. Jeje was told he was guilty of assaulting and threatening a priest. Then he was walked down from the temple grounds where a beast-drawn wagon waited by the marble balustrade that kept vehicle traffic from the holy grounds. The round-faced draft creature nuzzled a marble pillar in front of it, hoping, perhaps, that it was salt. She had as much knowledge of where they were going as Jeje.

$$\mathfrak{D}O\mathfrak{C}$$

Maede was given a key to Hitra's apartment. She held it close by her breast, and congratulated herself constantly, with a touch to its smooth brass shape, on not taking undue advantage.

She had half expected to find Illoe sitting in the front room, wasting his time reading filthy books. But of course he wasn't. He was, as the arbiters had put it 'in protective custody'—which she suspected meant being corrupted by state-subsidized atheist miscreants. She searched his room, found that he really didn't have any decent clothes, and what was more, he had a collection of dirty, broken pottery. She tossed that out the back door. Being reduced to cleaning a servant's room gave Maede the martyr-like satisfaction she so greatly craved.

Dusting off his prayer mat—which obviously hadn't been used since it was purchased—Maede noticed a glittering object under the bed. She pulled it out and ran her hand over it, though there was no dust. A brass scroll case, embossed with designs of flowers. She opened it, and her eyes played over the first line of text.

Much in the same principle that even an empty clock is correct once a day, Maede's sluggish mind stumbled on a few simple truths; the first of which was that she had the name of Illoe's mother, and the second of which was that a mother always knows where to find her children.

Maede then sat on Illoe's bed, trying to make up her tiny little mind. On the one hand, she wanted desperately to have Hitra indebted to her, especially now that she was poised to become truly famous. More than that. A new prophet! She had to become Hitra's best friend. It was the only option, the only reasonable path available to increase Maede's personal power and influence.

On the other hand, she imagined Illoe's mother as miserable, mannish, and possibly disease-ridden. What other sort of mother would sell her child?

In her simple, clumsy way, Maede was doing what I was supposed to do. Scheming.

I'd learned something from my observations: Emotion was the easiest, most natural way to control and influence someone, and Maede was a woman who all but bowed to an inner altar of her emotions, without ever wondering where they came from. So I massaged a little covetousness into her—it wasn't hard. Like forcing a child to take candy. She wanted Illoe like she wanted a pretty bracelet in a shop window. I reflected that want back at her. It wasn't hard; I wanted him, too. I should want him. Not to protect him and talk with him. I should want him like Darian, like something to carry off.

I could be me. If Maede could, I had to.

Much to my surprise as well as her own, Maede actually formulated a plan. She arrived at yet another truth: she could have her personal advocate call for her. The advocate would endure the unpleasantness of interaction, and Maede could still claim the hardship for herself.

The Arbitration Council (Temple District) had not, in fact, contacted Loata Middlemount concerning the incident and her son, but as soon as they did, Ele was the first person Loata contacted. It was then a simple matter of making Maede's disinterested advocate think she'd closed the connection when she hadn't, which resulted in her hearing more than she or the Arbitration Council intended.

Discreetly closing the connection, the advocate sighed and wondered why it made her depressed every time she had good news for Maede Faydehale.

Chapter Eleven

Penance

A single shaft of morning light made it into the holding cell, having survived the sun's assault on the bathhouse, the courtyard, and finally the portico that was the continuation of the closed-off hallway of the arbiters. It just happened to hit Hitra's face and burrow through the thin skin of her eyelid. She winced, rolled over, and then, slowly, awoke to the sight of a sand-brick wall.

Arel coughed and she turned to find him sitting on his bunk, his hands in his lap, his stubble-chinned face hanging low. "Good morning, Priest," he said. After she sat up and the rustling of the straw subsided, he added, "I'm sorry I lost my temper last night. It really wasn't like me, if you can believe that. Please, accept my apology."

So much for being moved to another cell during the night. Hitra considered telling him to shove off, but she was too sore to fight. "We've all been under unusual stress," she said, and even managed to sound concerned. She grabbed hold of the edge of her bed to stretch her back. She felt her vertebrae move slowly. Her wrist popped.

"Will you want to pray this morning?" her cellmate asked. "We can push the beds back. There should be plenty of space for you. Well, if you brought chalk."

Hitra stared at him as though he was speaking a foreign language. "Chalk?"

"Did I tell you I'm a sectarian?" He squinted at her. "Oh, I guess I did. It's all right; I won't stop you from praying your way. We each have to find our own path to the gods."

"After..." she rotated her wrist and tried to come up with a word that could describe the sum of her recent experiences. "After everything, you can sit here and calmly talk about chalk?"

He shrugged. "I've been awake, thinking about what you said last night, about faith and proof. Your god appeared to you, and it caused you to question your faith. The gods refused me, and I questioned my faith; don't you see? It's all quite simple. The gods choose to test each of us where we are lacking. Me and my need for proof, and your need for...well, I don't know what you need. Mystery?"

"Oh," she said. "Good." Thinking, exactly as I did, that Arel was an idiot. Her body complained to her as she crawled off of the bed. The floor was stone, as cold as spring water on her bare feet. She hopped to the bag Maede had brought. Sure enough, there was the gaudy orange mirror-tiled chalk case her grandmother had bought her. Maede really had a gift for picking out her least favorite possessions. Hitra let it fall back into the bag and climbed back onto the bed. It itched, but at least it was warm. "Maybe later."

There was a knock at the cell door. Hitra jumped up, but of course, the door did not have a handle on this side. It opened, and an arbiter nodded to her. "Good morning, Holiness. Citizen Nereshore, you're being transferred to the Municipal Holding Facility. We'll be back in about ten minutes. Make whatever preparations you need to."

The door closed again and Hitra looked at Arel, who hadn't moved. His violence the night before contrasted with this defeated calm. She didn't trust it. "What are you going to do?"

He shrugged. "What I can."

That sounded to Hitra like he was about to blow up a school or something. She rolled her lips inward. "Do you...I mean, you really think you awoke the gods?"

Arel was unaware how sinister he sounded, or that Hitra was trying to talk him down. He felt hope. This was what he could do: preach the truth and urge others to prayer. "We reached our consciousness toward the heavens. We felt...something...it was...." He couldn't describe it. "We felt a mind in the heavens. A month later, the pillar of fire appeared."

"So you think you contacted the gods, but they waited a month to respond?"

He blinked, his eyes glistening. "It wasn't like us. If it was.... it was...I don't know what I experienced."

"Then why…no, forget that." For a moment, the two priests leaned toward each other, like conspirators. Hitra couldn't believe she was getting pulled into this. "What if what you connected with was not our gods? It could have been the Anichu god, Xushem, or something else entirely. Something that is now pretending to be Wenne, and Revestre."

Arel smiled. "But I don't believe in Xushem, or any other non-Casu god."

Hitra leaned back. "No, I guess not. I mean, I don't, either."

They sat in silence together, waiting for the door to open again. I wondered why I hadn't considered the existence of other gods.

))O((

Illoe awoke confused by the texture of the wall before him and the bed under him. He rolled over. Blue plaster all around him, and under him a lumpy, narrow mattress. He stared at the pattern of cracks in the ceiling and memory returned to him like a falling cobweb. "Ugh. Right."

He listened at the door, and peeked out at the front room. Sunlight fell from a narrow, curtained window across the wooden table and the visible arm of the couch. He stepped back, let the door creak shut again, and looked around the tiny bedroom for a sign. Two days until Harvest Home. One day left to change his contract, and his only hope was that Hitra would find time in the middle of an arbitration, in the middle of a religious crisis, with him not there to remind her.

There was always next year. He was trying to accept that, but a year was such a terribly long time to a boy his age.

He shrugged out of his tunic and into the one his brother had given him to sleep in. Changing clothes was at least a normal thing to do in the morning.

There was a bang. Illoe looked out into the front room again.

"Oh, hey!" Tara said, and separated her back from the apartment's front door. She had a basket of plums in her arms. "I was wondering when you were going to wake up." She was wearing a bright green tunic, the slit sides exposing long expanses of calf as she crossed to the table. Her hair had been gathered haphazardly into three puffs, short hairs sticking out around the edges. It was somehow messier than when she'd had it loose.

Illoe stepped into the room and watched her set down the basket and select two plums from the top. "You live here?"

She set the plums down and opened a high cupboard over the small apartment's diminutive fire pantry; it was really more of a fire *box*. "Of course I live here." She brought down one plate and a paper parcel. She set these on the table as well, and noticed the look of near-panic on her boyfriend's little brother. "I know you work in the temple and all, but you aren't some sort of ascetic, are you?"

"No. I just... thought Ele would tell me there was someone in his life."

She opened a drawer in the table and got out a knife. "Well, he didn't tell me how cute his little brother was, so we're even." She sawed at the fruit, mutilating its flesh.

"Stop. Gods, stop!" Illoe cried out in horror. She froze. He grabbed for the knife, but she held it tightly. "Let me do that," he said.

She held the knife out at arm's length until he stopped reaching. "Just because I'm a woman doesn't mean I can't be domestic." She smiled. "But who am I to stop a man from making me breakfast?" She flipped the knife and handed it to him handle first.

Illoe sliced the plums properly, so little juice was spilled. "Is that bread?" He nodded toward the paper parcel.

"Why," she unfolded the top, "yes, it is!"

"Are you going to marry my brother?" It popped out of his mouth unbidden, rude, but necessary.

Her arms were quite muscular when she crossed them. "By all the gods and their children combined! You just start out with that? Ele told me his family was old-fashioned."

"So you aren't?"

Tara laughed at how serious young Illoe looked, and then at how quickly his expression darkened. She had to control herself before the conversation spiraled out of hand. "Maybe. Why is the world so afraid of men not marrying? Like there's not a pitiful shortage of men!"

That made Illoe uncomfortable. He went back to separating out the plum pits. "Ele told you I work at the temple."

Tara tore hunks off the loaf of bread and scattered them on a plate.

"Yes. He's very proud of you. Heck, I'd be proud too, if I had a little brother with a job at your age!"

Illoe laid the fruit slices on top of the bread pieces. "Did he tell you what I do?"

Tara shrugged and licked the crumbs from her forefinger. "Laundry or something? Someone's got to take care of all those pale robes dragging in the dirt."

"Yeah." Illoe rolled two plum pits with the tip of the knife. What, he wondered, had Ele told her about his current visit? "It's not as hard as you'd think. The floors are pretty clean." He watched Tara sprinkle herbs over the plate of fruit and bread from a small jar he recognized as his mother's work. "What do you do?"

She grimaced. "Nothing right now. Failed the entrance test for Arbitration School. I can reapply in another month."

Illoe watched her pick up bread and fruit with her fingertips and shove it in her mouth. How far did he have to go from Temple Mount not to be surrounded by adepts?

Tara licked her thumb and reached for more herbs. "Is something wrong?"

"No." He set his hands on the table edge. "You and Ele must have met at the academy, then."

"A sordid dining-hall romance. You want the details, or would you rather torment your brother for them?"

He shook his head.

"You can eat some of this too, you know." She leaned over the table, looking sideways at him. "What is it? I know you got into some kind of trouble. Relax. The Arbitration Council exists to help people. And I'm sure the temple district arbiters are the best. They'd have to be. In a couple days, whatever went wrong will be right again."

"That's really not what I'm worried about, but thanks." He scratched his head. "And...thanks for not reading my mind."

"Gods. Is that what's got you jumpy? Do Temple Adepts just run around touching minds? You're not supposed to do that. Not ever, without permission. Wenne's tits! We got that rammed into us for an entire month before field training."

He stared at her. She scooped up more food with her fingers. "Come on, eat. Then you're coming to the wharf with me. It's not much, but it's the kind of entertainment we can afford. I figured we could skip some stones, watch the barges coming into harbor, then swing back through the market and catch Ele on his lunch break, but that's four hours from now, so you'll want food in you."

Reluctantly, he picked up a piece of bread carefully by its edges. He felt some juice on his fingers. He tried to be neat about it, but the structural cohesion of the dish was such that he ended up pushing his fingers into his mouth. The sweet, dry, and spicy mingled nicely, though, and the messy, pungent quality of it seemed appropriate for the dim, dusty apartment.

When he'd had a few handfuls, and the plate was getting too sloppy to dare, he wiped his fingers on his hem and said, "I don't work at the temple. I'm indentured. Our mother sold me to pay for Ele's school."

Tara stared at him as though he'd insulted her. "How did...I mean..."

"The usual way. Just the noble family that paid for me sent me off to the temple with their daughter."

She opened and closed her mouth, frowned, and shook her head. "No. Wait, why are you telling me this?"

"I thought you should know."

Tara licked her fingers. Illoe took her plate and his and set them on the fire-nook. He tried to turn the spigot and found it wouldn't budge. He pressed and twisted, his fingers turning white and pinched.

"I'll get it," Tara said. They jostled, elbows and curses, until she got him to step back and with a glare twisted the spigot the other way. "It was put in backward," she said. She rinsed the two plates and set them atop the fire grid to dry.

"It's not that I thought you couldn't do it," Illoe said.

"Right."

The awkward silence was broken by a knock at the door. They stared at each other a moment, as children might when caught doing something they shouldn't.

"I'll get it," they both said, and then stared at each other again.

The knock repeated.

"Your hands are wet," Illoe said, and took the few steps to the door.

The man at the door was Maede's chauffeur, Aedeareal, a tall, bored man in the old-fashioned clothes of the nobility. Illoe blinked at him. "Can I help you?"

Pushing past Aedeareal, Maede grimaced into a wad of embroidered fabric she held to her face. "There you are, young man!"

Tara had both hands on the table. She shouted, "Hey! You can't barge in here like that."

Maede gasped in horror. She clutched her other hand to her chest and looked liable to pass out. "Illoehenderen," she shouted, finally removing the sachet from her mouth. "What are you doing in this dreadful place, alone with a…" She pointed angrily at Tara. "A barely dressed hooligan!"

Illoe bit on his lip to keep from smirking. "Lady Faydehale, this is my brother's apartment, and as he is not home at the moment, I have to ask you to leave."

"Who is she?" Maede continued to point at Tara.

Tara was the only person present with their name on the rental agreement, and she put all of that into the tone of her, "Who are you?"

"Please, Lady Faydehale…she's my sister-in-law."

Tara cringed at the false-feeling so strong it was almost audible from his untrained mind. "You didn't just say that."

A shriek came from Maede and she tottered back. Aedeareal slid nervously past Illoe to take hold of Maede's arm and ask her if she was all right. Maede repaid him for this service with a swat. "Lying. To me! What sin haven't you committed, Illoehenderen? When I think of poor Hitra and all you've put her through…"

"All I've put HER through!"

Tara pulled Illoe back. "Stop it, both of you. There's an arbitration taking place and for whatever reason, Illoe's staying with us until it's finished. If you have a problem with that, I suggest you contact your local arbitration office and a personal advocate."

Maede surged with professional glee, now that the subject of arbitration and advocacy had been brought up. "Well! I have contacted the arbiters, and they have given me temporary custody of Illoehenderen. Why in the name of all the gods else do you think I would come all the way down here?"

"She's crazy," Illoe said.

"Il-lo-e-hen-der-en," Maede said, turning each syllable of his name into a richly accented remark of its own, "I will be waiting in my carriage. Aedeareal!"

With that, like a narrow but proud ship leaving port, Maede made her slow way back down the apartment corridor, her sleeves carefully gathered up, lest they be dirtied by the poor quality of the wainscoting.

"I have no idea what she's up to," Illoe looked to Tara as his only hope, "but it's not philanthropy. The woman hates me — she wouldn't ask for custody of me!"

Tara scratched the back of her neck. "I'm checking now. Hold on." She wasn't good at talking and thinking at the same time, but she also had direct contacts in the form of her friends who had passed the arbitration exam.

Illoe pressed his fists into the edge of the wooden table, watching Tara's blank expression turn confused, and then irritated, as Maede's story held up.

I wasn't enjoying seeing the scheme come together. Maede was awful! But I was supposed to be awful, too. I had a duty to do awful things. There was something exquisitely awful about Illoe climbing into Maede's carriage under his own power. When she accidentally-on-purpose dropped her hand on his thigh, he just ignored it.

I should be proud, or at least smug. I felt a strong need to be somewhere else.

☽○☾

They came for Arel. He stood at the lead arbiter's gesture and walked out with them. They silently informed him that he was being moved to a higher security "waiting area." Hitra stood automatically when the door opened and remained standing, ignored, until it closed again.

Later, an arbiter brought Hitra a bowl and pitcher to wash with. The water was cold and the cloth they gave her loosely woven. It was a far cry from the delicately scented, perfectly heated baths Illoe drew for her. She stopped searching through Maede's bag for soap and reached out with her mind to the officer on the other side of the door.

May I make a call or two? I mean, am I allowed?

The response was slow in coming. She could hear the arbiters walking around their office. *Not now, ma'am.*

I just want to contact my office…

Not now. The arbiter's mind was tinged with irritation.

She tipped the bag over and found the soap, wrapped in an oilskin. It was one of the decorative blocks she'd gotten from a patron that felt like oil and smelled of ill flowers. Which was why she used them to decorate the windowsill and used the soap Illoe bought instead.

The thought of Happy Sun Spice Bush soap made her miss Illoe like he'd been ripped from her skin. She slipped her robe off her shoulders and started to wash. The cold water didn't rinse the sticky soap easily. It felt like washing in the dormitories. She hadn't noticed before, but the holding cell had the same smell as the dormitory rooms. She wondered if she could pretend she was a neophyte, undergoing the rigors of her final year of ascetic training. Washing in cold water. Wearing only simple robes. She looked up at the ceiling, still dancing with reflected light.

A knock broke her reverie. *If you've finished washing, Holiness, there are people here to speak with you.*

She wriggled back into her robe. "Yes?"

One arbiter held the door for two others who crowded the room. Hitra spilled soapy water moving the washbasin away from the door.

"I'm sorry," she said. "I'm not really prepared to entertain."

Her half-hearted smile was the only response to the joke. The two visitors, Asta and Der, regarded her with solemn expressions and waited for her to take in the magnificence of their white robes, marking them as members of the Queen's Adept. Not because they were vain, they simply knew from experience that people needed a moment.

Asta said, "If you don't mind, Hitra, my associate would like to perform a brief screening of you. Strictly a high-level look at your current emotional state and stability."

Hitra sat down on the hard edge of the bed. Der was a dour-faced man with receding white hair, a little too much like her grandfather, who had spent what few interactions they had railing against children in general. She tugged and tucked her robe around herself so the overlap front covered more of her skin. "I don't see how I can refuse."

"You can always refuse a probe; as a citizen you have a right to privacy." Asta spoke with the assured calm of a schoolteacher, her hands clasped in front of her. "You also have a right to request that an advocate-adept of your choosing be present to assure that no harm is done to you. I am sixth level, my colleague is fifth; I can provide you with a list of seventh level adepts if you wish."

Everyone in the room knew that list was mighty short. Only fourteen seventh level adepts existed in the city, and the Ritual Celebrant and the Queen wouldn't be making house calls.

"That won't be necessary." Hitra re-tied her sash and then set her hands on her lap as though preparing to meditate. "I trust you."

Almost deferentially, she felt the touch of Der's mind, a delicate sweep over the surface of her consciousness, no more invasive than a brush of the cheek.

"You'd be surprised how many people are afraid to submit to a routine scan," Asta shook her head in bemusement. "As an adept yourself you understand the strict control we are under. No one capable of considering using her gifts malevolently would be allowed to keep them."

"Someone like me," Hitra said. Her skin felt thick and numb as she contemplated losing her ability to touch minds.

Asta had a serene smile. "The arbitration council has already determined that you acted under duress on the first charge and in self-defense on the second. You are not a threat to yourself or others. You needn't worry."

"Then why am I still here?"

"We aren't attached to this arbitration, so I can't provide you with information concerning your release."

Hitra frowned. "Then why *are* you here?"

Der spoke for the first time. "To offer you a job."

Asta smiled to her partner, always to be relied on to get to the point. She took a seat on the other bunk. "We suspect from the arbitration report that you have the potential to train up to the sixth rank. It's hard training and not everyone who enters succeeds, but we're hopeful. This could be a wonderful opportunity for professional and personal advancement."

Hitra looked at Der. He shrugged. Hitra shook her head. "It is my intention to continue my service to the temple."

"They don't want you back," Der said.

Asta shot him an annoyed look for his bluntness. His eyes tightened at the corners, a smile only she could detect. To Hitra she said, "The Temple Adepts are debating whether to allow you to return to your position or not. See it from their perspective—it was only last week you claimed to have spoken directly to your god."

"We didn't actually speak."

"You are something of an involuntary celebrity. Recent events have people desperate and confused." Asta was calm and assured, and very pleased with how her argument was flowing. It wasn't often the Adept of the Crown had a chance to swell their ranks at the expense of the Adept of the Church. "You are being watched too closely. If the church reinstates you, they may be accused of turning a blind eye to power-abuse when the accused is one of their own. However, if enough time were to pass, after you worked for the crown for a while, they could take you back without fuss."

"This is stupid." Hitra stood. The queen's adept stared at her in confusion. "I want to talk to Forthright Jeje," Hitra said. "I want to apologize and see what I can do to help him. The man just wanted to see his daughter."

"I don't see what that has to do with anything."

"That's why I'm here. This arbitration is between me, Jeje, and Illoe. I need to sort things out with them. I don't see how talking to you is going to help me do that, and I have no interest in becoming a government adept."

Asta was perfectly still for a few moments. She couldn't imagine anyone not wanting to be a part of the government. Der sent her a wordless nudge. He knew when more words wouldn't convince someone.

Asta rose. "As you wish," she said.

"We'll let the arbiters know," Der said, and waved to her in farewell.

☽○☾

The entryway of the Faydehale manor was decorated with a lurid mural. Darian held one stiff arm up between the two gods, who were an exact depiction of what women thought men thought was attractive. To Illoe, they resembled sleazy politicians. The depiction was the moment Darian had resolved an argument between Wenne and I, by offering to sacrifice himself. For some reason, it was a popular motif for establishing homes. The three mythic figures were surrounded by flowers of all seasons, a dozen different fruits growing on one spidery tree rendered in broad strokes of color. Money cannot buy taste.

Maede stormed through the atrium, her flapping sleeves rippling the surface of her reflecting pool. "All right, young man, first let's get you into some decent clothes. One of my son's old tunics should fit you."

Illoe glanced back for the driver, but he had already closed the front door between them, and was probably putting the carriage away. "Lady Faydehale, you don't have to do this. I'll be perfectly fine at my brother's, and Hitra is probably already being released."

"How dare you talk back to me!" She settled herself in front of him, a vapid pillar of black velvet. There was something undeniably permanent about her when she stood like that, perhaps it was just that her skirts covered her feet, but Illoe got the feeling that he would sooner beat his way through the mural than get past her. "I have taken you into my home as a charitable favor to dear Hitra. Honestly, what more can you ask of me?"

"I'm not asking anything of you."

"Then be silent!" She waved a hand overhead, her sleeve streaming like a flag. "Ondra!"

Maede's front hall opened into two identical parlors: two fire nooks, two sets of sitting couches, two ornamental racks of glass figurines, as though the one served merely as a backup should the other be indisposed at the moment. Dusting the right-hand collection of glass figurines was a dour, thin woman in a threadbare tunic a decade out of style. She stood tall, however, and could just as easily have been touching the vacuous birds and beasts with a blessing staff. She turned with glacial patience, resting the duster against her palm.

"Ondra, see if we have any of Erti's old clothes. I cannot bear to have this indecency in my house." She waved a hand up and down Illoe. "Just look how she let this boy dress. Like a prostitute!"

Ondra inclined her head the exact minimum amount required to keep Maede from calling her disrespectful and walked unhurriedly to the stairs.

"Oh, of course! Erti's room." Maede flapped and fluttered a few feet, then turned to glare at Illoe, fairly quaking with excitement. Illoe was her new expensive possession, and she couldn't wait to show him off. "Come!" she said, hitting her skirts with her open palm.

With a grimace and a force of will, Illoe followed. He told himself it was all too absurd to be fully insulting.

Ondra opened a dusty room that smelled of disuse. With surprising strength, she lifted large piles of fabric from a wooden chest. She spread tunics on the bed in faded colors merchants probably called "harvest gold" or "sunset brown" but the dyer called "end of lot."

"Yes, they look almost a size. Of course, Erti had a better figure." Maede grasped the air, as though her gestures directed the precise placement of clothing upon the bed. "You should take advantage of this opportunity, Illoehenderen, being around real, proper servants for once in your life. You are going to learn to be silent, respectful, and decent."

Ondra was annoyed that she didn't say "like Ondra." Oh, they were both so delightfully awful.

A large, older man stepped into the room, assisted by a finely crafted cane that was a little too short for him. "Dearest, what's going on?"

Maede glanced very quickly over her shoulder, as though afraid to lose track of the hierarchy of ugliness on the bed. "Oh, hello, darling. I've had the most trying day! Hitra—my priestess friend who is relying on my help right now? Well, she needed me to take on her servant for a few days."

Illoe raised one hand in greeting. "Really more like a few hours."

"Dear?" Lord Faydehale leaned over his cane. "Could we have a word in the hallway?"

Maede had not considered her husband in these matters and had rather naively hoped he wouldn't notice Illoe's sudden appearance.

She pointed at one of the tunics. "That one," she said, and made a clearing wave. "Get the rest of these put away."

"Dear?" Lord Faydehale repeated.

"Not now. I have so much to do! Also, Ondra, before he's dressed he should be bathed, preferably with lye. Heavens know what he's carrying."

Lord Faydehale tapped his cane, hard, twice on the tiled floor. "Dear," he said, like it was an insult, "were you going to consult with me before bringing strange boys home?"

Maede threw her hands up in the air. "Fine," she said, and stomped out of the room.

Lord Faydehale smiled and nodded to Illoe. "Nice to meet you, son. You're welcome to stay as long as you like." He followed his wife, hoping Illoe would be gone for good within the hour.

Illoe turned to Ondra. "Now what?"

Ondra shoved the bundle of tunics against his chest. "Don't talk to me."

He followed her out into the hallway, holding the mildew-smelling clothes in front of him like a particularly nasty and effective talisman. "I'm not your new slave," he said. "I'm staying here as a guest, because of an arbitration."

Ondra turned on one heel. "I may not be Her Ladyship, but I am a free woman. I earn my keep here, boy, and I deserve your respect."

Illoe blinked. "I...sorry..."

"Never mind setting m'lady and m'lord at it. They'll be arguing until midsummer. I don't abide indentures. Take honest people's jobs and can't get fired no matter how lazy they get." She returned to her unhurried walk down the glass-inlaid corridor. "Now don't talk to me. Bad enough I have to give a strange man a bath."

"I can bathe myself!" But he followed Ondra to an enormous bath, set with a ceiling of curving glass and mirror tiles, like a frozen starry sky. She directed him with grunts and hand waving to wash the old tunic he was carrying in the sink while she filled the bathtub.

"I'll be back when that's full. Don't let it overflow!" She twisted the water-knob once more for good measure and walked out of the room in the same imperious manner with which she had walked into it.

Illoe rinsed dust from the tunic and wrung it out and slapped it against the tiles and hung it on a bar. Unwillingly. He had this cold feeling he'd be doing a lot of unwilling things while he was in this house.

Maybe it was all right, to have done this. To have manipulated things at last. Not for Maede's benefit, but my own. Motion in any direction was better than standing still, wasn't it?

Illoe undressed. I touched him, a brush down the small of his back. He shivered and ignored it, thinking it was a trick of his mind, but I knew better. I was on my way to making him mine.

Chapter Twelve
Mortal Sins

Sorrow's Market at midday was a cacophony of sight and smell. Long, low stone benches older than any other structure in the city smoked and sizzled with cooking food. Their sides were beige, their tops brown and black, cut with divots and parallel marks from knives. Old men squatted, feeding and fanning the flames in their shallow holes while women threw down handfuls of meat over them. Copper domes were set on items that required a while to cook, and a thin but pervasive smoke curled around them, under them, and up to the brightly colored awnings that competed with each other to block out the sky.

Tara sat on a block of wood, roughly formed into a chair—one of countless like it scattered throughout the market where workmen and -women took their lunch. Her back rested against the eastern leg of the Sorrow Market arch, the right foot of Nolumbre over her head like a storm cloud. Two meat buns burned her hand through the napkin she had wrapped over them. The little wood-block chair was not comfortable, nor was it stable, one stout little leg being demonstrably shorter. She teetered on and off it rhythmically.

Ele did not like her to contact him telepathically while he was at work. Not even if she scanned ahead and waited for him to be available. Her mind reached out over the marketplace and felt minds: jumbled, strange, boring minds. Not Ele. Succulent meats charred nearby, tugging at her entire digestive tract with their promises. The grease from the meat buns had already stopped burning her, growing cold in her palms, when finally she felt him approach. Her eyes moved to where her mind directed, and she felt the satisfaction, still a surprise after years of schooling, of a mental probe solidifying into reality. She stood so he could see her more clearly and held up the napkin-wrapped buns together like breasts in her hands.

Ele dragged a wooden seat close and fell on it. "Where's Illoe?" He reached for a bun.

Tara wiped the grease from her free hand on her lap. "He ran off with some deranged noblewoman, said she knew his mistress." She let that word hang and looked at Ele to see if he picked up her annoyance.

He was stuffing his mouth with bun. *What a day. What a week. I can't believe he told the arbiters he'd stay with me. He could have gone to Mom's. Mental traffic is just nuts. We finally calmed down from the panic, and now the holiday's coming up. We need more people.*

"You know, I think it's disgusting using your mind to talk just so you can eat at the same time."

He rubbed the back of his hand across the corner of his mouth. "What, are you a husher now?"

"Why didn't you tell me your brother is a slave?"

Ele's hand fell to his lap and small bits of meat fell to the ground under him, attracting the attention of some bold feather-rats. He kicked them away, but others came, gathering up his crumbs and squawking at each other. He gestured wide, seeming simultaneously to be losing his grip on his seat, his lunch, and the battle with the rodents. "Indentured," he managed to say, and held up one finger to underscore the difference in the two words.

"Well?" Tara asked. "Seems a pretty big deal, doesn't it? Didn't you trust me enough to tell me?"

"That little..." Ele lifted off his seat, straining to look over the crowd. "Listen, Tara, it's not my fault, what he and my parents did. I'm tired of apologizing for it."

"Hey!" Tara grabbed his tunic sleeve. "Sit down. I'm not asking you to apologize. When he told me, I was unprepared. That's what I don't like, Ele. You have to prepare me for dealing with your family someday, or are you going to continue to pretend they don't exist?"

Ele turned to her tugging and squinted at her. "I can't find him," he said.

"Who?"

"My brother. If he's anywhere in the city, I should be able to find him through the network, but he's not there. None of the routers have heard traffic from him all day. Where did he say he was going?"

Tara sighed. She let go of Ele and leaned against the cool stone behind her. "He ran off with this ancient bat. Will you please sit your butt down? Maybe he's blocking you."

"Illoe can't block." Ele sat down, though he kept glancing across the market, up the hill. "You just let him go?"

"I didn't exactly *let* him. This woman had official custody of him. I checked."

"That doesn't make sense. Who was she? He could be in trouble. The contract could be in trouble…do you have any idea how crazy my dad will get if the indenture money stops coming?"

"Am I still in this conversation? Will you listen for a minute? I can tell you where they went. It was Noble's Hill."

Ele squinted into the distance, ignoring her. "They're going to blame me. Somehow, my parents will blame me for this."

"I can't compete with your brother," Tara said, and stood. "See you when you come home."

"Tara!" She didn't look back. He followed his sense of her through the market and sighed. He was a fool, not following her, when a single kind word or expression would turn her thoughts. She wanted to be turned. But Ele was more concerned with his own sense of martyrdom.

☽○☾

Forthright Jeje spent the intervening night in the public corrections house, near the palace of the secular government on Main Avenue. It was the Sanadaru section of town, as the Casu saw it, though the people here were not Anichu, like him. They were mostly foreigners, Grostens and Northmen. All of the city was once the Sanadaru section, and the streets still bore the names Anichu had given them when the city ended at Sorrow and High Street and Temple Mount were raw mountainside covered in spice bush and reed-cedar.

Jeje saw a past where his people ruled all the land to the top of the blue hills on the other side of Lake Chagrin, and a history of the world that started here, created by gods I had certainly not met.

He was reflecting on the unfair pendulum of fate, but his musings gave me pause for different reasons. Did their deity not exist because it was male, or because it was Sanadaru? I had noticed the absence of any male gods. Darian was not the only male of our pantheon, just the most prominent. His absence alone could be explained, maybe, by his half-human nature, but where was the comical fertility god and that fellow with the tall head who ruled over the realm of bureaucracy?

Besides that, how to explain the different history?

Jeje's world was created by a god named Xu as a gift to his partner Shem, who was simultaneously one and the same with him. This part of their mythology made no sense and they knew it, building shrines to Xu, shrines to Shem, and shrines to Xushem with statues of three deities split into two personalities.

There was more: how this two-in-one god made the plants and the rivers and then Lake Chagrin itself as a sort of nursery for mankind—the details don't matter. No mention of Wenne pulling the world from the sun, or even of Sanadara founding their race. How could you miss that happening? It was supposed to have happened far south of here, in the holy river delta.

I made myself visible. I wasn't sure how good I looked—I hadn't done it in front of a mirror yet, but I'd made some modifications since the Ele test. There were robes falling around me on the floor, and two hands I could stretch out and use to stroke his back. I whistled behind his ear.

He didn't move. In his mind, I felt my complete non-presence.

It was stunning. Every mind I'd felt had some sort of conception of me, of the dark, of fear personified as me, whether they thought I was a real, breathing god, a myth, or something in between. More people were convinced of my existence than Wenne's! I was not even a myth to him.

I asked, "Is it just me, or does one of us not really exist?"

The door to his cell opened. We both started from our reveries, turning ironically as one to watch Hitra step in, her hands folded before her, bowing like a penitent. Two arbiters in the full purple tunics of municipal rank stood behind her. I faded into the wall, and only one of them noticed me, but dismissed the sight as a trick of shadow (albeit a disturbing one that haunted his thoughts the rest of the week.)

The one who hadn't seen me said, "Forthright Jeje, Priest Hitra has requested a visit with you. We will be monitoring her for your safety, but otherwise you may speak freely."

"I don't want to speak to her," Jeje said, but the arbiter was already closing the door.

Alone then, except for the tangible pressure of the arbiter's inexpert scanning—and my own observation—Hitra bobbed her head in another little bow and tried a soft, "Greetings, Citizen Jeje."

"I don't want to talk to you," he said.

"I understand," she said. "But I want to talk to you. I've come to apologize."

He started to turn back to the window, but felt too vulnerable with his back to the adept. He circled the room instead. "Why? I attacked you, you attacked me; I *thought* we were both in jail."

"We are. I was only released to talk to you."

He turned his eyes resolutely away from her.

Hitra wore her kindest, most careful expression. "Although I acted in what I felt at the time was self-defense, it is inexcusable that I used my power as an adept against you." When he didn't respond, she fidgeted anxiously with the tie of her robe. "You aren't going to be held much longer. The arbiters know what happened, and why. I've taken full responsibility. The law works."

"I'm sure it works great, for Casu."

"It does work. Slowly, though. We're prisoners of paper, that's all. When our paper selves have been approved and stamped and filed properly, we'll both be able to return to our lives as they were. Maybe better." She really believed this, having never been in an arbitration before. "I'm speaking to the arbiters on your behalf. I know why you came to me, why you were driven to fight for your rights as a father. I don't understand why you chose to do so with a threat of violence, but these are anxious times. They have been for me, for my fellows in the temple. I can only imagine how recent events have impacted your life."

Hitra was proud of herself. She'd rehearsed her words a great deal, yet she felt they were coming off genuine, even a little vulnerable, light and feminine in the thick, male surroundings of the jailhouse.

Forthright Jeje, however, smugly noted to himself that no one used words like 'impacted' off the cuff. "Used to be the official people—the smooth-talking priests like you—didn't come right out and call our religion false to our faces. Used to be you saved that for your sermons."

She had hoped he had forgotten about that. "Forthright...may I call you Forthright? I have been questioning my faith. I have been seeing events that could only be called miraculous, and an apparition claiming to be my god. You can understand, can't you, the stress that brings? The confusion?"

"I'm never going to see my daughter again. I don't see how anything you say is going to change that."

What was a daughter, Hitra thought, compared to a god? She pushed down her anger. No, to a father, what was a god compared to a daughter?

"A god is a god," I said. "That's what!"

She flinched. Jeje took it to mean that the arbiters were talking to her, perhaps ordering her to hurry it up and placate the heathen already so they could go home.

There was a bench, silver with age, against the near wall of the cell. Hitra approached it with one hand out, as though afraid she would not make it all the way. Once she was seated, feeling the reassuring reality of the rough wood, she said, "Our questions have the same answer—that's the point of arbitration, to find one answer to two questions."

"I don't want to sort things out with you. I don't want anything to do with you. I just want to serve my time, and go home."

"I know exactly how you feel," she said, and the collapsing sound of it made Jeje's heart soften a touch, though he doubted very much that she knew exactly how he felt.

He accepted that she would listen, though. He tried to sort the mess of his life into a story. Where to begin? "I lost my job, and the divorce.... It costs a lot to un-marry. I was losing my home, and they threatened me with deportation. I only had a few days to try to see Bota before this shipping gig...it might have saved me. Well, that didn't work. Now it's a sure thing. Immediate exile. For threatening you. Did you know that?" She shook her head mutely. He pressed one fist into the wall as if to test its solidity. "This is my city; my fathers' fathers were all born here. Don't know what I'll do in another country. I don't even know how to talk Grosten. That's your Casu justice, though, right there. They think the problem is that there're people different than themselves around."

Hitra shook her head more vehemently. Forthright raised his eyebrows, and that was all the argument he needed. She could feel his honesty, they both knew that.

"No," Hitra said. "I won't let them do that. It's absurd!"

"It's been coming. Won't be the first time my people were given the shove from their own land."

"I'm sure the arbiters just want to separate you from your wife...I mean from the temptation to come back to the temple. Justice is supposed to be personal."

"It feels personal, all right." Jeje held out a hand to Hitra. "Well, thanks, anyway, for coming to talk to me. I'm sorry, too. I shouldn't have taken things out on you."

Hitra didn't take his hand but got up on her own, awkwardly ducking aside. "I'll see what I can do, about the exile." She walked to the door, reaching out to tell the arbiters she really needed to go home, now.

"You know," Jeje took a sidelong step toward her. "That column of fire...it didn't have no signature on it from no Casu god."

It didn't need one, Hitra thought. "I know," she said.

Jeje shrugged. "It's nice to hear one of you admit it."

"Coward," I said, "tell him what you're really thinking," but Hitra kept her flinch internal this time. She walked as fast as she could, her head down to watch her hem, mincing her steps behind the arbiters, who led her away unhurriedly, their minds already elsewhere.

I lounged in front of Jeje and willed myself visible. He turned and stood as he had been, before the window. He let out a long exhale.

I hadn't realized how much I relied on that inner eye to "see" me when I manifested. With Hitra, with all the Casu, I'd been half cheating. Their mental ear picked up the suggestions I gave them, and they saw what they expected to see. Heard what they expected to hear. With Jeje, I had to rely only on the physical, on vibrations of air for sound and light for color. I regarded the elegant fall of my robes and flipped the skirt to expose one well-turned calf.

He continued to stare blankly out the window of his cell, thinking meandering thoughts. What he should have said. If he'd said it right. If the priest had even understood him. If it mattered. His non-regard felt personal. Instead of wasting time bending light around myself I pushed him, hard, through his skin and bones to his heart. He fell back and clutched his chest, fear rising in his mind; fear of hospitals, of the unseen progress of life's limit.

I conjured a breath and felt him register it, felt him shiver and draw the thin blanket off the bed to cover his arm.

Warm panic spread through him, around him, almost coloring the stones of the wall itself. He rubbed his chest deeply, awakening the pain with each pressed finger. His thoughts were on age and organs and the secret ways disease creeps up inside a person.

"Heathen!" I whispered. He heard a soft, unformed sound, a huff. I focused on the purity of sound itself. It took more doing than saying, but soon I was able to push air fast enough to make something of a whistle. It meandered in pitch and location.

From soft to sharp to cold, he followed and reacted to the sound, heart racing. I wrapped myself around him. I reached through the fabric of his clothing with my hands—running over his stomach and chest while I pressed my lips to the back of his neck. His skin tightened, puckered up each small hair, and for an exquisite moment, I could feel him, the warmth of him, the soft hairs of his chest bending and springing up around my fingertips, the throb of his heart. He was still, balanced on the knife's edge of horror.

He jumped up, arms and legs flailing randomly to dislodge himself from what he sensed as a spider's web, dirty, invisible, the memory of my touch clinging to his skin like thread.

He fell against the opposite wall, gibbering, convulsing, unable to draw breaths as quickly as the sobs came. He feared he had gone mad, from some unexpected side effect of Hitra's attack, or from the unfelt interference of his Casu guards. Or from nothing at all. He was sane, though, and deep down, he knew it.

I tried to vibrate the air inside his ear...it was altogether difficult and frustrating. It's one thing to speak words, it's quite another to pick apart their shape in vibration, pitch, and quivering air.

"Puh," he heard and "Ugh."

In the scriptures, I was the one who took the ability to speak with the mind from the children of Sanadara. How could I have done it? I didn't see how it worked in the first place. Something in me seriously doubted this was the handiwork of a vengeful me, and again I uncomfortably thought of Darian, who ought to be flitting about causing trouble like the rest of us.

I didn't want to think about it. And, looking down at the broken man, in his heart quite morally decent, I felt not just guilty but humiliated.

$$)O($$

Not far away, Arel sat in a little sandstone cell in the heart of the municipal complex. Molestable, Casu Arel. His cell had small windows of thick glass blocks which were placed oddly, one low to the floor, two high, conforming to a pattern on the outside of the building, the open hand of justice. Some hours ago, he had been told that he faced possible treason charges. He had just eaten stewed roots and pastry. The metal plate was licked clean; it had been a good, if bland, meal.

He was content, his belly full, and writing. The arbiters had provided him with stylus and paper, and so he was furiously filling scrolls with letters trailing from the haste with which they were pressed.

The tip of his tongue flicked over his teeth twice, and he drew the back of the stylus through the last three lines he had written, smearing them. He wrote another paragraph, and then he crossed that out too and crawled to snatch up an already written-over curl of parchment lying against the wall. Sitting on the floor, he read a sentence he was particularly fond of and smiled, looking up at a point of space some three hand-breadths from the ceiling, he mulled over what it was he was really trying to say.

I rested my hands on my knees. Being in human form took less concentration with practice, and Jeje had given me good, hard practice. I suspected I had made a much more interesting, less cliche avatar than Wenne, too. I said, "What makes you think you have it all figured out, little man, when I don't?"

His palm landed flat against the floor directly in front of my toe, and he stared at me, completely frozen. Every square of him quivered, his muscles tensed for fight, as he crawled slowly backward. Yes, to him, I looked like a god.

I made myself invisible and he jumped. He stared as though he could resolve my form from empty air through sheer will. I circled around him to the other side of the room. "Hey!" He wheeled on his knee to face me. I clapped. He held his hands out at his sides, feeling like he was blind. I let him crawl his way toward me.

It was too easy. And a little too much like what I'd just done with Jeje. I sank into the sandstone and sang to him a ditty I'd heard an old man humming as he took down laundry the sunset before.

Arel brushed his fingertips along the wall's surface. He sat upon his heels and let his hands drop in his lap. "God," he said, "if god you are, let me see you, let me hear your words."

That was more like it. Adoration. Appreciation.

He curled his palms upward and closed his eyes. "I...do not ask for my own glory, or because I need to hear you to believe. I offer myself, quietly, patiently, for whatever use you have."

He stayed that way, his heart and mind open, his defenses, physical and mental, carefully lowered, waiting.

What use would I put him to, then? Had I a heart, it would be pounding blood spiked with sharp expectation.

And fear. Arel was starting to wonder if nothing was about to happen.

The door to the cell opened, the shadow of the jailer moving aside to admit the glittering form of the Ritual Celebrant. She was wearing her morning robes still, though the sun had set. Silver threads couched around squares and circles of mirror caught the overhead lanterns and scattered fingerprints of light over the drab cell walls. Normally, she'd have had two costume changes by this point in the day. She pressed her hands flat against the embroidered panel that ran down her front and said, "Excuse the intrusion, Revered Arelandus Nereshore."

Arel was caught like a man mid-leap, believing himself to be soaring toward safe landing when the other side of the divide crumbles, leaving him treading insubstantial air. He squinted and worried that somehow she might be a sign or representation of a sign from the gods.

Reha leaned forward. "I said 'hello,' Reverend Child of Darian."

"I've not been an acolyte of Darian for many years."

She took a few steps to the left, glancing around the room. "Prodigal child of Darian, then. We forget the gods; they never forget us. You've been writing?"

"Tell her to go away; we're having a moment," I whispered in the heart of his mind, where even she could not overhear.

Arel's eyelids fluttered, trying to cover his twitch at the sound of my voice. "Please go away."

"Don't be foolish," she said. "I didn't come all this way to say hello and leave."

"What are you doing here, Reha?"

She gave up her search for a place to sit down and turned to him. Her hands folded, her head back, and she closed her eyes. "I'm here to question you."

"Has the government no arbiters willing to interview a Speaker of the Sectarians? Or is this some scheme of yours? Have you come to 'protect' me again?"

Reha shook her head. "Her Highness does not wish to risk having anyone but the highest level adept in the city interview you. It is not about us, child. It is merely a question of power. The Palace suspects, as I long ago did, that you are not merely fifth level. They want you tested. Don't worry; I told them you wouldn't agree to it."

Arel stood. "Who are you to put words in my mouth?"

Reha tilted her head. "'I will not take the sixth test, Reha; I will never take the sixth test.' Don't you recall? You were almost in tears."

"That was when I cared what happened with my 'career,' what others thought of me. I am a prisoner, Reha, and I would rather they knew me and respected my power."

Slowly, she folded her hands into her sleeves. "My apologies. I'll amend that after I leave."

"Please just leave." Arel tried to avoid looking at Reha as she carefully arranged her white satin robes and sat on the stone floor opposite him. She was still a captivating woman, all these years later.

"Arel," she said, "we have both seen some pretty astonishing things, and I'm not talking about columns of fire. I always believed you were destined for greatness."

"What I am destined for is not your concern, your doing, or your undoing." He was in near-panic, thinking of the unknown god waiting for him to achieve the test of getting Reha to leave when Reha didn't want to.

I wouldn't blame him, though. Not even I could do that.

Reha said, "Destiny is not driven by what you will be but who you are. That was never my doing or undoing. You came to me the man I knew you could be."

He calmed. "I can't believe I used to think you were wise when you talked that garbage."

To Arel, I said, "Your defenses are back. What happened to 'I offer myself to you'?" I managed to push his shoulder. He stared blankly forward, so as not to show Reha that he heard or felt something she could not.

The clearly involuntary motion worried Reha. "Very well. We've neither of us an epoch to waste." She straightened her back, holding her knees through the thick embroidered fabric of her skirt. "You told the arbiters that you were responsible for the column of fire—for the miracles we've been experiencing. Arbiters aren't in the habit of missing a lie, which leaves us either with the possibility that you are telling the truth, or that you are mad. I don't know if I'm prepared, Arelandus, for either."

I said, "Oh come on, tell her I'm here. You want to. She'll be jealous. No gods are talking to her."

Inside him a steely resolve grew to ignore me until I revealed which god I was. This of course meant until I revealed I was any god but myself. Which, okay…I could lie. Did I want to?

To Reha he said, "You'll believe as you wish, you always have."

"That's not an answer. Do you understand what your little proclamation has done to the council? They want to know how it was done, and why, and with whom as an accomplice."

"I'll tell them—and you—nothing of how or with whom. As for why, I've written as much as I can to explain that." He gestured at the papers around him.

"This isn't a game, Arel. I have been ordered by the crown to pull the information from you, by force if necessary, even if it drives you mad."

"You will fail. I will protect the identities of my fellows until you drive the last coherent thought from my head. How will it feel to have my death on your hands?"

She raised one eyebrow. "You aren't that good."

"You mean *you* aren't that good."

"It's not a question of strength. Arel, please..." Her shoulders sagged a moment, and she looked directly at him, hoping he could see the compassion she felt. "I have no intention of forcing anything from your mind. I wouldn't make a man betray his friends. The queen can take my title and possessions and sit on them for all I care." She set her elbows on her knees and peered upward into his downturned face. "Arelandus, I want to know why you said what you did to the arbiters. For myself, as your friend, your mentor — whatever it is I was to you at one time. Help me understand."

Arel folded his arms tightly and stared at the lowest of the cell's small, square windows.

Reha sighed. "What did I do, dear man, to make you so angry with me?"

"Nothing that I can explain here, now."

"There are times I could have helped you, could have used my influence to your advantage, were I the sort to do so."

"That's not it," he said.

"Is it that I didn't approve of you leaving us? Seven years, Arel, is enough time to forgive a woman for standing behind her convictions."

Very, very carefully, I dragged my fingertips up his spine, and I could feel the impulses fire along his nerves...He shivered. "I awoke the gods, Reha." His eyes were wet when he looked up at her.

They held each other's gaze for a long moment. Reha's lips parted. "You've gone...farther than I can help you."

Arel quivered under my touch. He wanted to tell her, then, of my words, of the lines of sudden, unexpected touch. Instead, he said, "There was a time I believed in you...believed in you as no man should another mortal. Believed that if I could just follow you, I would always be in the right...and the world would step aside."

The tiny mirrors on Reha's sleeves chimed against the floor as she raised her arms and drew them around him. "Sweet Arel. That's a terrible burden to put in any mortal shell." She held him while he cried softly on her shoulder.

The water clocks declared one day ended and the next begun. I neither felt nor imagined myself as passing the sphere of the world from Dioneltar to Nolumbre.

Chapter Thirteen

Confessions

Illoe passed the night in a cold cell in Maede's basement, sleeping on a folding cot. His skin was itchy and dry from the caustic bath he'd endured at the hands of Ondra. She had grabbed hold of his hair and scrubbed him down with hard strokes like he was a cooking pan caked with grease. He might as well have been one, for all she listened to his objections.

But the degradation, the cold, the itching, the lack of a proper blanket, and the mildew smell were all secondary to one overriding horror. Again, as he had done every hour of the night, he reached out with his mind for the local router.

There was no local router.

Illoe could feel the four—no, five—people in the mansion, but nothing beyond, as though a curtain had been drawn across thought. As soon as the other minds stilled into the fuzziness of sleep, Ondra being the last wakeful presence—a projection of sore feet and aching joints in the kitchen—he crept out of his cot and up the basement stairs. The door at the top was locked. He jiggled the handle and heard the iron latch clatter. His chest constricted. He scurried down the steps and felt around the basement like a rat. There was a metal chute about a hands-breadth in diameter over a wooden box, and a metal door set low in the wall, only knee high and arched like a furnace entrance. It was bolted shut. Illoe got filthy digging through corners for holes and openings, not finding anything more useful than a stack of folded pasteboard.

He flexed each piece until he found the strongest and went back up the stairs to try wriggling it between the door and frame. He felt the latch, but it wouldn't lift. Despite the cold, he sweated. He tried using more force, and the pasteboard crumbled.

He leaned against the wooden door, pressed his body hard against it and tried by muscle alone to propel his mind further, out, beyond the house.

Nothing.

His brother would have seen what he could not: the private router for Maede's mansion, a luxury reserved for the most appallingly rich, feeling and intercepting Iloe's probes, creating not so much an impenetrable dome as one skilled hand with a flyswatter, batting down his errant thoughts.

The private router was not enjoying the game, and he hoped that Maede would compensate him for the sleepless night. He never wondered why the boy was being blocked. That wasn't his job. He was also one of those men who assumed other men were the worst people.

Illoe was sore with exhaustion, and he didn't want to rub his eyes, while his hands were sticky with old dust. He paced, internally lecturing himself as he might Hitra. Calm down. Think it out. There *is* a router. We aren't that far from the temple. He turned in what he thought was the direction of Temple Administration and tried scanning, not for broadcasting routers, but just wakeful minds nearby…he thought, maybe, he felt something, and concentrated on it, but then it was gone. It was the private router, unprepared for a split second to cover his wakefulness.

I wondered if I should do something, for or against. I'd succeeded in moving Illoe from one custody to another. Now, how to use what I'd learned to move him into my custody? What would that even look like? I didn't have a consistent body, much less a house to put him in.

Mentally and physically drained, Illoe returned to the top of the stairs and curled up, resting his head so he looked directly at the crack where the door would open.

Dawn light started to filter in. A pair of floating shadows distinguished themselves in the door crack. Ondra unlocked the door and snorted at the picture he made. "Wash your hands," she said, "then get me some firewood."

Ondra stepped to the side, leaving him a path into the kitchen.

Illoe stepped uncertainly into the strange light of this new day. "Wait. I...Where?"

Ondra answered his questions with a smack to the back of the head and a finger pointed to a water pump.

Illoe was too eager to be clean to disdain washing in cold well water over a laundry tub. Ondra followed him, silent and angry, as he went into the side yard where the woodpile was. The yard had a great high wall around it, whitewashed and hung with small planters. It was as if the house had always been designed to be a prison.

When the fire was set and the water pots filled and set to boil and, Illoe presumed correctly, Ondra had simply run out of orders to give him, she sent him up to the bathing room to have a real scrub.

Illoe went to the front parlor first. Maede sat on a delicately carved stone bench, reading. He couldn't believe he actually felt grateful to see her. He knocked on the doorjamb to get her attention, but she didn't look up. "Hey. Look, your house...there's no way for me to send a message out. Your router won't talk to me."

Her mouth kept working at silent words, rather like she was nibbling them off the air. Having reached the end of a sentence — he could tell by the pause, the draw of breath, and the confused expression, she glanced up at him. "Gossip and chatter are the gateways to sin, young man."

"It's not like that. I need to make a call. It doesn't have anything to do with...with my being here or the arbitration, even. It's family business."

She gave him the smallest push with her mind, all she could muster at the moment. He flinched, feeling rough warmth under his skin.

Illoe forced himself to talk gently. "Lady Faydehale, there's a contract negotiation that needs to take place today. Just let me speak to my mother?"

Her saggy cheek convulsed in a half smile. Illoe leaned forward to see what she was reading, and she pulled the scroll closer to herself. "Illoehenderen," she said, teasing, as though he had just tried to flirt with her, "you are supposed to be in the kitchen."

"You don't understand. I don't know where I'll be a year from now. It has to happen before Harvest Home, and that's tomorrow, or it may never happen. It's my..." Her eyebrows tightened and he lost his breath of his own accord, remembering the power she had.

Maede released the scroll, letting it curl up on her lap. "Were you raising your voice to me, young man?"

He clenched his fists and looked down. "Sorry," he said.

"That's more like it. Now go to the kitchen."

Stiffly, Illoe turned on his heel and walked back to the kitchen.

☽ ○ ☾

No arbiters followed Hitra into her apartment, but she somehow knew they had been in it. The air felt breathed.

She placed her hand against the curved glass of the dining nook, gazed out at the paper shrines left on the grass and pebble path below. A figure by the tanglewood shrub rose and came toward the window with upraised palms.

Hitra retreated to the fire nook and tried, unsuccessfully, to start a fire. She knew the oil reserve should pour out into the fire pan, and then the flint would ignite it; she could operate both, but ended up with the acrid smell of cold sparks and an unlit pan of oil. In the end, she searched the cupboards until she found some dried fruit. She went back to the sitting room and took a book at random from the shelf.

Hitra felt the weight of the book on her lap—familiar. She recognized the peculiar hand this tome was printed in. She knew each of the illustrations. Yet it felt as though she had never read scriptures before. Had they always been this awful? Words seemed to have slightly rearranged themselves, or perhaps it was just what was said in the white space between them that was changed.

The door-chimes sang. She called for Illoe, then remembered he wasn't home.

Who is it?

"It's me, Hitra," Reha called, her proud orator's voice penetrating the wall between them easily.

Hitra bit her lip and thought petulant, teenage thoughts of wanting to just be left alone for once. She set the book on the floor and walked to the door.

Reha was wearing the plainest of her day-robes and a simple headscarf. "May I come in?"

Hitra couldn't help peering behind the Ritual Celebrant.

"Oh," Reha said, "they're there. My guards, my entourage. But don't worry. They're busy keeping *your* entourage at bay."

Hitra backed into her foyer. "I swear I've done nothing to encourage them."

Reha shrugged and followed her in. "It wouldn't be a crime if you had. Their sort of faith isn't moldable by doctrine or dogma. They believe as they choose to, until it can be believed no more." With a sigh, she stopped. "Still, it's a shame you never gave that speech."

"My gods, the speech…" Hitra closed the door. "That seems a lifetime ago."

The Celebrant bent over to read the title of the book on the floor. "It's always the case at the top, Hitra. Nothing gets done if it isn't done today."

Hitra hurriedly picked up the napkin lying next to the book. "Illoe hasn't been back and I haven't had time to—" She shook her head, stopping the apology. "What are you doing here?"

Reha took the book and sat down with it on her lap, unknowingly taking exactly the position Hitra had just vacated. Reha had an odd look on her face. "I used to think our biggest threat was secularism. The academy…you know how it is. The more people learn, the less they can take on faith."

Hitra started for the fire pantry with a mind to get them both tea, but then remembered her earlier failure with lighting the stove. She turned to Reha like a proper hostess and asked, "Would you like some wine?"

"I think I should like nothing better," Reha said.

Hitra opened the wine cupboard and found only two bottles. She selected the higher quality of the two and a pair of cups.

Reha said, "You're reading the Apologia."

"Taking comfort in old favorites," Hitra said, without emotion. She poured the wine and set the full cups and bottle on the tea tray.

"Really? I always found it a dreadful book." She squinted at the spine. "It makes a fetish of regret, without a single decent sin to inspire it." Reha had hoped for a smile, to cut the tension with her slight vulgarity, but Hitra's face was like stone.

Hitra set the tea tray on the carpet at Reha's feet and sat herself next to it, cross-legged. "What are you doing here, Ritual Celebrant?"

"I'm not here to take away your job," Reha said, and picked up one of the wine cups. She held the Apologia in the other hand, one finger tucked into its pages. "And I'm not here to offer you mine. So there are the extremes taken care of. I am here to see a priest who has gotten in trouble and may need my help, and I am here to see a friend who may help a pontiff no less in need of assistance."

"I know the church may not want to continue my commission," Hitra said. "I'm prepared to wait for the council to make its decision."

Reha sipped her wine and set the heavy religious tome on the cushion beside her. "Forget about the council. They're too slow for either of our purposes."

"Are you here," Hitra asked, "to ask me to resign?"

"No," Reha said. "I wish to the stars I knew what I needed. Then I could do it and be done." She took another sip. "I believe you, now, about seeing Revestre in your tub. These are definitely days of miracles. There are more being reported. Stranger, smaller ones." She thought of the stack of reports she'd gotten. Some were explainable: a garden wall disassembled overnight could be eager pranksters. Likewise wheat growing in the middle of a street. Some less so: a libation cup rising from an altar in full view of a congregation, a live fish suddenly appearing inside a block of glass (and quickly dying).

Hitra was irritated by Reha's far-off look. "Thank you, but believing me would have been handier when I first came to you."

Reha threw up her hand more like a frustrated acolyte than the head of the church. "What am I supposed to do? How do I preserve the temple as it is when there's a new potential schism-causing miracle every day? Sometimes I wish I'd already died, and could molder away in my sepulcher, unaware that my world is changing. Irrevocably changing. We won't recognize the faith in ten years, I guarantee that."

Reha ended her speech by draining half her wine.

Hitra took a small sip, herself, and wished she didn't feel self-conscious doing it. "I don't have any answers for you."

"No." Reha sighed. "I didn't think you would." She finished off the cup and looked for the bottle, which Hitra obligingly moved from her far side. Reha poured, then tilted the bottle toward Hitra in silent offer, but she shook her head. Reha handed the bottle back bottom-first. "They've arrested a man, an old, dear friend and enemy of mine; he is being charged with creating illusions, of making us believe the gods awoke. Of course it's rubbish. I can't imagine even the crown believes it, but the odd thing is *he* does."

Hitra regretted sitting on the floor. Her knees were already aching, and getting up to sit next to Reha on the sofa would feel like agreeing with her. "I don't care how this started. It could have been a wish on a breaking fire-log. What does it matter?"

Reha frowned, disappointed. "Don't you realize the importance of that? They may kill him. I've just come from a meeting with the crown, and I am almost certain they've decided to. He would have been the first ever man to test seventh level, I'm sure of it. And now... Cold hearted bastards." She frowned at her cup. "The trick, however, is this: the crown will announce why they have killed him, with their ridiculous charge that all these miracles were his. What then? Even if we never experience another unexplained event—and that isn't going to happen—our faith will be divided into those who believe the crown, and those who believe Arel. He may be revered as a prophet, a martyr. And then! If the miracles do continue? What then, for the crown? For the Casu temple and all its children? What then for the Secularists, the Hushers, the Monotheists?" She realized she was sermonizing and reeled herself in. "I need you to help me save him, so that we may save the church. Whatever role either of us plays in that church in the future, this comes first."

Hitra looked to the cold fire pantry, wishing Illoe were there, bustling about, ready to come in with a polite word and a subtle joke. She shifted her legs, which were already tingling and bloodless. She thought about two conversations in a holding cell. That same Arel? He had been above fifth level, for certain. That zealot holding the fate of the church? Even if he was, even if she could do something to help, she wasn't sure she wanted to. "I can't do anything."

"Everyone can do something," Reha bent to whisper, "And you have a devoted following." She flicked her eyes to the narrow window by the door.

"What are you saying? That I should preach for Arel's freedom?

Won't that cause the same fracture? 'Attention, everyone, the crown is going to kill the man who awoke the gods?' Oh, that will calm everyone down!"

"All I am saying is that there are people who have chosen you to lead them, whether you like it or not. That's power. And an innocent man, a godly and good man, is going to be killed. What you do is up to you."

"What about what you do? Can't you preach for your friend?"

"I can. And will. We will present a united front. I will speak for the church," Reha reached for Hitra's hand. "And you will speak for the gods."

Hitra saw a new political party forming behind Reha's earnest smile. Hitra pulled her hand free. She got up and walked to the fire pantry and set her half-full cup of wine in the washtub. "Ritual Celebrant," she addressed the fire grate, "please go."

"We each have power," Reha said as she stood. She straightened her robe. "I'm doing what I can with mine. What will you do with yours?"

Hitra didn't feel particularly powerful. She didn't return to the front room until she heard Reha leave.

Hitra picked up three throw pillows that had fallen off the couch. She started to set them back but stopped. She dropped them, side-by-side, on the floor. Jeje. He was going to be deported because of her. Arel. He was going to be killed and she might prevent it. Illoe. He'd asked for her help, and she'd promised it.

She couldn't save all three.

"If I'm going to speak for the gods, it would be nice if they told me what to say."

That was my cue. I should really say something. But what? That I wasn't sure what I was? That I couldn't do half the evil a noble idiot could?

Hitra went into her bedroom and changed into her ritual costume. *I…had not expected that.* The autumn robe was still dirty from its last wearing, so she put on the summer one. She liked it better, anyway. She gathered some ritual objects and went into her bathroom.

Hitra felt the smooth, cool tile through the thin fabric of her summer robe. She steadied the flimsy headdress of paper and wheat. For a moment, she got it straight on the top of her head, but it resumed its leftward cant as soon as she let go. She gave up and continued the ritual cleansing. She dipped a whisk of rye grass into a golden plate filled with purified water, then brushed it over the floor in front of her. The ritual words of blessing came out of her mouth like a broken nursery rhyme. "Wash free tomorrow and make today new. Wash free the mind and make the soul new."

She felt indescribably stupid.

She waved the whisk over the damp floor, urging it to dry. Then she set it down, adjusted her headdress, and picked up her chalk. "Since the days of the ancient covenant, we pray first to Wenne, on all occasions. May the god of wisdom mediate over this summoning."

The chalk marked thick and easy on the wet tile, a brilliant line of yellow. She watched its edges bleeding out, fraying like yarn. She didn't want to turn around. With a sigh she stood, dusted her knees, and knelt in the other direction. "Since the days of the ancient covenant...damn." She held her hand over the tile. It wasn't considered polite to call upon two gods with the same words. "Senne, this one's for you, and balance."

She dedicated both side lines to Revestre, calling her both Golden One and Lady of Harvest. She knew the litanies of Revestre best; that was understandable.

Turning again to the front, to the western wall of her bathroom, she set the chalk down parallel to her first line and held her hands out at her sides in supplication. "Revestre, I'm calling for you. Talk to me. I've dedicated this space..." she looked anxiously around the bathroom, its mundane fixtures, the floral towel rack, "to your service. I am ready and prepared. Please, tell me how I might serve you."

We both waited. Hitra's knees ached, her calves were squished against her thighs and the small of her back began to feel the strain of sitting perfectly upright.

Revestre was more or less in the marketplace on Denisen Cove, the very edge of town where the mountain's arm stretched out to touch the lake, where farmers from the lands beyond brought their produce and city grocers brought their wagons. It was a flatter, more open place, with buildings only one or two stories high and patches of rough weeds between them.

"Hey," I said to Revestre. She noticed me, but with irritation, and went back to watching a small child place her hands on the swollen bellies of fresh gourds that a farmer was transferring from his cart to a low stand. Revestre was admiring the simple, delighted thoughts of the child.

"Belly!" the little girl cried out, and laughed so hard she doubled over. Then a new gourd was placed and the child ran up to it, both hands slapping the firm flesh, she cried, "Belly!"

Yeah. That was what caught Revestre's immortal eye. "Your priest has summoned you. Full ritual with purification and everything. I think she even fasted a day beforehand." I tugged at Revestre's essence. "Shouldn't you *feel* that or something?"

Revestre didn't answer me. She wasn't interested in answering me. She thought I was being insufferable. Hitra was her failure, and I was bringing it up to be mean.

It's amazing how even telepathic beings can be so caught up in their own minds they can't see others.

I pulled myself back to Hitra. Together, we sat in her cold bathroom and began to worry.

Okay. I could do this. Dispense godly advice. But did I go with something evil, or what I was really thinking, which was that Illoe had the hard deadline, among the three men in trouble. Also Hitra and I liked him best, didn't we? Maybe that *was* evil, since it was self-interested.

I wasn't sure being evil was necessarily an argument for doing something. Maybe I wasn't an evil god? Maybe I was just misunderstood.

Through the open door to the bedroom, Hitra could see the discarded robes she had worn the day before laying on the floor with the towels and washcloths she had used cleaning the ritual space. "I need," she said, with sudden confidence, "to make up my own mind."

"Yes," I said, "How do we do that?"

Not the godly advice I had hoped to dispense. And yes, Hitra heard me. She felt a moment of shock, a frisson, and then turned her back toward me. If that was the voice of Revestre, she didn't want to hear it. She rose with a sense of purpose, action, and plan. Hitra washed away her chalk lines and threw her ritual gear, the washrag and the hat all together in the laundry hamper. She went into her bedroom and gathered up the dirty clothes and tossed them in as well. Then she straightened the books on her shelves and returned those she'd left scattered across the front room. Finally, she returned to the bedroom and emptied the contents of her clothing chest, searching for something un-vestment-like. She wrapped herself in a summer gown, a gift from her mother for wearing at the family vacation house on the far side of the lake, where dressing as a priest would have been weird and a little rude.

Without bothering to stretch her mind out to the local router or the arbiters or anyone, she marched briskly out the door, into air that bore the sharp tang of winter and blew straight through the summer dress as though it wasn't there. She ran back into the house.

Right. It wasn't summer anymore. Her only cloak was too much like a vestment. She took a blanket off her bed and fastened it over her shoulders with a cloak-pin.

Even with this additional layer, her cheeks grew red and numb and her nose ran. It felt good, like a slap in the face, clarifying.

The most faithful of her petitioners arose from their watch posts, but Hitra walked past them without acknowledgement, and they, not understanding how to react to a prophet clad in a blanket, let her pass unmolested.

She went straight to the arbitration office.

Her mind was racing through steps, rules, and paperwork to file. It was impressive to see her professional mind at work, but she wasn't starting with Illoe. Jeje could be deported at any moment, so she considered him the priority. Illoe had the rest of the day before his contract deadline, and Hitra assumed he was safe, happy, even, wherever he had gone.

)O(

Maede's voice carried through the mosaic-inlaid walls of her home like the incessant buzzing of insects. She sat in the white upper parlor, the most feminine room in her house, all spindles and flowers of pulled glass. Across the delicate tea table from her were two equally delicate women, all nose and cheekbones, their heads and hands protruding like branches from their thickly folded robes. Maede liked these friends for being even skinnier than her. She set her tiny teacup down. "And we ought to be able to issue fines, to protect our interests and authority. Who will listen to us if we can't do something about it when they don't?"

"But Maede..."

"I know what you're going to say, Lady Plaingrove, but there's nothing in the charters against a committee levying fines."

Illoe was in the kitchen, two floors below and a room's breadth to the left of the parlor, scraping the ashes from the large wood-burning ovens and muttering to himself with each draw of the ash rake why a woman as wealthy as Maede couldn't upgrade the ancient behemoths to something less labor intensive.

The chauffeur, Ael for short, was back in the stable and almost as absorbed in his book as he had been when Maede had ordered him away from it. He had been posted in the kitchen to stand vigil over Illoe after his most successful escape attempt, which had ended with Ael snatching him off a high garden wall. But it had taken the fight out of the boy when he saw that what was on the other side of the wall was another, deeper mansion garden.

Ondra was washing the breakfast dishes, a task she abhorred, but not as much as scraping out the wood-ashes. Where Maede's mind was currently a torrent of agitated glee, Ondra's was as placid as the surface of a deep well.

Ondra was a religious woman, in the quiet, classic sense of the word: she prayed three times a day, gave a portion of her meager earnings to the church, and generally didn't say anything about it unless the topic came up.

Illoe smacked his knee against the sharp edge of the oven, and the rake clattered. He leaned his arm against the lintel and sighed, a deep, heart-felt sigh.

"Hey," Ondra shook the excess water from a cleaned bowl, "you can take a break after that. Sounds like you need it."

Illoe rubbed his face and too late realized his hand was covered in soot. "Wow, that's almost considerate of you."

The bowl clattered as she dropped it on the drainage board and Ondra made a saintly effort, in her own opinion, not to rise to his sass. "You can use the time to pray. There's supplies in the closet. You didn't have chalk with you last night."

"Not that it will matter to you," Illoe wiped his face with the hem of his tunic, "but I don't pray."

Ondra snatched the kitchen towel from its hook and stared at him, waiting for him to repeat his blasphemy.

Illoe almost laughed at her expression. "Come on, you can force me to clean the oven, but you aren't going to force me to pray. You'd have to be a hypocrite."

Ondra did not pause to think about why it was hypocritical to force someone to engage in prayer without faith, simply hearing the worthless indenture insult her. "I never!" She marched from the room.

Illoe made one more drag with the ash rake, just in case someone was listening, and gently placed it next to the bucket. That had probably not been the way to ingratiate himself. He tiptoed after Ondra. She wasn't in the hall.

He bit his lip and considered his options for half a second before making a mad dash for the front of the house.

Where Lord Faydehale was just coming in the front door.

"Excuse me," Illoe said, trying for bravado, and did his level best to act naturally as he pushed his arm between Lord Faydehale and the servant who was following him.

"Hold on," Lord Faydehale said, taking Illoe's arm. "What's got you in such a hurry?"

"Uh...Maede ordered me?" Illoe met the servant's gaze pleadingly, but the other man just closed the front door and, with an unhurried motion, locked it. It didn't take a first level adept to hear that lie.

Illoe said, "Lord Faydehale, please, I need to go. There's an urgent matter that needs my attention."

Lord Faydehale was not under any illusions as to why his wife had brought a handsome young man home. It wouldn't be the first time. He tried not to blame the boy. "Easy there! You're covered in soot. We can't let you go outside like that."

"It's my contract—my indenture. Please, sir, just let me go. I'll be back before you know it."

Lord Faydehale leaned forward, his hand moving to rest paternally on Illoe's shoulder. "That sounds like something you should let the ladies worry about for you, son."

"There's no time!"

"Now, son…"

Illoe cut him off. "No! Maede doesn't give a damn about this. She won't even let me make a gods-be-damned call!"

Or, Lord Faydehale reflected, the boy was a little shit and completely to blame. He let go of Illoe's shoulder and straightened to his full height. "I try to be nice," he said.

"Just get me through to the local router," Illoe said. "Please."

But Lord Faydehale shook his head. "You are going to go back to the kitchen and clean yourself up. Then you will wipe up every speck of soot you dragged through my front hall."

Illoe lowered his head. "I…sorry. I will. After—"

"No. Now. And if I see you anywhere near the doors, you will get a thrashing you won't soon forget."

Illoe turned, not expecting but hoping there was someone else in the room he could appeal to, and saw Ondra had paused coming down the stairs to point at him. "Atheist!" she proclaimed. "In our own home. I'll not work with him, m'lord. Not in the same room. Not in the same house!"

Lord Faydehale grew very quiet. His face took on a red flush. He silently recited the prayer for patience, which his pastor recommended to him as a cure for his temper after the last incident.

Ondra strode down the steps continuing to point at Illoe as she listed off all the gods, demi-gods, and historical prophets who should join in condemning him.

In an exceedingly quiet voice, Lord Faydehale said, "I want to come home to a peaceful house."

Illoe took a step toward the kitchen. Lord Faydehale's hand was strong and hard on his arm, pulling him around and into Lord Faydehale's fist, still clutched around the top of his cane.

Chapter Fourteen
Passion Play

In the second floor parlor, Maede held perfectly still, hoping that if she pretended not to hear the shouts and muffled violence in the front hall, her guests wouldn't notice it, or at the least, would join her in willing deception.

Lady Plaingrove, however, had already tilted her head in rapt attention, straining all six senses to make out the intimate and embarrassing details.

Illoe was as startled as a bird flying into a glass pane. I was startled. Lord Faydehale's fist descended again. In his mind, the older man was still reciting the prayer for patience and blaming Illoe for it not working.

"Beat the evil out of him!" Ondra shouted, clear enough to be heard in the next mansion over.

Maede lifted her napkin and dabbed her lips. "Excuse me a moment, ladies," she said with forced gaiety, and walked serenely to the top of the stairs, where she belted, "What do you think you are doing? The Flower Ministry Council is here, and I won't have them disturbed by your noise!"

Illoe twisted his arm out of Lord Faydehale's grip and pelted up the stairs. He slipped past Maede before she could react.

He ran through the house blindly, finding another stair and going up it. The third floor of Maede's house was a ballroom, little used and little furnished. Illoe found a spot between a large potted plant and one of the tall, narrow windows where he could hide. He could just make out Maede screeching in indignation one floor below.

It was stupid, hiding, but he couldn't come up with a better idea.

Maybe he could hide long enough for Hitra to remember him.

The drama unfolded neatly under him—the exasperated Lady, the boiling mad Lord, the gleeful guests, all unwilling to let go of their particular piece of misery.

Illoe pressed his forehead to the cool glass. These windows faced the downhill side, the rear of Maede's home, and afforded a magnificent view of the city: nicer buildings closer and more detailed, white stone giving way to yellow and brown brick, marching down to the sparkling haze of the lake. On an exposed stretch of Penitence Street, a tiny figure stood atop a tiny ladder, attaching garland to a store's awning. It was the day before Harvest Home, past mid-day. Illoe had no idea how he could get out of here before the sun set, locking him into the agreement his mother had made for another year.

The ballroom door opened. Illoe startled like a small prey animal hearing a twig crack. He cringed behind his potted plant, heaping angry epithets upon himself for not finding a place to hide that also had an escape path. Ondra's heavy footsteps cleared the distance between them in a firm straight line. She could see his foolish reflection in the window. "Come on, you'll only make it worse by dawdling."

Lord and Lady Faydehale were waiting together, a united wall of anger at the foot of the stairs. "You have ruined my meeting," Maede said. "And upset my husband. It's beneath his dignity to chase after a bastard like you."

"Is it beneath his dignity to hit me?"

"No. And if he doesn't, I will," Maede said.

They all had some power over him—even Ondra. There was nothing Illoe could do but walk to the wall as directed and put his hands on it. Lord Faydehale braced himself against the decorative pilasters in the front parlor and laid into Illoe's back with his walking stick until his face streamed with sweat and his breath was ragged.

Sore and certain he was bleeding somewhere, Illoe was locked in the basement again, with chalk and not very vague threats about what would happen next if he did not use that chalk to pray.

He twisted around in the dim light of the basement's only oil lamp, lifting his tunic gingerly. There were places of softness and swelling which he closely examined, but which stoutly refused to look as bad as they felt.

This wasn't fun anymore.

)O(

Hitra's throat was sore from talking calmly over the urge to shout. She had at last gotten her appointed time with the officer on duty, in the same tiny room at the front of the arbitration office where she'd waited to be interviewed and arrested. People came and went, passing from one door to the other in the office, and Hitra felt squeezed by their presence.

"You have to file a complaint," she said to a very tired Uelo.

With his hands spread before him on the little stand that served as a receiving desk, he said, "Your Holiness...this arbitration is over. That's it. You go home. We've got other people's problems to handle."

"It's not over if they're going to deport him!"

Uelo rubbed his hand over his eyes. It was only partially an act of exhaustion. Though his shift had just started, he'd not slept well during the day due to a loud bird outside his bedroom window. Birds did not appreciate the night worker. "Forthright Jeje was slated to be deported before this. He only had citizenship because of his marriage to a Casu woman. A marriage both he and his wife had filed to legally end."

"But that's preposterous. We don't deport Sanadaru for being Sanadaru."

Not for the first time, Uelo wondered how those with the keenest mental hearing couldn't use their ears. "Holiness, your concern is touching, but there's really nothing I can do. Go home. Please."

"No!" Hitra smacked the little stand, which shook like it would fall apart from the slight assault. "Drop the...what do you call it? The charge."

Uelo feared for the structural integrity of the ratty old desk and held it firmly on each side. "Madam priest," he said, in a carefully neutral voice, "either calm yourself or we will forcibly calm you."

Hitra snatched her hand back. She'd been 'calmed' only once in her life, when she was twelve and inconsolably furious at a friend for...something she didn't even remember. She did remember the

204

heavy wet quicksand feeling when the school arbiter buried her emotions and how she felt like a stranger in her own mind for the rest of the day.

She blinked a few times before she spoke. "I...I'm sorry. But please, can't you lodge a complaint for me? It's been established he never meant to hurt me."

"Are you a warranted arbiter," Uelo raised one eyebrow, "to determine this man's motivations throughout the assault?"

She had to hold herself back a moment, lest she be threatened again with forced calming. "I know he doesn't deserve to be sent to a Sanadaru prison."

"It's not your decision," Uelo said, and with real sympathy he added, "or mine." He took a step around the little stand. "There have been a lot of deportations lately. Truth is, he'd probably have been deported in a month or two, even without the divorce. He didn't have a job."

Hitra felt exhausted and helpless. "But this is my decision. I've decided to save him. I have three men I'd like to save tonight, and his situation is the most critical—and the most my fault. What...what if I hired him?"

"We'd know you're only doing it to save him."

"Why do intentions matter when you're helping someone, but not when you're punished for hurting them?"

Did she really think that was in any way close to his pay grade? Uelo just stared at her.

Hitra tried one last tactic—being obstinate. She drew on all the wealthy upbringing she had, lifting her chin and hardening her expression. "I'm not leaving here without a promise that Forthright Jeje is not leaving this country."

Uelo wasn't intimidated. He was also completely without ideas. Hitra could see it in his eyes. She touched his pedestal, a gentle, supporting touch. "Here's what we're going to do." She tapped out a pattern on the worn edge of the lectern, like she was pointing to agenda items. "Give me the chain of command for the deportation, and I will address every step, every clerk, every official. I'll make sure it's more trouble to fight me than give in."

Uelo, for his part, believed her. There was also a line forming behind her, and getting less patient. "I...fine. Yes. Whatever."

Hitra felt fierce glee. The church and the gods themselves had deserted her, but bureaucracy was just how she'd left it. "This will go faster with paper."

$$)O($$

The afternoon was chill, morning frost clinging to edges of the paving stones. Hitra felt oddly unprotected, walking alone after so long in the custody of the arbiters. She was on her way to the central arbitration authority with a list of names and offices. She could make polite inquiries about Illoe and Arel while she was there, and plan her next steps as time and space dictated. She only prayed the offices didn't close early because of the holiday tomorrow.

Hitra caught the water car in High Plaza, where Penitence became Center Street. The water car traveled down the center of two cobbled lanes, one smooth for cart traffic, one with occasional steps for the ease of pedestrians. On either side of the road, the shops and homes bore stalks of wheat and wheat-like grasses as well as signs declaring "Closed tomorrow."

Technically, you had to enter and exit the car at regular stops like the plaza, but it slowed at intersections for safety, and people took the opportunity to jump. "I'm so relieved the holiday is finally here," a woman exclaimed as she hopped lightly on in front of Hitra. She was looking back at her friend, who had to scramble the last step, but she laughed in agreement.

"I can't wait. We're taking the kids out of the city."

Harvest Home had started a week ago for Hitra, and she was sick of it. It was different for lay-people. She didn't want to look at the decorations. She pressed a map of the city against the shaking passenger-railing and studied it as the car lurched its way downhill. There was an office for Sanadaru Affairs not far from the water car off Meridian, and from there it would be a short omnibus ride downhill to the jail Jeje was being held in. If all went well, she'd be leaving that jail with Jeje before dinner, which she would eat on her way to the Middlemount's house. Lost in thought, she missed her stop and had to pay her fare at the dockside station and wait for the car to be turned around on its wooden track to catch once again on the cable being powered by the water wheel far up under Penitence Square

She was frustrated by the delay, but it didn't make that big a dent in her plans. She was making progress, moving forward, one task at a time. I felt good, soaking in her hope and confidence.

Then the water car was held indefinitely at Low Plaza as a funeral procession took precedence.

It was the funeral of a popular old father of the quarter, a man with many children and grandchildren and great-grandchildren, and so they filled Low Street. There were so many funeral torches that Hitra could feel the heat of them passing almost a carriage-length away. The mourners were uncomfortable, the soot marks on their faces blurred by sweat into stripes down their cheeks and necks.

It was then that Hitra was contacted by her assistant Jante. *Hitra? Holiness?*

It was as if she'd been contacted from another life, another universe. *Yes? What is it, Jante?*

Don't you know what day it is?

Hitra counted on her fingers. *Cassiaday?*

Harvest Eve! We need to start the ceremonies.

Hitra rolled her head against the back of the hard wooden car bench. *Oh gods. Does anyone really want me to lead that?*

Of course we do! Jante's mind was fit to explode with righteousness. *It's your ceremony. You planned it. The whole staff has agreed you should lead it. We NEED you.*

Hitra balked. She did not feel remotely related to the sort of person who would lead a religious rite. The car lurched in preparation to start again. She was still two stops short, but afraid she'd miss again. She pushed her way through the irritated standing passengers to disembark the water car. She could take care of Jeje, send a note to Loata, and ask her to meet before sunset when the ceremony ended. *I have something I need to take care of first. How late can we start?*

Hitra elbowed a man out of her way who glared at her openmouthed as she failed to apologize.

We need you here by fifth hour.

Hitra scanned the shops for a clock. *What time is it now?*

It's half past.

Hitra bit her lip and stifled the irritation that might leak through her mental connection. *Half-past what?*

Three. What have you been doing all day? Nata has been trying to get in touch with you since…

She'd forgotten that the arbitration office blocked incoming thought traffic when you were talking to an officer. *Gods, what I'd give to stop time. Look, get everything ready without me.*

The congregation will revolt.

They are coming to worship – they will worship. They may complain later, but, Jante – they don't NEED me. They want me. I have to take care of needs before wants.

Hitra? This is a responsibility. You are the high priest!

I know, Jante, and I'm sorry – but it is your job today. You are ready to lead. She could feel the answering anger, disappointment, abandonment. She steadied herself on a street corner wall. *If I can be there by five, I will be. If not, I will make it for the evening service after sunset, I promise. Build me up as a treat if you have to.*

She felt Jante's sullen acceptance. *Oh, also you need to contact your mother. She's been calling for you non-stop. Claims you told the routers not to forward her?*

Hitra's stomach ached as she hurried up Center Street. She *had* told the routing authority not to forward traffic to her. It was a perk of her station she'd never used before, and she was mildly surprised it worked. Surprised and guilty.

"Forget your mother," I said. "Illoe's the one who needs you."

"After Jeje," she said, "and who asked you?" She didn't look where I'd made myself jog beside her. She recognized the bodiless voice and assumed it was still bodiless. She jogged faster, and I gave up on manifesting because it was easier to keep up without thinking about feet.

The Sanadaru legal system was a pit of demons to her, a blind beast fumbling after the truth with paper, unwilling to hire a Casu adept to properly probe the facts from minds. With Jeje's name on a paper saying he was guilty of assault, that was how he was going to be treated – and she had heard stories about how the Sanadaru punished each other. Brutal tales of vindictive laws that gouged the eyes from a man for leering at another's wife or cut the tongue out of a man who lied. And there was nothing she could do about it.

A quick glance at the memories of the nearest Sanadaru told me that their punishments were actually much more mundane—mostly fines and prison sentences. I should tell her Arel was in more danger in the custody of the Casu, but then, I was most concerned about Illoe.

☽○☾

Illoe knelt, staring at the bare stone floor. It looked like a perfectly happy bare stone floor, and who was he to make any mark on it? He rolled the unfamiliar chalk between two fingers. Even when he was a kid, he'd never felt right about praying. He considered it talking to one's self. He'd watched his father have *arguments* with himself over an intricately drawn square.

Illoe dragged the chalk limp-wristed over the floor, making a crooked, broken line. He struck the breaks in the line to join them. For all he knew, Maede would be checking on him. Or else Ondra would be down to inspect it. She could probably tell how a chalk line had looked by the scattering of its dust. He sighed. He couldn't pretend not to know the first words to say. "This is for Wenne, queen bitch of the gods." The words hung stupid in the air. "No," he said, and retraced the line, stronger, straighter. "This is for Senne, the evil bitch god. Oh no, I'm praying to Senne first. Come on, end of the world!" He looked up at the corners of the room. "Not coming? Well, then this line," he drew hard, crumbs of chalk spattering out, "this line is for Senne also. And so's this one. And what the heck, this one too. Why pray to four gods at once anyway? Senne, if you hear me, send me a hefty stack of gold coins, a decent outfit and, oh, I don't know, a way out of here. One immortal soul on the line. No waiting. Take your time."

It was the perfect entrance. I even had the perfect line prepared. "No," I said. "I'll give you nothing."

Panic shot through him. He twisted around and I obligingly made myself visible, starting at the feet and filling in upward, to show off my slit robe, my plump calf, the sweet roundness of a belly under draped fabric, then of course, a perfectly wicked smile on top of it all.

"Holy tits! Lady, you scared the crap out of me." He started to stand, then looked down at the summoning-square and the chalk in his hands. Feeling foolish, he started kicking the lines out. He hadn't noticed my slow reveal. It hadn't been slow enough for human senses. I'd have to work on that.

I walked up to him in what I hoped was a seductive sway. (Borrowed, I'm ashamed to say, from that lecherous groundskeeper). "I should have felt something, don't you think? Summoned like that?"

"Don't joke around. They take religion seriously here." He looked away, unafraid, to dust the chalk off his hands and the knee area of his tunic. "You're not an idiot, so I'm guessing you aren't a Faydehale. Please tell me you're here to take me home."

"That hurts, Illoehenderen. I'm Senne. The god." I reached out to touch his cheek. He flinched away from me. "I've been watching you." I grabbed his arm near the shoulder. It worked! How lovely the feel of his skin, of his muscles straining under my fingers. He twisted ineffectively and stared at my hand, shocked that I was so much stronger than he was. He had a thought he half-believed that it was only that he was weakened by hunger and sleeplessness. And many people were stronger than they looked.

What did I have to do to prove myself more than human? "Don't I look godly to you? Something magical and indescribable?"

I didn't. "Let go of me," he said.

"Come on! Revestre barely tried, and Hitra was all over her. I worked very hard to make myself beautiful for you. You have no idea how difficult it is to make hair. There are literally thousands of strands!" I shook him, perhaps too hard. His eyes bulged and his heartbeat tripled.

He raised his open hand, placatingly. "Yes. All right. You're pretty. You're also really strong," he struggled, mind churning for ideas and failing, "and pretty. Let me go? You're very beautiful." He knew calling me a god would calm down this strong, likely insane woman, but he couldn't bring himself to say it.

"Don't you feel a divine hand in your life? Haven't things turned unnaturally dreadful? Hitra's forgotten you. Maede's going to have you scrubbing her toilets until you hit a ripe old age. Did you think it was random chance? I've made your life terrible so you won't feel bad throwing it away to be mine." This made my plans sound more consistent than they were, but he didn't need to know that.

Through his struggles and my gentle care to maintain the contact of our skin, we ended up against the damp basement wall.

He pressed his cheek to the filthy, damp wall to stay farther away from me. Wasn't I pretty? Did my skin not feel right?

He straightened, trying not to look afraid. "You want my immortal soul? Take it in exchange for getting out of here." He would gladly trade something he thought didn't exist.

Admittedly, I had not seen any evidence of what a soul was, much less how to take one, but it would have to be a start. I picked him up to fly away. His senses blanked a moment as he hit the ceiling. I had to let him down gently on the floor. He blinked at the stars before his eyes. Gathering him up again, I moved not up, but out, pouring like water, as I did when I traveled alone, not through the walls or around them but without them.

I wasn't sure it would work, and the thrill that I might lose him was intoxicating. I wasn't sure he was still there, if he could follow. But he was there, and I re-formed myself in his grasp. We rushed through the skies and he clung tightly to me, hot and desperate.

Over the temple complex, there is a mimic carved in the mountain peak, archways and columns carved into the living rock of the mountain to make it seem as though the temple climbed all the way to the top. Devoted workers had to ascend with ropes and metal picks driven into the cliff face, two days up and two days down. The resulting sculptures were called "The homes of the gods." It seemed like the place to go.

They weren't very homey. Balustrades and colonnades gave way to shallow niches. One cupola was the only real roofed space, a round dome carved in-situ with a natural spire atop it. Fat columns supported the roof, but the inside was all rough stone, even the inside edge of the columns.

Illoe shivered and fell, curled against the low wall of the balustrade. His breath came in rasps and gasps. His muscles convulsed and shook. He felt burnt by the cold, in an odd contradiction of nerves.

I curled around him and realized I had no body heat. But heat is an easy thing to make, just jiggling particles. Soon the tiny particles of ice inside the stones were melting, then evaporating, warmth radiating out from the area directly around Illoe.

He sweated—his face red, but his breath was still coming uneasily. There was something he needed in the air that wasn't there, no matter how much he pulled in.

This was terrible. I had to make it work. I kissed him, but the touch sensation was vague, slippery. He didn't even move in response, just shaking and staring. "But where else could we go? I don't know if you'd survive as pure consciousness in the heavens..."

Somewhere below the mountain, there was a sound loud enough for me to hear, a crack. It was terribly loud, echoing on the stones around us, echoing in my mind.

Illoe screamed as I flew with him from that high perch. His lungs burned. His fingers grasped helplessly, digging into me with less control than before as he stared at the city opening up below us. I hoped he liked the view, but it didn't register for him. The lake was a mirror from this height, the far shore which was invisible to most of the city was a fuzzy curve, like crumbles of sponge.

As we lowered, Illoe's breaths came easier. He panted and clung to me, thoughts a rush of *We're flying don't fall we're actually flying not gonna fall we're flying.* I kept myself solid for him, and he was grateful.

We landed in a less densely populated part of the city, full of modest homes with stone-walled gardens. Something had happened here. Dust rose in tendrils between boulders the size of houses, heaped atop each other at the base of a clean cliff face, new as a baby's cheek. Beneath the boulders, life ebbed out of crushed bodies, and where life was long gone, warmth bled in its stead.

I set Illoe on a convenient precipice. He curled into a ball, gulping fat mouthfuls of air.

Your fault thought Dioneltar and Telumene, simultaneously. Quivering with rage, their grasping parts clenched, having just wrestled over the stone which they were both sure would not have broken if the other hadn't interfered.

"Not this again," I said.

Before I could get into their tiresome argument, I felt someone still alive under the stone...a child barely ten, she'd been so happy to get a chance to go to the market. She'd begged and pleaded to be allowed to go, and went to that long boring church thing and didn't even fidget. She'd carried her basket just like Daddy did and she remembered exactly what to get and counted the change and felt so grown up. Then she saw the mountain fall, so slow she was sure she'd escape it. She didn't. She'd sobbed her lungs out. She couldn't move. Her legs were crushed. She was terrified the eggs were broken, and she'd never get to go to the market alone again.

All the contents of her basket were broken. The basket itself was half-crushed, the handle still around her arm was disconnected from it, but she didn't know. She didn't see how little time she had, the blood seeping from her. There was only so much blood in a human, and she was a small one. I attached myself like a frost to the boulder above her and put all my soul into it. The boulder flew easily.

The boulder hit a home two blocks away. Two of the three occupants were killed instantly. A dentist and her wife. Their adult son, who was visiting for the holiday, happened to be in a doorway, and so was buried but alive, a tray of sweet buns still in his hands, covered in stone dust. Exposed to the air, the girl with the crushed legs gasped, smiled in hope at the sky, and died.

We began to panic — by "we" I mean "I." I tried to get the boulder again, to fling it up on to the top of the mountain, but my control was terrible. It hit the broken cliff and fell again atop the pile at the bottom, with additional rubble it had dislodged on impact, a scattering of which struck the girl's still-warm corpse.

I felt like I was breaking.

Dioneltar and Telumene were amused at my efforts. They had much better control over rocks, having practiced nothing else. They lifted and danced them around me. "It's easier to destroy something than set it right," I shouted at them.

They didn't care where the rocks fell, or who was under them. Why should they? The scriptures made it clear that it didn't matter if humans died, only that they said their prayers.

Mortal observers — the survivors of the initial fall, those who had been near, those who came to dig out the bodies and those who stared in horror from nearby homes and dear Illoe — saw stones flung up and down the hill, rising and falling again. Once or twice, I managed to stop a stone from falling upon a victim, and so they saw boulders hang in the air, spinning a moment, change trajectory and crash...I was as effective as a giant toddler trying to clear damage from an ant's nest. There was control needed, patience I didn't have. By the time I got the hang of moving rocks sensibly, it didn't really matter if I did or not. Those underneath were dead, and Illoe had crawled down to the road where he was limping away from me.

"Illoe, wait! Let's start over." I tried to follow him, but a current caught me, a strong pull. I fell as if into a drain.

Chapter Fifteen

Scriptures

"This has got to stop."

Wenne gathered us at the Homes of the Gods. It was a useful meeting place for us non-corporeal beings, unable to freeze, not needing to breathe. We lounged around as clouds, as concentrations, or, in the case of myself and Wenne, as fully formed women in trailing robes. I noticed a direct correlation... how clear we were in the average mind and how clear we were, here.

All of us were here, such as we were: the ten major female gods, four minor, and one undefined divine something that hadn't decided on its name yet.

With the combined will of all of those who had not yet figured out that the old laws meant nothing, the Queen of the Gods dragged us here. It felt like having my feet stuck to the floor, right when I most had something I needed to do.

Someone I needed to save.

"We don't belong here," Wenne said. "It's clear to me that we need to leave mortal affairs alone until we are stronger."

I let them all see what I'd just seen. "Any stronger and we'll be tearing down the mountain." Lives, ending, permanently. We could break, we couldn't repair.

Dioneltar curled herself around a pillar. "That was you."

"No, I was trying to put the mountain back. If you didn't have your head transposed with your ass —"

"Ladies," Wenne made herself glow, a soft yellow woman of sunlight. She turned her head, catching each of us in her gaze, in the touch of her essence. She'd been watching Reha. "Who here can disagree

215

that we are not ready? Perhaps, yes, 'stronger' was an inappropri-
ate word. We need to learn to control our power. We need to refine
ourselves. I propose we leave the city, and all mortal habitation altogether, return to the heavens and work it out there."

There was a despondent lull. Revestre said what most were thinking, "There's nothing up there. We'll be bored."

I said, "Entertainment isn't worth human lives." I was impressed
with my maturity. The others weren't. They thought I was a hypocrite. Yes, I remembered casually killing a man two weeks ago. How
ignorant I'd been! I regretted it, hugely. That didn't mean I was ready
to accept a cosmic time-out.

Someone, I think it was Nolumbre, thought but did not say, or try
to say, that a god's entertainment was worth any number of human
deaths.

There was a divide in us, on this issue, on how important individual human lives were. The argument turned non-verbal, memories
and emotions passing back and forth. It seemed everyone had knocked
a human over trying to touch them. Chubby toddlers who wailed the
injustice with innocent purity, businesswomen who sprained ankles
in the middle of carpeted offices, and one elderly woman who fell like
wheat before the scythe on a red marble floor, and turned out to be
the queen. She insisted she was pushed, but her advisors assumed she
was lying to cover for the frailty of age, and it infuriated her to know
they thought that, as she begrudgingly ruled from her bed, nursing
broken bones she feared would spell the end of her rule. The pain was
deep and hot and made her patience run thin.

Scriptural accounts joined in with memories of witnessing or
causing human pain. Stupid scriptural accounts.

"No," I said, "dead is dead. There's no reviving them or bringing
them back. There's no taking them to heaven, either. I've tried."

Ijawitar, always hopeful, said, "Maybe we just don't know how
yet."

"Honey, if any of us would know, it would be me."

Dioneltar glowed smugly. "You didn't see her boulder-throw-
ing." Like she'd tried half the things I'd done.

"It was embarrassing," Telumene said.

Now they had something to agree about.

"But it is harder to move large objects," Ijawitar offered. "It's not like making words."

The cow. I didn't need defending; I was the second-most powerful goddess!

"Exactly my point," Wenne said, half to my thought, half to Ijawitar's. "We're not ready. We don't have the basic skills to move a rock. You laugh at poor Senne's distress—"

"Please don't call me poor or distressed."

" —but none of you could have done better. We are all-powerful, yet we lack the skill to move a single stone!"

"Could it be that the mental world is separate from the physical?" Dioneltar asked, which was the most foolish thing I'd ever heard. We all knew the making of words was physical, everything the mind did was physical, and hence, able to be altered.

I had to stop myself, as my thoughts had already been heard and a debate was warming up. Was there, perhaps, a second layer to reality? One that we just needed to access for things to make sense? Or was the physical not completely known? Telumene had noticed something tiny deep inside particles smaller than grains of sand.

I didn't shout so much as wipe out all their thought waves with my own. "Who cares? Am I the only one who remembers the void?"

There was an uncomfortable silence, in minds as well as words. They remembered the void.

Wenne said, "The Heavens are a forbidding place, yes. That doesn't disagree with scripture."

"In the scripture," I countered, "it's a forbidding place with furniture."

"Human writings are of necessity interpretive," Wenne said, but already Jestina and Solinumbe were ready with counters, defending the scriptures against a noncompliant reality.

"But I know who did it!" I said. No one listened. So I flew up to the arched ceiling of the cupola we were in and made myself bright and made my voice boom so the rocks around us shivered. "I said, 'I know who did it!'"

"Did what?" Wenne asked with an undertone of "you don't have to shout."

"Woke us. I'll show him to you. He touched our minds, with help.

He did just what you did, Wenne, joining many together to be more powerful. And, well, I think he told us we were the gods…maybe it was the start of everything. Come on, you can see the whole thing in his memory…"

I was halfway down the mountain when I saw that none of my sisters had followed me. How could they not be interested in this? I floated back.

"Senne, we just don't have time for theoretical questions," Wenne said. They didn't believe a human could "wake" us, and they didn't want to believe we hadn't always been gods. They found it more likely an entire pantheon had lost its memories and powers than that we were something else that had woken up, splintered itself, and was figuring it out as it went along.

"Why are there no men?" I pointed around the room. "It's because we were one entity, and we picked female, because all the best gods are female."

The less-solid, less-sure gods sank, felt deep shame, clung to each other. Oh, I'd missed something there.

"Complete rubbish," Wenne said. "Now please, can we vote on the matter at hand?"

A murmur of agreement. Yes, yes, the matter at hand. Nolumbre raised a hand, "What is it, again?"

"We return to the heavens. We'll join together, be as one. It will be safer," Wenne said.

I felt the others consider this, the allure of safety. They'd had their belief in themselves shaken over the past two weeks. They didn't want to try anymore.

Oh hell no. I flew as far out of the cupola as they'd let me with their grasping, pulling wills. "You want me to vote to stop being me?"

"It's not like that. We are all one substance, aren't we?" Wenne's essence touched my own, tried to grab on.

I had to get out of there. I could feel us collapsing, becoming one thing, but that one thing wasn't what we were before; it was Wenne.

No. I was me. I was mischievous. I loved watching complex emotions and pretty men. I…what defined me? I felt myself unraveling. I felt Wenne's smugness.

I searched for a strong mind, like an anchor, found one, grabbed it, and pulled myself toward it, releasing like a rubber band. I shot down into the city. I didn't look back; I was too afraid to.

☽○☾

It was Reha, of course, and she wondered at a sudden chill, or itch, which was me wrapping myself firmly around her and holding on.

Reha approached the government complex, afraid that she'd tarried too long, but the jailer took her name and led her down the same corridor as last time, without the slightest change in demeanor, and Arel was still sitting on the floor, writing.

The guard left her inside the door and barred it behind her. She waited for Arel to pause in his furious writing. When he lifted the tip of the stylus to his lips, she asked, "What is that you are so ardently laboring at?"

He rewarded her with an upward glance. "Just...words I ought to say."

"There are a lot of them." Reha smiled.

He looked at the scrolls spread around him in confusion. "I don't know how much time I have. This isn't half of what needs to be said." He smoothed the one he was working on, blowing on the ink. He began to roll some up to make a clear space on the floor for his guest. "You can read them, I guess. Just...wait for my death. Some of these are about you, and I'd rather you didn't read them while I'm living."

Reha squashed her panic about just what he'd written about her. Now was not the time. "They aren't going to kill you, Arelandus."

"Maybe not now, but they will." He gestured toward the cleared floor space with a bundle of scrolls, urging her to sit. "I'm a heretic. Perhaps a prophet. I have thousands of truths to speak, Reha, that haven't been spoken in a long time. At some point, they will have to kill me to silence me." His thoughts were racing, but I caught bits of what he was writing. It was mostly useless minutia about interpretations of specific scriptures, said with all the fervent authority of a thousand such scrolls in the archives.

Reha folded her legs under her. The plain brown slacks she wore made the act of sitting on the floor far easier than it had been in her previous visit, but they offered less warmth against the stone. She rubbed her knees. "I blame the confessional texts," she said. She studied him hard, trying to predict how he would react to what she had to say. "Arel, our government does not execute heretics. They haven't in centuries. The Arbitration Council and the queen have decided it is more humane to silence you."

A corner of Arel's mouth jerked up. "They can't silence me. I won't be..."

"Silenced," Reha repeated, placing her palm flat on the scroll Arel held. "Surgically. A mind doctor will be called in, before the day is done, to remove from you those gifts you have already forsworn as a Husher."

They both looked down: Reha slowly, Arel with a sudden jerk. Reha said, "Perhaps, for you, it won't be so bad."

For him, he felt it would be worse than for anyone else. He'd rather die. He had *planned* on dying. "They can't do that!"

"They can. It is allowed, in cases of insanity, and Arel, they think you are insane."

"No...I..." He curled his scrolls against his chest. "I need to be able to speak to the gods."

Reha was uncomfortable seeing his emotions, feeling them slip his control and fill the room. "You need to prepare yourself. I have tried every avenue open to me to change their minds, to convince them you aren't a threat."

"But I am a threat! Reha...the time of secular governance is ending. Our people need to remember the gods!"

Reha stared at him, and he could see he had lost her, could see fear and disappointment, as surely as he felt them ripple over her consciousness. She stood. "I haven't given up hope of a delay. Keep writing. Perhaps the words will come to you that should have come to me, when I spoke with the queen."

She left him a frightened man. For all his careful non-use of his powers, he knew them, felt them like a favorite ring on his hand. There were those senses he could not turn off, like a second smell, and he could not imagine that sense forever numbed, cut from his mind like a malignant tumor.

It was extraordinary, his fear. It consumed him, made his heart beat faster, his blood surge through his veins filled with useless adrenaline. His hands shook, and he could not think of a single new word to press to paper.

Wenne had not come after me, yet. And Arel was as strong an anchor as Reha. I settled into her vacated spot. "So, are you insane, or the only one who knows the truth?"

Perhaps it was the fear, or the chemical balance of his blood, or a sudden appreciation of the vigor of a limb about to be cut off, but he wasn't afraid. He looked directly at me. "Who are you?"

"Who do you want me to be?" He glared. Some people have no sense of sport. "The Moon at Zenith, The Sun at Nadir, Trickster, Artist, The Joyful Darkness…"

He scrambled to his feet and threw his wadded paper at me. "I did not summon you! Begone!"

The paper bounced off my chest, because I thought a second before it hit to make myself solid. "Oh dear, sweet man. If that worked, Wenne would have been through with me long before Darian was born."

"I'll make no bargain with you."

"Did I say I wanted to bargain? This isn't a story."

He covered his eyes with his hands and muttered, "Wenne, Queen of Light, my soul is yours, Darian at your right hand, guide and protect me…"

I was mostly sure that Wenne wouldn't hear his summons. No one had so far, but still I cut him off a little louder and more breathlessly than I'd intended. "Relax, Arel. Shush." I continued with more outward calm, "Your soul's slightly worn, and I don't think it's quite my size. I don't want it. I want the truth, if you have it, about what I am, what we all are — the gods."

Wenne was like a breeze over my shoulder. *So that's the one you were talking about?*

Shit. She'd found me. I pulled myself tight, imagined being hard to grab onto. *Wait. Watch. He knows something.*

Wenne doubted that, but not so much that she was pulling away, or pulling me away.

Arel said, "I have nothing to give you and you have nothing that I want."

"We both know *that's* not true," I said, before I could stop myself.

I'd spent too long coming up with good flirty villain lines. "Just be-cause there are some stories where I play the villain doesn't mean I'm automatically out to destroy everyone I talk to."

He was quietly, and without moving his lips, praying to Wenne. It was only making her smug. I rolled my eyes, basing the expression on the eloquent way Illoe did it. "All right, a bargain, since you're so desperate for one. I want you to remember the day you contacted us. Remember it in detail, the boring parts you weren't paying atten-tion to as well as the moments you keep flinching away from in your mind. Remember it for me right now, and whatever you want in re-turn is fine. Think up all the clauses and addendums you want."

He assumed there was a trap, but couldn't see it, which made him certain it was a terrible trap, more complex than any in scripture. Ugh.

"Why?"

"Because that is what I want. I want to understand what hap-pened that day."

He looked down, his eyes searching back and forth for some clue how to deal with me.

Back me up, I pleaded with Wenne. *Yes, fine, he trusts you and not me. Don't you want to know?*

When Arel looked up again, he gasped. Wenne stood beside me, her hand on my shoulder. For her, he felt awe.

But then the awe vanished, like a light extinguished. "This is a false image." He swelled with pride. "A real god would know what happened. That isn't Wenne."

I tried to calm down, to marshal my strength. If I could be seen by an atheist like Illoe, I should be able to smack some sense into a true believer!

"He doesn't know anything," Wenne said. "You're wasting our time." She pulled me, heading back to her debate club, like her hand was glued to my shoulder.

No! Arel reacted to her words! He was really thinking! *One more damn minute!* But Wenne had done, she thought, more than enough for me.

She faltered...she wasn't as strong as before. She felt me feel it, and a flash of embarrassed memory showed me other gods breaking free when I did, Revestre and Nolumbre weren't keen on not-being either. More were slipping away even now.

I thought of Hitra. Good, solid Hitra. None of the gods were as sure about what to do as she was when she threw her headdress in the laundry. She would be anchor enough.

☽〇☾

Hitra stood at the door to Ele's apartment. In my absence, she had contacted important people, signed forms, and gotten receipts. She hadn't been allowed, as she hoped, to take Jeje with her from the jail, but she felt he was safe enough now. Like all noble families in Chagrin City, hers had controlling interest in a glass works. Jeje had been a glass blower. He now had an official job offer. She felt powerful and strong. In her element. Solving things.

Until she reached this point. She'd gotten Ele's address from an arbiter grateful to get rid of her and, finding Indy Street not that far from the civic center, had decided to breeze by and see Illoe. A few words with him would help her with his mother. Maybe he would even have already arranged a meeting.

But now she was here and knew she wasn't technically allowed to see Illoe and also that he might not want to see her and she felt frozen and foolish. She brushed the chimes like she was afraid they would break. Of course Ele did not hear the gentle sound they made. Besides, he had successfully acquired Tara's forgiveness for previous episodes, and they were reading a book together, arms and thoughts entwined, lying lengthwise on the couch. They weren't paying attention to anything else.

Hitra turned and walked three steps back down the apartment corridor, feeling like an intruder. She turned back. She retreated. She contemplated the very long trip awaiting her, all uphill, back to the temple.

"This is your woman who can figure things out?" Wenne asked.

If I had a heart, it would have skipped a beat. *Don't sneak up on me like that.* I very pointedly wrapped myself tight around Hitra and gave her what I hoped was a non-verbal prick of bravery.

Hitra returned to the door and struck the chimes more forcefully.

Ele had a start of panic, and he and Tara ended up entangled as both tried to get up and answer. Tara laughed and rolled over him, kissing his nose. "A moment!" she called out.

Hitra was no less startled to have the door answered by a young woman with ruffled hair and blushing cheeks. "Is this Eleteralenil Middlemount's residence?"

Ele set his hand on Tara's shoulder and said, "I'm Eleteralenil."

"Oh, good," Hitra relaxed. The brother. She could do this. "I'm looking for Illoe. I know I shouldn't be here, but I just want to talk to him. You can...well, supervise, if you like?"

Ele's eyes narrowed. "And who are you?"

"I'm sorry," Hitra reached over her bare arm to catch the robe sleeve that wasn't there. She then touched the makeshift cloak pin at her shoulder. "I'm Hitra," she said, "I'm Illoe's...well, I'm Hitra."

Tara raised one eyebrow at Ele, silently asking if he needed her to invent an excuse to close the door. But Ele's scowl lightened a little and he said, "Oh. The priest." He blinked again and held out a hand. "It's something, to finally meet you."

Hitra shook hands with Ele, both of them feeling awkward. Hitra, at least, had some training in awkward situations. "I don't know how much you know about the arbitration, but I'm told there's a few more procedures to be gotten through and I wanted to talk to Illoe about, well, about where we go from here."

Ele looked at Tara.

Tara drew him back. "Illoehenderen isn't here. You should contact your local arbitration office."

Hitra frowned. "Where is he?"

Ele started to speak, but Tara interrupted. "If you have a right to see him, the arbiters will tell you."

Hitra shook her head, unable to form a response.

Ele said, "Tara, why are you being like this?" His family depended on money from Hitra, and he was terrified of offending her.

"The arbitration council separated your brother from this woman for a reason." Tara turned to Hitra, "Please take no offense, but we don't know if it's best for you to see Illoe. That is the arbitration council's decision."

Ele said, "God's bods, Tara! We've never met this woman."

Tara threw up her hands and retreated into the apartment. *Don't tell her,* she sent to him. *It's an arbitration.*

Hitra shook her head. "Please...I want to know he's safe. Illoe has been through so much..." she stopped, seeing the bright edge of guilt in Ele's eyes. "He wanted me to renegotiate his contract before the deadline. I don't even know if it's still possible. The deadline is today, I was distracted and..." Hitra trailed off, realizing that she was asking for forgiveness Ele couldn't give. "If you won't bring Illoe out, can you contact your mother for me?"

Ele was horrified at the idea of contacting his mother. "Sorry," he said, then put his head down and grabbed the door.

Hitra didn't move as the door closed. Ele raised his head once, guiltily, watching her earnest face become obscured by wood.

He rested his forehead on the closed door.

"It was an assault charge," Tara said, sitting back down on the couch. "You can't be sure, Ele, that her intentions are kind. She didn't even look like a priest."

Hitra was in the dim, dusty corridor, thinking about Arel, how she had no real plan there, about Harvest Home and how long she had until the evening service. She had always been gifted at setting goals and achieving them, even in spite of her mother's plans. How much, she thought, does it cost to see a god?

Ele, on the other side of the door, felt her emotions, remembered the innocence and sorrow on her face, and sent a quiet, quick packet of words to her mind. *Some noblewoman ran off with Illoe. Maya Fad-something. He knew her. She took him.*

He stayed leaning on the door. He used all his power to keep his thoughts contained, but emotion crept out.

Tara wrapped her arms around him. "Honey," she said, misunderstanding his guilt, "you did the right thing."

Hitra strode purposefully down the apartment hallway, steps getting louder and firmer as she went. Arel first, she reminded herself. He was in more danger.

Wenne tugged at me. "She doesn't have answers. She's just doing what we're all doing, running to the next problem." I fought her. She was getting desperate. "Senne, I need you! The others will come back if you're there."

Thanks for the reason not to go.

She huffed. "You know they're back off doing terrible things. We need to stop them."

"Go, I'll follow."

Wenne was disgusted. "Like I'd believe that."

"Whatever. I need to check on the boy."

"And you think you're different than the scriptures make you out to be." Meaning that I was a boy-crazy lech of a god, as advertised.

She could believe what she wanted. I left Illoe far from his home near cliffs that were damaged and could still be unstable. I spread myself thin and wide until I felt him. Wenne dropped out of my awareness, I hoped for good this time.

)O(

Humans, with their blood-fed muscle and sinew, were doing the work I'd failed to do. Residents of the neighborhood where Telumene and Dioneltar had fought, as well as emergency personnel for the city and county, cleared rubble and tended the wounded.

The place was called Terrace Heights. The cliff face that had attracted my sisters was natural, a break in the mountain's western arm caused by a weaker stone and a swift turn of the Chagrin River. Below the cliff, a flatter expanse of ground sloped gently to the lake shore and had been prosperous farms before the city encroached and converted almost every available parcel into homes. Still, the homes were among the most widely spaced in the city, with walled gardens on streets with strange, non-Anichu names like Marble Cleft and Brick Lane.

Illoe was on a rough wooden bench along Farmer's Track, the main road back toward the city center, on the outskirts of the now-ruined produce market. His face had been washed, and his knee, where his worst scrape had been bandaged. Still, he was covered in rock-dust. His throat was sore all the way down into his lungs from the sharp not-air of the mountain. He held a gourd dipper that had been full of balm-grass tea, given to him by the rescue workers. It had felt good while he was drinking it, and he was coughing less, but he chose to ignore that evidence and think it had done nothing for him.

Illoe was sulking. The shadows were lengthening, and he couldn't do anything about his contract now without contacting a router, which would reveal to official channels where he was, and that would get him back in Maede's custody, he just knew it. Or in trouble for running away. It was going to be hard to explain how he'd gotten out of the basement, much less ended up on the far west side of the city.

I sat next to him. "Sorry about the mountain...I keep forgetting how fragile you are."

Illoe dropped the gourd and scrambled to his feet. He limped desperately, grabbing onto benches and stall-fronts as he passed them. Like I was going to hurt him!

Well, I had hurt him. I moved myself in front of him, which made him almost fall over as he lurched to a stop. "I mean it. I'm sorry about everything. Let me fly you back home? I promise I won't go so high that the air doesn't work this time."

He pulled himself upright with the help of a sign post that held a tilted 'closed on Harvest Home' placard and leveled a glare at me as imperious as a prince. "Leave me alone."

"But I can literally fly. Don't you want to take care of that contract? I could have you, Hitra, and your mother together in a clerk's office in a matter of minutes."

Stiffly, he let go of the post and walked around me, trying and failing to hide the limp.

I took a careful look at the insides of his legs, reassuring myself nothing was broken, just bruised. It was still painful to watch him march stiffly up the rubble-strewn road. I picked him up.

"Put me down!"

He flailed, striking me hard in the face. If I were human, he'd have damaged my nose or eye for sure. People were staring at this woman holding a nearly full-grown man and walking down the street with him. "If you won't fly, I'll walk you where you need to go."

"You bitch. Let go of me!"

Now he was flailing so wildly, trying to twist out of my grasp, that he was going to hurt himself. I sighed, stopped walking, and, after he paused to rest, set him down. "Do you not understand you have a god offering to do anything for you? Forget about the contract. We can leave the city altogether. Go to the southlands, where it never snows. I'll wave my hands, catch a few people on fire, and we'll be revered as gods together."

He raised one eyebrow at me.

"Come on, what's wrong with that plan?"

"Go away." He spotted a sheltered bench, the sort at which omnibuses stopped, and started lurching toward it. "I'm catching a wagon home."

"To Hitra? Or your awful parents?"

"Not really your business." His mind said Hitra.

He sat down on the bench and stifled a sigh of relief. I sat next to him, resigning myself to riding a wagon. It would be a novel experience.

He stared at the road in front of us. "If you're Senne, why are you dressed like a priest of Revestre? Senne's clergy wear blue and silver."

I looked down at my gown and it flickered and fluttered as I tried to get the hang of color. It was blue for a second or so. I laughed. "I look ridiculous, don't I? It's harder than you'd think, bending light. But I really am Senne. At least, that's the only name I know for myself." It felt really vulnerable, to say it that way. I bit my lip, realized I couldn't feel it, and tried again.

"I don't believe you are a god." He looked right at me when he said it. "And I'm not going to. Whoever you are, whatever your game is, leave me out of it."

"But I'm trying to apologize! To help you."

"You want to help? Leave."

He meant it, so I did.

☽○☾

Hitra secluded herself in a tea room off Penitence. Maede had Illoe? She was confused, but also horrified. It was like the last clue in a word-cross, and she'd filled in the letter to spell out something terrible.

"Don't leave me alone with her," Illoe had said.

Maede had always been hinting that Hitra shouldn't have such a young and attractive servant. Lingering on his youth and beauty. Like a covetous cow.

Hitra knew what she had to do, but it took all this time to calm herself down so that when she contacted Maede she didn't blurt out all her suspicions or just scream at her. That wouldn't be best for Illoe. Maede could take things out on him.

Hitra took a sip of her third cup of calming blend and reached out for Maede's mind. She had prepared a reasonable excuse and opening statement. *I was wondering if you were coming to the ceremony tonight?*

As usual, Maede's mind blanked, startled, like she'd never been contacted before, but unlike usual, this was followed by a spike of rage and suspicion. *Holiness. I was just, er...well...*Maede didn't have the power to lie in thought, and her words carried the overtones of what she didn't say, like a caption under a picture. She was just about to NOT call Hitra, because she had lost Illoe! The suspicion then was that Hitra knew this.

An uncharacteristic desire to be cruel moved Hitra to affect a casual, friendly tone and send, *And I was wondering if you'll be bringing Illoe? It shouldn't be a problem, for the arbitration, if we aren't left alone together. You understand.*

The flare of panic was delicious to both of us, though as Maede struggled to respond, Hitra began to worry just where Illoe was, and if he had escaped or been taken by someone else.

No, Holiness, Maede finally arrived at the only non-incriminating truth. *I simply can't get away tonight.*

Hitra felt mean, so she sent, *Well, then, perhaps I'll stop by before sunset. Just to wish you all well.*

In her front parlor, Maede's hands shook, and she almost dropped the glass of hard spirits she was using to calm her nerves. *I don't think that's a good idea, Holiness.* Maede's husband was pacing angrily, complaining loudly about the arbiters who had visited and said they couldn't begin searching for the run-off boy until he was gone for a full day. What were they paying taxes for?

Maede seized on a fuzzy idea. *Of course I would LOVE to see you, but, well, considering the, well, the admiration and exposure Your Holiness is experiencing lately, perhaps, well, it wouldn't be prudent to be seen with him?*

Hitra wondered how prudent it would be to rush straight to Maede's house and strangle her. *Oh really, I must insist. My friendship to you is more important than my public image.*

Maede's husband noticed something was wrong with her. "What is it? Did they find the bastard dead or something?" He hoped that was it.

Maede held up a hand and hissed, "I'm on a call."

To Hitra, she sent, *And I care more about your career...I mean image... I mean YOU...than your friendship. I...didn't mean it that way. Than a visit.* Maede growled audibly, trying to pull her thoughts together and away from what she didn't want to say. *It isn't like I'll keep him from you. I understand the appeal of having a virile young man about, and the temptation is great when men are so naturally drawn to power and flaunt their legs and their arms...*Maede seemed to do her best thinking when lustful. She suddenly had a great idea; it would buy time to find the boy, and secure him in her care. *Let me keep him out of sight for you, until things calm down. Then we can arrange discrete appointments, somewhere unassuming.*

Hitra never expected to hear such things talked about so blatantly. Maede thought she wanted Illoe kept like...like some...

"Kept boy," I provided. Really, how hard was that phrase to come up with?

Hitra flinched, told me, "Go away," and felt a headache starting. *I have to go,* she sent to Maede, and severed the connection.

She stared straight forward for a long moment. She felt too disgusted to move, like her skin was surrounded by filth. If Illoe were a free man, Maede could never get away with this.

She couldn't, she realized, renegotiate the contract like Illoe wanted her to. In her mind, a neat line went through that entire plan.

"What?" I materialized in the chair opposite her. "No, you have to."

She glared at me. "Who are you? You're not Revestre."

"Senne," I said. It came out apologetically, which I hated.

That figures, she thought to herself, which wasn't flattering. She stood. "Leave me alone. I have things to do."

She walked out of the café thinking about Arel.

$$) O ($$

Loata Middlemount was in a mild state of panic, wishing the holiday had not arrived so quickly. Her pottery orders for the Sanadaru festival were all completed and shipped, but she'd done nothing for her own religious holiday. She was supposed to bring Illoe a gift—they always gave him a gift at Harvest Home, which was the anniversary of his contract, and she had not thought to arrange anything. She hoped something would come to her in the midst of panic. She didn't really want to go to the temple. Illoe would be unhappy about the contract, and she would rather wait until he'd forgotten about it.

Uja was in a better mood. He thought his wife's nerves brought on by happiness, and he had spent a lot of time preparing for the holiday. His and Loata's clothes were freshly pressed and mended. He was particularly proud of how he had turned and reattached Loata's collar, finding the interior fabric a beautiful, brilliant shade of melon. It made the whole tunic look new again. He'd picked a tunic for himself that almost matched and was packing a picnic dinner to eat after the trip to the temple and before the evening ceremony.

Loata dashed in and out of her studio. It would be easy to catch her. I'd give her a good god-scare, short and sweet. Something like, "Change Illoe's contract! And tell him Senne said to and you're welcome." I lined myself up.

The front door of the apartment slammed open. "We need to talk, now," Ele said.

Uja's good mood dropped. "We're late for the temple."

"Hoping to see Illoe there? Because he isn't." Ele crossed his arms, blocking the entrance to the apartment. "He's in an arbitration. I'm not blaming you for not knowing; I'm just pointing it out."

"Arbitration?" Loata sank into a chair. She tried not to show that she was relieved to have an excuse not to go to the ceremony. "What happened? Tell us everything!"

Ele started to explain that he couldn't give details to an active arbitration, stopped, and considered confessing that he didn't know any details, but instead just skipped to why he'd come in the first place. "You need to help him. Help Illoe. Now."

Loata feared this was about that contract again. "There's nothing we can do," she said, and hoped it was right. Damn it. He'd scared her defensive and now nothing I said would work.

Ele was incensed by his mother's twisting hands, her weakness. He barely kept from shouting. "I've spent the past four years feeling guilty about what you did, because it was for me, but I was a kid, too. It's your responsibility."

"Don't speak to your mother that way!" Uja stepped in front of his wife. His son flinched. His wife whimpered. He wondered what god had cursed him that he did everything right and his family couldn't do their parts. He tried to lower his voice and almost succeeded. "Whatever this is about, it can wait until Dioneltarsday. Now help me with the basket and stop upsetting your mother. I just want a normal holiday for once."

Ele groaned, loud and obnoxiously. "You think I don't want that? Just say you'll do something so I can get home to my girlfriend."

"Your *what*?!"

"Girlfriend?!"

Both parents erupted into questions and demands at once and...I wasn't going to do any good here.

Chapter Sixteen

Martyrs

The sun was setting. Illoe had made it to Dockside, and was waiting for the water car to come take him back up the mount. He had a few coins the omnibus driver had given him out of pity, thanks to his bedraggled appearance, and hoped they were enough to cover the fare. Illoe didn't normally take the water car. He hadn't had an errand that took him downhill of Meridian since…ever. The last time he'd been here was as a child, visiting the shore with his family.

He had fond memories of his father teaching him to swim that he didn't want to admit he treasured, and the rotted fish and scum smell of the docks brought them to mind.

I decided to give him some space and materialized a few paces away, leaning against one of the posts that supported the roof of the shelter Illoe sat in, with a half-dozen others hoping to get uphill before night, on eight evenly spaced benches in two rows. It was like a little school room.

I was still trying to decide on the best opening line when his gaze happened to fall on me. He sighed. "I thought the 'and never come back' was implied."

An old woman on the other end of his bench glanced at him, then me, then moved farther away.

"I don't get it." I dropped my seductive pose. "Aren't you even a little bit afraid of me?"

He gaped. "Yes. I'm a lot bit afraid. You are terrifying. Will I be any safer if I run around screaming about it?"

I took the seat the old lady had vacated, still giving him plenty of space. That didn't stop him from leaning away. "Even if your mother and Hitra got together now, it's way too late to find a clerk to certify the changes. And I peeked in on both of them, and they are not getting together."

He rolled his lips inward and looked uphill at the still empty car track. "Thanks. I wasn't despairing already."

"I'm trying to say, why not run away with me? If you go back to Hitra's apartment, the arbiters are just going to find you there and drag you off to Maede, and you do not want to see what's in her mind." I could feel him deciding what sort of no was the most emphatic and cut that off. "You don't believe in the gods. You don't think I'm Senne. You aren't saying no to avoid giving in to evil. Explain to me why you won't take what I can give?"

He looked at me, at last, and he was so tired it was painful to think, but he had to think carefully how to answer me, because of his very justified fear of me. Finally, he settled on, "You'll want something in exchange that I might not be able to give you."

All I wanted was gratitude and affection and...oh shit, he was right. He relaxed with a quiet little smile that showed he saw me realize it.

For an all-powerful god, I felt pretty helpless next to a nineteen-year-old boy. "Could you at least accept that I'm Senne?"

The smile deepened. "I don't doubt you have the power to kick my body into a stain on the pavement. But you're not Senne, not the Senne in books. She's too stupid to be a real person."

"Stupid!"

He waved one hand. "Not stupid herself, I mean her story is stupid. You don't think about it if you focus on the heroes, but I always rooted for the bad guys. If you read the story of Darian from Senne's point of view, well, it makes no sense. She's supposed to have all this knowledge to make people able to hear thoughts, right? So she knows about brains and skulls. If the stories were true, she'd seen seven generations of men since the all-mother before she kidnapped Darian, and she's supposed to be surprised he doesn't immediately fall in love with her?" I felt as if I'd been punched. That was...a little close to home, but Illoe was talking to me like he might to Oke, open, gesturing with his words. "And then, instead of just letting him go, giving him a choice, or hell, taking him on a date? She panics and locks him in heaven so Wenne can come to the rescue?"

He had a point. "I don't remember doing any of that stupid stuff. I like to think the better bits are true, though…like how I invented the stars."

"You can't do that. It's all the same sources, the same authorities…if you doubt one, you doubt them all." He'd actually moved closer to me on the bench.

I swatted his arm gently. "You're no fun."

"Good! I don't want to be 'fun' to someone who throws boulders around."

He meant it as a joke, but the memory was fresh and raw for both of us, and it effectively destroyed the playful mood. "All right," I sighed. "I'll see you when you're home." I let myself vanish, and felt as I parted a deep shiver of relief from him.

I sat there a while, soaking in the disappointment as the sky deepened to blood-orange, oozing over everything like a freshly-broken yolk.

☽○☾

Hitra was back at the Temple Mount arbitration office. Uelo was not, having this evening off, and his replacement stared in disbelief at this priest who thought the temple arbiters were some sort of information service for mad, idealistic quests. "Even if I could tell you the whereabouts and sentence of a person undergoing arbitration, you wouldn't be able to do anything. The magistrates aren't at work." She pointed out the door, indicating the very obvious twilight. And a holiday twilight, at that.

Hitra wished fervently that Uelo didn't have nights off, which wasn't very grateful of her.

I made myself visible outside, to be polite, and walked in the door, one hand raised in greeting. The arbiter set her lips tight. "Please wait outside until the current client is finished."

"It's fine, I'm here to take her off your hands. Come on, Hitra. You're not going to get anywhere here. I can see it."

The arbiter thought I was some self-important priest who considered herself above the law, but gestured Hitra toward me anyway. Hitra turned with a shocked expression. She had no idea what to make of me.

I made a placating gesture. "If you feel like telling me off, I'm afraid Illoe did it already, and more eloquently than you can imagine."

That settled her. She followed me out of the office (to the relief of the night-duty arbiter). "You know where Illoe is?"

"I left him at the Dockside Water Car station."

The words had hardly left my mouth and she was jogging toward High Plaza, the highest and nearest Water Car station. I followed. This was exciting! We were going to do things together. Like a team. Friends. Best friends. "Make sure you tell Illoe this was all my idea. I kinda want him to like me?"

She gave me such a look when she finally stopped at the station. A look that said we were not going to team up and become best friends, or even acquaintances. "Stay away from Illoe."

She imagined I wanted to do...much of what I had wanted to do. "I'm not like in the stories."

"I don't care." She shrugged. "It needed to be said. That's first. Leave Illoe alone."

"But you're going to save him, right? He can't go back to Maede."

She dismissed the thought, as if Illoe were already saved. She hadn't done a thing! But she had a plan and thought it would be easy. I'd heard that before. Before I could object, she pinned me with a glare. "If you do have power like you're pretending to, you can save the man who created you."

She was scanning down the tracks for the car, considering my godhood, and scheming what she could get from me. This lady was good. I had to show her I was just as good. "No one created me."

"His name is Arel."

"Oh, *him*." I felt embarrassed. "Right. They were going to silence his mind."

"And?" she asked, expecting me to fill it in like one of her students. *And you can stop it*, she thought.

"...and I wanted to see that. Thanks!" I didn't want to give her the satisfaction. I stopped, halfway to the prison, and returned to Hitra's presence. She was bristling with her next demands, mad I'd fled because who knew if she'd meet a god again? It felt good to be demanded of — it meant she really saw me.

$$\mathcal{D}\bigcirc\mathbb{C}$$

Arel was terrified. He lay on a table, held down with stout bands of leather. He'd made the short walk from his cell and down three flights of stairs under his own power, trying for dignity, but he had started struggling when he saw the clean, orderly room, and the table. He was still struggling, though his muscles and joints ached and the fear wouldn't sustain his efforts much longer.

The only sound in the room was the creek of leather and Arel's grunts of exertion. Five arbiters ringed him. As I watched, their minds touched his, smothering his into stillness. The body followed the mind, hands unclenching, breaths slowing. That was how much they feared him, Arel thought. He tried to take comfort in that.

What an ass, but I was here to save him. I concentrated on the arbiters, but they didn't know what they were doing. They knew there was a chamber, a little grape of fat and oils behind the ear, filled with tiny connections. They knew that they could move it. They moved it. Rapidly. Pulping it against itself while Arel screamed in pain.

"Senne," he cried. "I'll take the deal. I...I'll take it. The bargain. Please, please not this." He would do anything, if I only asked. He would be my slave.

I'd have saved him for a lot less. I slipped between him and them. I tried to make a barrier. Flow like water. Everything was so *small*. I wasn't used to small. I had barely done well with large.

They were wielding a power that could draw masterpieces on his eardrum like it was a cudgel. I couldn't do better, but I could see how it could have been done, the microscopic connections, yes, this was how it worked.

Arel wasn't speaking anymore, but his mind, incoherently, was still begging.

Back off. Slide in. Pour myself around the little hairs, push back against the arbiter's pressure.

I felt Arel realize I was there. I felt him notice me, feel me with my hands in his head. A fierce, shameful hope suffused him, and then I felt the awareness fade and vanish. They'd done the damage already. The operators were exhausted and confused.

"He had some fight in him," one said. "Must have been more than seventh level."

They left Arel to rest, and cry. I stood over him a long while. I could see the damage, but I was no finer a tool than the arbiters. I could see how it had been, and how it broke, but not how to put it back together again.

"I'd give up half my power to be able to fix one thing," I said, but he was no god to offer me a bargain, and even if he were, he didn't hear me. He couldn't see me. He could never see me again, not as I was.

)O(

Illoe was on the water car heading uphill past Meridian Street when he saw Hitra leaning out of the downward car, waving frantically at him. *Stay on,* her voice echoed in his head, *I'll hop and catch up.*

Don't you'll hurt your — It was too late. He saw her duck back inside and then leap onto the road with a billow of...was that her blanket? Illoe switched to a seat on the other side of the car so he had a better view of her running up the street, trying to catch up. *Hitra! You weirdo. What are you wearing? We're still in an arbitration.*

No! I took...wow that thing is faster than it looks...I took care of it.

She was adorable, running too fast to think straight. The car was slowing for Sorrow's Market, and Illoe stepped off to save Hitra some dignity. She dropped her hands to her knees and heaved heavy breaths. *I would have caught up.*

And I'd have suffered watching you do it. It's better this way. Illoe's legs were stiff from sitting, and he was sore in too many places, but his walk became a little less of a hobble the closer he got to Hitra.

He still got to see her expression go from excited to dismayed. She held her hands out, wanting to touch him but afraid to hurt him. "What happened?"

He closed the distance and wrapped his arms around her. "A really long story. I was dropped down the mountain by a flying woman who claimed to be a god." He pressed his cheek against hers. She smelled sweaty and a little musty from the blanket and exactly like home. "Okay, not that long of a story."

Hitra felt tears welling. "I think I met her. She's a bit insecure for a god."

I tried not to take that personally.

They were both crying, and Hitra insisted on supporting Illoe as they jointly stumbled to the nearest café. It was closed, but they didn't care; they just wanted to sit down. Sorrow's Market opened out east from here, the giant arch facing them. Neither of them had ever seen the market closed, the cook-benches clean and all their implements packed away. The scattered stools told stories of groups gathered and vanished.

They were both chuckling like drunks. "Not that I'm not so, so relieved to see you," Illoe sobered, "but it's not like you can just take me home."

"You're right, but not how you're thinking." Hitra reached across to take his hands and she looked so serious Illoe was afraid she was about to tell him bad news. "While you're still indentured, you need a guardian, and Maede got herself named that, somehow, so...I stopped the payment on your indenture. I'm in violation of the contract as of now."

He felt a spike of outrage. Of all the things he took care of for her, he was always conscientious about his own debt. To undo his work was insulting! But she was looking at him, steady, like there was something he was missing. "What...what does that mean?"

"Well, I'll have to keep refusing to pay for a while, and my credit is going to be destroyed, but the contract will be nullified, and my personal advocate says we can treat it as void starting right now." She ended with a smile that was, frankly, evil.

She'd really done it, and it *had* been easy. With no more power than a normal human, she'd saved two out of three.

His hands tightened on hers. "You mean I'm free?"

She was suddenly shy. It felt too big to say out loud. She nodded. "And you should know before you decide anything that, well, for some time now, I've...I've..." There were simple shorthand phrases she could use, "I care for you" or "I love you" or "I have feelings." She rejected them all. "I can't imagine my life without you. But don't let me hold you back. I'll keep my emotions in check, and I understand if you'd rather go to your parents' house, or to your brother's. I promise I won't feel bad."

That last sentence was a lie and we all knew it. Illoe pressed his lips to her knuckles. "Hitra, let's go home."

☽○☾

The morning dawned bright and clear on Harvest Home. Ele and Tara sat on a braided rug of Tara's. A pace away his parents were picnicking on a canvas tarp folded smartly by Uja, who was hyper aware of Tara and exactly how close her arm was to his son's. Loata was quietly whispering that Jante wasn't handling the blessing quite as well as Hitra did. "I do hope Her Holiness is safe."

"She'd better be. The bank transfer didn't go through this month."

"Darling, shh." Loata didn't approve of looking like you cared about money. "I'm sure Her Holiness was just distracted, and you know how clerks leave early on holiday weeks."

Ele, who had talked to his brother earlier that morning, and shared what he knew with Tara, winked at his girlfriend who shook her head in mock disapproval. *Let them have today,* she sent to him. *They put up with you bringing me with.*

Ele decided not to tell her that his parents had insisted on meeting his girlfriend immediately, and just squeezed her hand in agreement. It was better than he feared, being here, with them and Tara at the same time.

His father made a choked sound, and Ele turned to see him glaring at their interlocked hands. Ele carefully disentangled and moved his hand back to his lap. *Fine, but I can't wait to tell them tomorrow.*

☽○☾

Illoe walked across Hitra's front room with a folded great robe in his hands. He set it in a basket on the sofa. Hitra came down from the dining nook with a stack of plates. She set these in another basket on the floor.

I didn't let them see me.

"What about the candlesticks?" Illoe asked.

"Leave them. I'll pick my favorites. Oh, we should drain the water clock."

"I'll do it after I take down the stove."

Their minds were full of plans and motion. They were going to an apartment in the city that Hitra had rented but not seen yet. Her advocate's cousin was the owner and it was assured to be comfortable, sunny, and inexpensive. Hitra felt light with the lack of ambition, almost giddy to think of nothing more complicated than taking care of her own immediate needs. She had enough savings to spend some time just existing, waiting to decide what new career she should take on, and she had Illoe by her side again, as a friend, not a servant. She hadn't realized how much she needed that.

"You're sure?" she asked, for the eightieth time. "We could find you your own place."

Illoe suspected she kept asking just for the pleasure of hearing him say, "Yes, I'm sure. I don't want to have to worry about what a mess you're making of your life without me."

He was right, she loved hearing him say yes.

I called for Wenne. I felt her shock that I would. Felt her hesitate just to make me wait.

She came. She took my cue and stayed invisible. "These two again? Honestly, what is it with you and that priest?"

"I think I figured that out. We need to be more like them."

Wenne huffed. She felt stretched thin, frazzled. "Mortal? Tiny? Powerless?"

"We're that already. I mean we need to be responsible."

She snorted, thinking that was what she had been saying for over a week. "We owe it to them to leave. People are dying."

"We owe it to them to stay. I know it sounds weird, but they are like our parents, and we aren't fully grown yet." I felt her thinking *what does that even mean* and answered, "No one else can show us how to be who we'll end up being. But we have to do it responsibly. Children need rules, right?"

Illoe threw down a pile of bedding with an exaggerated gasp. "No. Absolutely not."

Hitra was holding up one of Illoe's old tunics, which had fallen behind the clothes-press. It was tiny and also hideously out-of-fashion. She laughed and balled it up. "I'll destroy the evidence."

Wenne wasn't convinced, but she also wasn't going anywhere. There was something defeated in her. I sighed. "Fine, let's go back to your void."

There it was. A spike of fear and embarrassment. I held in my glee, just barely. "You tried to go back? You couldn't, could you? There is no heaven to return to."

She threw her hands up in the air. "It's a void. We...we were fine existing there before, but I think it's because we weren't thinking? I can go there but..." But she couldn't stand it, not for a minute, and she'd tried twenty. "There has to be a back if there's a forward. We'll figure it out."

"Oh shush. Just...just look into Hitra. See how she helped Illoe, and Jeje? She did good things, on purpose. She gave me the job of saving Arel, and I failed completely. What powers does she have that we don't? Let's...let's start being better gods."

In the apartment downstairs, a man pulled down holiday decorations, keeping the trailing grasses free of the grasp of his baby daughter, watching raptly at his feet. Across the street, a woman lifted the cover on a dish of leftover beans and sniffed to see if they were still good. Down the hill and to the east, Jeje walked into a glassworks, unsure of his future but comforted by the familiar smell of iron tools and scorched leather.

Wenne pulled me back to Hitra's apartment. On the grass outside, not far from where Wenne had dropped her fire column, she formed herself solid, holding my arm, looking intently into my eyes, which I formed reflexively from her insistence. "Senne, you're supposed to be evil."

"Maybe I'm misunderstood." Which wasn't the point. "Evil works better in stories than reality. Let's forget the stories. Haven't you figured out that we aren't the stories? There aren't any gods. There's just whatever we are, and we have to take responsibility to be that."

Wenne looked back toward Hitra, who was comparing two candlesticks against the space in a basket. Wenne frowned. She'd gotten a pretty good frown developed. Her shoulders dropped and she nodded. "You're right."

Illoe stopped halfway through the archway and watched Hitra gathering plates. The unspoken was gone between them. Their eyes met, and there was nothing that needed to be said.

Wenne and I hugged, but did not merge. It was a start. Only thirteen gods to go.

About the Author

Marie Vibbert has sold over 80 short stories to places like *Nature*, *Analog*, and *F&SF*. Her work has been translated into Vietnamese and Chinese, and has been called "...the embodiment of what science fiction should be..." by The Oxford Culture Review. Her debut novel, *Galactic Hellcats*, was longlisted by the British Science Fiction Association for 2021. By day she is a computer programmer in Cleveland, Ohio.

Marie is also a member of the Science Fiction Poetry Association, SFPA. She was nominated for their Rhysling Award in 2015, 2021, and 2022, won second place in the Hessler Street Fair poetry contest, and once sold a rhyming poem to a magazine that had "no rhyming poetry" in their guidelines.

~

The lifeblood of every author is audience feedback. Please consider leaving a review (of whatever length) on Amazon, GoodReads, or your favorite platform.

Acknowledgments

Mary Grimm guided this book in its infancy in her graduate seminar on novel-writing at Case Western Reserve University. The first draft of the book was lost on a stolen laptop, and while never recovered, I owe a debt of thanks to fellow CWRU IT workers, especially Kevin and Eric Chan, Tod Detre and Tom Trevlik, who tried to help track it down for me.

I owe a lot of my atheistic education to my high school biology teacher, Mr. Walters, and to CWRU physics professor Manu Singham.

Members of the Cajun Sushi Hamsters writing workshop read most of the early drafts, and friends in the SCA Barony of the Cleftlands provided much encouragement, especially Sir Ephraim (Ken Robinson).

Finally, I owe a lot to my wonderful child, Jennifer Vibbert, who put up with me spending a lot of her formative years staring at a screen and yet managed to become a smart and kind young adult.

About the Publisher

Founded in 2019 by Galactic Journey's Gideon Marcus, **Journey Press** publishes the best science fiction, current and classic, with an emphasis on the unusual and the diverse. We also partner with other small presses to offer exciting titles we know you'll like!

Also available from Journey Press:

Sibyl Sue Blue - Rosel George Brown
The *Original* Woman Space Detective

Who she is: Sibyl Sue Blue, single mom, undercover detective, and damn good at her job.
What she wants: to solve the mysterious benzale murders, prevent more teenage deaths, and maybe find her long-lost husband.
How she'll get it: seduce a millionaire, catch a ride on his spaceship, and crack the case at the edge of the known galaxy.

Kitra - Gideon Marcus
A YA Space Adventure

Stranded in space: no fuel, no way home... and no one coming to help!

Nineteen-year-old Kitra Yilmaz dreams of traveling the galaxy like her Ambassador mother. But soaring in her glider is the closest she can get to touching the stars — until she stakes her inheritance on a salvage Navy spaceship.

I Want the Stars - Tom Purdom
A Timeless Classic

Fleeing a utopian Earth, searching for meaning, Jenorden and his friends take to the stars to save a helpless race from merciless telepathic aliens.

Hugo Finalist Tom Purdom's *I Want the Stars* is one of the first science fiction novels to star a person of color protagonist.